Evil Among Us

by

Matthew W. Vaughn

Evil Among Us
by Matthew W. Vaughn

Printed in the United States of America

ISBN 1-59781-262-5

www.xulonpress.com

1 ⌀⌀

This book is dedicated to the two women in my life who encouraged and supported my writing efforts from the beginning: First, to my mother, *Marjorie Vaughn*, who saw my hidden talent and so pushed and nudged me towards writing at a very early age. As often is the case with youth, I resisted her encouragement and direction, and it pains me to say that she did not live to see this work completed. I can only pray that she can now look down from above and celebrate her dream come true through the publishing of this book. To my wife, *Jodee Vaughn*, who stood by me in the best and worst of times and who has always been my biggest fan. It was with her support and vision that this work began. I love you and hope that you will accept the completion of this book as a small token of the depth of my love and thankfulness for all of your support along the way. Your love is an enormous blessing to me.

I also want to offer a profound thanks to my friend, *Jeff Michaelson,* for his support and counsel throughout this literary endeavor. He was a great help, and is a wonderful friend.

Thank you to all of my family and friends for your unending support and overwhelming encouragement.

Matthew W. Vaughn

Chapter One

Fear consumed my whole being as I drew closer to our agreed upon meeting place. It was past dusk, but not fully dark yet. The shadows played eerie games with my head as they moved about and repositioned themselves in anticipation of the coming nightfall. The abandoned warehouse they had chosen as a meeting place sat alone at the end of the block near the water's edge. It was obvious why they had chosen this site. It was dark and deserted. No one would see or hear anything that came from this place. There were no other active businesses operating within blocks. I pulled down the street and approached the building with my lights on as instructed. I was gripped by fear and I could see my hands trembling on the steering wheel. This would all end tonight. Death was in the air. I could smell it. My only hope and prayer was that it wouldn't be my own death I was foretelling. I exited my car and realized that I was wet with perspiration, yet the air was cool and dry. I had to regain my composure. I needed to get control of my emotions, especially the fear that was trying to consume me. There would probably only be one opening, one chance of surviving this, and it would require all of my wits if I have a prayer of pulling it off. I walked into the vacant front office through the open main entrance and worked my way to the warehouse area in the back as they had ordered. The darkness played with my head and affected my sight. The sound of a man's voice startled me, and I turned to see the voice's owner standing in the middle of the warehouse waiting for me. Upon catching sight of him, my fear immediately turned to anger. They had devastated my family, killed my friends, and still they wanted more. This will end tonight. There are no options left to explore. Enough is enough!

It seems as though this nightmare began months ago, but, in reality, it has only been days. Time as I know it has come to a stand still. Terror has a way of disrupting reality. Tonight terror is reality, and tonight will mark the end one way or the other.

* * * * *

It was a Tuesday night when I met the person that would quickly turn my world upside down. I was on my computer killing some time while waiting for my wife to finish bathing the kids. I clicked on to a chat room entitled "Looking for Christians." I felt pretty excited about meeting someone else who was in search of fellow believers. It turned out that I was the only one on the site when I entered, except for the room host. The host was named "Searching for Truth." I sat quietly in the room for a short period, disappointed because I was looking for a lively chat with other followers of Christ. When it seemed obvious that no one else was going to log on any time soon, I moved my mouse towards the exit key. A message jumped up on the screen as though the host knew I was about to leave.

"Are you who you say you are?"

"I haven't said who I am yet." I typed.

"You entered this room. Are you a real Christian? Are you a true follower of Christ?"

"I'm a believer yes......I was hoping to find some fellow believers here to chat with."

"Well, you found me instead. Are you going to run and hide or stay and chat?"

"Who are you? Why would you host a Christian room if you aren't Christian?"

"I am who I am. I host because I am in search. Christians seem few and far between these days."

"Well, I only know of one "I am," and I'm pretty confident you're not him. As far as "few and far between," I think you are hanging out in the wrong circles. There are believers all over the world, and they grow in numbers daily."

"Right now I am only interested in one believer and that's you! What gives you the confidence to think you know who I am and who I am not? Do you think you know God himself? Do you think he will reveal himself to you in a conventional way and that you will recognize him? I think you are naïve. I think you are foolish. I think you should go now. Run back to the safety of your ignorant flock."

I sat for a minute or two thinking about his comment. His attitude took me aback. I didn't really like the way this was going and the host seemed more of an antagonist than someone "Searching for Truth." My gut told me to sign off and go check to see what my wife and kids were up to, but I just sat there watching the screen, wondering what this room was all about.

"I see you haven't left yet."

"No, I haven't...not sure why though....you seem to have quite a chip on your shoulder."

"Ahh...is that what you think? I am only in search of truth. What are you in search of?"

"An intelligent conversation would be good.....what do you say we try again?'

"Now who has the chip? Am I to understand that anytime we don't see eye to eye, it will be interpreted by you as unintelligent? I seek the truth; not the road most traveled."

"Well, tell me about what truth you are looking for. I

assume you want to know more about Christ and God because you said you were in search of Christians. How can I help?"

"You say you believe in Jesus as the Christ....what makes you so sure he is the way? What makes you so sure you are not headed down the wrong path?"

Ok, now it looks like we are going to get into the meaty discussion I had hoped for. This is obviously a guy who is searching, searching for "truth" as he calls it. I'll bet he is also listening to Hindus, Muslims, and anyone else who will talk to him. He obviously needs some help, and maybe I can share the truth with him, as I have come to know it.

"I do believe that Jesus is the Christ, and I have no doubt that he is the way, the truth and the light. I know this because God's word tells me. Do you have a Bible? I have confidence in my beliefs, because his word is trustworthy."

"MMMMM.. The old "Because the Bible tells me so" argument huh? Well, what if the Bible isn't what you think it is? What if it isn't "God's word," but instead, just the ramblings of some dying desperate men? Do you have a foundation for your beliefs that will stand even if the Bible is proven to be less than what you envision it to be?"

"Well, I have confidence in the truth of the Bible. I do believe it is his word and I believe that it is the same yesterday, today and forever. I believe that many have tried to prove the Bible wrong, but all have fallen far short. Many that set out with this goal in mind have actually been converted to Christ by what they have found. Why don't you read it and try to see if it might reveal the very truth you are looking for?"

"Read it? Read it? I can quote you chapter and verse......I know its truths and its fiction....I know its grandeur and its lunacy........Read it??? Maybe what you should do is read it with the open mind that you were given at birth! HaHaHa"

"It sounds like the chip on your shoulder is back. Glad to hear that you know the word of God so well. Now we just have to find out why you are so confused about your beliefs."

"Oh my friend, you have made a big mistake in your assumptions.....by the way, you sure seem to assume a lot.....I told you I have read the Bible and know it chapter and verse. I never told you that I know the "word of God." You are the one that jumps to the conclusion that the Bible is the word of your God. I have no such conclusion. In fact, I believe that it is a far cry from it. It may actually lead many people down paths that they wouldn't go down if they actually knew what it really was. It is interesting, it is entertaining, but the word of God????? That's your assumption, not mine. As far as the chip on my shoulder is concerned, you know nothing of me. Do not judge what you do not know."

I had to take time to rethink this discussion. This guy is obviously a well educated individual who has spent time reading the Word. Something has set him off; something has hurt him. Where do I go now? What would Pastor Steve do with a character like this? I try to think through these questions and keep coming up with just one thought, RUN!! Run and hide! Pretend you were never here and lose this chat room link. Then my thoughts move to a much larger question. "What would Jesus do?" I know he wouldn't run and hide, and I know he wouldn't side step a discussion about the truth with a lost soul. I need to figure out what makes this guy tick, and I have to see if I can get him back on the right track. I should go check on Sarah and the kids first. They have been pretty quiet for a while now.

"I need to go check on my wife and kids, but if you hold on a few minutes, I will be back and we can continue these discussions."

"I await your return with sweet anticipation.....and by the way, say hi to Sarah for me."

I head off upstairs to see what the gang is up to. By the time I reach the landing it hits me that this guy knew my wife's name! How was that possible? I just met him in the chat room. How can he know anything about me? I use the name "Jesse James" as a chat room name, so how could he know who I am? I need to check my computer profile when I get back downstairs. Maybe I mention Sarah there. That's probably it. I might have said something in my profile about Sarah and the kids. Maybe he took a look at my profile while we were chatting, learned what he could about me, and is now being cute by sharing some of the details back to me.

Upstairs I find Sarah just settling down to read to two wet headed kids who have big smiles waiting for me. Tyler is six, and he welcomes me by bounding up and grabbing me around the neck. Jodie is four and just laughs at her big brother. Sarah is having a laugh too, but she tries to calm the kids down so that they will go to sleep sometime before we do.

"What are you up to downstairs, Jason?"

"I'm on the computer talking to a strange guy about God. I'm trying to get him to understand why we believe that Jesus is the Christ, but he seems a little resistant."

"Well, that seems like a worthwhile endeavor. I'll just stay up here and read to the kids."

I look at her sitting there in her jeans and sweatshirt, soaking wet from the baths, and my heart fills with warmth. "Sure, stay up here and read. There's nothing exciting going on downstairs anyway. I will wrap up with this guy soon, and then I'll come back up and see if I can get some of this attention you are tossing out to the kids." I look over at the two smiling children that God has entrusted me with and I just want to swoop them up and hug them to death. "Now you two be good for Mommy, and I will come up and check on you later. I love you both." I get an "I love you too, Daddy" in unison from the two of them. I give hugs all around and head back down the stairs to check in with my new chat partner. As I head down, I hear my wife ask the kids what story they want her to read, and they throw out four or five titles all at the same time. Smiling, my mind drifts back to my chat, and thoughts of how to approach this person and how best to help him. I wonder if I am smart enough to help him. Maybe he needs the help of someone far more trained in this sort of thing.

"I'm back Mr. Truth Searcher. You still out there?"

"Of course I'm still here, it's my room isn't it?"

"Well, now that you mention it, it's a pretty lonely room. We have been chatting for a while now and nobody else has even joined us. Maybe you scare them off???"

"Maybe, or maybe it's just that they are smarter than you. Think that's possible Mr. Jesse James????"

"Lots of people are smarter than me. I'm not the smartest and far from perfect."

"I know your next line......Not perfect, just for-given....is that it?"

"That's pretty much it......it is great to be forgiven, and it is great to know your destiny!"

"It is sad that you feel the need for forgiveness, and it is arrogant to think that you know your destiny. What if I were to tell you that you are destined for things that you do not know and things that you will not understand? Things that will frighten you, things that will devastate Sarah, Tyler, and Jodie. What would you say to that?"

There he goes again, using my family's first names. An eerie feeling wells up inside me and my body convulses in a quick shudder. How does he know my children's names? I quickly jump to my profile to see what I have listed there about me and my family. I must have mistakenly given out their names for some reason. My profile pops up and it doesn't say much. Male, 42, married, "love family, love God, love life"......Okay, he could figure out that I have a family, but how would he know their names? How could he possibly get that right? What is going on here? Who is "Searching for Truth?"

"Why do you use the names Sarah, Tyler and Jodie?"

"Why? Because those are the names of your family. What else would you like me to call them?"

"How do you know their names?"

"I know much....I know you....I told you. I am who I am."

This guy is beginning to scare me. How could he possibly know me? How could he know I would come to his chat room? Is this someone from the church trying to be funny? Nobody at church knows that I use the nickname Jesse James. They couldn't match up this chat name with me.

"You have not said anything for awhile, Jason. Are you taken back by what I know? You will see far more wonders than this. If you can be calm, if you can stay focused, I will show you many things."

"I want to know who you are. I want to know how you know me. I want to know how you know my family. Why have you set up this chat room?"

"I know many things. I know all about you: your likes and dislikes, your family, your faith....... I set up this chat room to meet you...In you I will find the truth, and with you, I will show it to the world."

Chapter Two

The next day I was consumed by the whole chat experience from the night before. I didn't share the details of it with my wife, as I knew it would have frightened her and I saw no point in that. By the time I had gotten off the computer last night, my wife was half asleep and she didn't ask for much explanation of my chat. Although I was bursting with anxiety and had a thousand questions, I did not share them with Sarah. I just kissed her and told her I met a stranger on the internet who had a lot of questions about Christianity. She seemed satisfied with that and drifted off to sleep. I was not so lucky.........I found no solace in sleep.

The next morning I awoke tired and groggy. My head felt as though I had regressed back to my old ways: as though I was hung over. But I had no hangover. There was no bar, no liquor to blame this on, only the computer. Only some guy who knew way too much about me and who seemed to have a very hostile side to him. I couldn't quite pinpoint what it was, but anger and hostility were what I observed as I read between the lines. He wasn't threatening: he didn't warn me of doom. He just said "In me he would find truth." It wasn't what he said, but the way he said it. Many of the things he said sounded as though they came from the Bible, but I don't think he's a believer, however knowledgeable. Could he be a believer that has lost his way? Maybe he needs someone to help him back to the family of

God? I'm just not sure I'm that man though. He has rattled me. His questions were forceful, and I think someone more rooted in the faith would be better equipped to help him. I think I had better talk to Pastor Steve as soon as I can reach him.

Sarah left for work with the smile and kiss she always leaves me with. I would soon be in the car with the kids on our way to the daycare and then off to carve my little niche in the world as well. My concerns ebbed and flowed like the ocean waves. I would think about this man's needs and how I could help him; and then I would remember how much he knew about me, about my family. I remembered how harsh he sounded and that he seemed to imply that he had plans for me specifically. "With you I will show the world," he said. What did he mean by that?

The kids climbed out of the car at the daycare center arguing about whose lunch was going to be better and who was smarter and who would be President first. All those funny things that seem so important to minds that are going 100 miles an hour. I doubt that they even heard me as I gave them my typical morning instructions, "Eat all your lunch, bundle up before you go outside to play, be nice, and be good for your teachers." Oh, they humored me by looking at me and nodding, but I hadn't stopped talking for two seconds before they resumed their arguments right where they had left off. They walked up the steps of the small commercial daycare center while I watched. They knew I was watching, because I always watched. At the door neither turned around, but I got a half hearted wave as though they were doing the required salute before they could go in.

They attend a great daycare that is run by a small Christian congregation. I believe it was originally formed to help hard working parents that really couldn't afford to provide the kind of daycare we all want for our kids. It had recently expanded, however, which gave other families with two working parents an opportunity to participate. Here they pay a lot of attention to the children. They feed them and comfort them and provide them security and transportation to public school for those who go. Tyler is in first grade this year and they take him to his school, log him in there, and then pick him up again in the afternoon. It is a wonderful service, and the price is so reasonable for what they provide. For the financially challenged, the costs are supplemented by the congregation as a missionary outreach program. For those of us who can afford the full tuition, it remains a positive influence and a great place to entrust our children's care. They require all of the children to participate in Bible studies, which require the family to work together each night on the homework. Regular parent-teacher meetings are scheduled so that the parents can understand their children's progress and teachers can track the progress of the entire family. This program has brought many new families to the Lord, and the school disciplines have also helped those of us who already know the truth to remain grounded through daily study. Our family does not belong to the school's home congregation, but our Pastor knew of and recommended the program. We were thrilled when an opening came up that allowed both of our children to attend.

Once Sarah was off to work and I had the children in school, I could begin to focus on my day. I hold the position of Plant Manager for a medium sized factory in town. We aren't the biggest employer by any means, but we are important and the community treats us that way. That means that I not only have to run the factory and all the fun opportunities that come with it, but I also play a large role in community relations. Community relations calls for breakfast meetings, lunches, attending city council meetings, and all the political side of life that I would prefer to ignore. It isn't anything that I enjoy, but it came with the territory when I was promoted two years ago. It still seems difficult to see myself in this role. I wasn't in line for this big job and was surprised when it fell in my lap. I was in charge of the warehouse, the logistics group, and reported up to the Plant Manager through the Operations Manager. When tragedy struck the Plant Manager, everyone assumed that Gene Rikes, the Operations Manager, would get the big job, but they placed me in charge instead.

Two years. It seems hard to imagine that I have been running this factory for two years. Joe Deener had the job before me, and I liked him a lot. Joe was a member of our church, and he was a big influence in my growth as a Christian. He gave me a lot of support both inside and outside of work. It was a wonderful experience to work in an environment where you could openly praise God and share "God moments" with other believers. Gene Rikes, on the other hand, was not a believer. Oh, Joe talked to him a lot and tried to bring him along, but Gene wasn't interested. He stayed to himself most of the time and just did his job. Nobody really knew what he did outside of work because he didn't talk much about his personal life. Gene never seemed to mind Joe's and my relationship, and I was very careful not to over step my bounds or side step the chain of command. He seemed to recognize that and respect it. But then Joe died. Well, he didn't just die, he was killed. Not just killed but murdered. Not murdered, sacrificed. His naked body was found at the local park laid out on the lawn as though he were hanging on a cross. His hands were nailed into the soil, and his feet were crossed and tied. The official report said that Joe bled to death. Someone had cut him open from the chest to the stomach and just let him bleed to death. Everyone thought it was a ritual of some type, but no body parts were removed, no sayings were carved in his body, nothing else to clue anyone into what lead to this. Obviously, the way he was laid out made it clear to everyone that he had offended someone and he had died because of his love for Christ. It has been two years since that day and we know nothing more about it. There weren't any ghosts found in his closets. No hidden torments or rumors. His wife stayed in town for a while but then left to be with her family in Toledo. No one has ever heard from her since. Although the police have kept the case open, they have had little to go on and aren't afraid to say so: no witnesses, no prints, no knife, and no motive. Just the body in the park left behind as a message that most of us couldn't understand. The city was devastated, the plant was shut down for a week, and the church was in mourning for months. We lost a friend, a mentor, a brother, and none of us knew why.

During this period of mourning and sorrow, Gene picked up the company reins and ran with them. He took charge of the plant and got things going again. He worked hard to get everybody's mind back on business and started focusing on things like efficiency and profits. Some thought he pushed too hard too fast, but I thought he did what he had to do, and he did it the only way he knew how. I tried to help him in every way I could. About two weeks after Joe's funeral, the V.P of Operations came to town and stayed for two days talking to some of the employees and to Gene specifically. Everyone assumed that Gene would take over, so we just kept our heads down and focused on work while their meetings convened. The second day of his visit, I was summoned to the office by the V.P. I was a little nervous. I didn't really know this guy, and he was really two layers above me when Joe was around. I walked into Joe's office and found him behind the desk. I have to admit that I felt a shiver go up my back when I saw him at Joe's desk. Gene hadn't even sat at that desk during the transition.

"Jason, sit down a minute. We need to talk."

I looked around and didn't see Gene. "Sure," I said.

"I want you to take this office and see what you can do with this plant. I know that Joe had the greatest regard and trust for you, and I think I want to take a chance and see what you can do."

"What about Gene? We all assumed he would get this job."

"Gene's a good man. He's just not the right man."

After a pretty sizable pause, I finally gathered some words together. "Well, I have to tell you that I have mixed emotions. I am thrilled to be considered for something I didn't even think was attainable, but I am torn because it is being offered to me because of the death of a good friend. I am also concerned about Gene. I think he did a pretty good job here, and I wouldn't want to be seen as a guy that side stepped the system."

"Well, Jason, I understand your concern. Joe was a good man and he was good for our company. We don't know why he was taken the way he was taken, but the facts are that we have to keep moving. We owe it to the rest of the employees, and we owe it to the investors. We have to put a leader back in this chair, and it is not going to be Gene. You can take it and give it a spin, or I will go and pull one of our boys in from another plant: either way, we are putting a new man in this office."

I sat silent for a second or two but didn't want to seem ungrateful. "I am very grateful for the opportunity. I'm just surprised by it that's all. I will need some help getting up to speed, and I'm not sure how thrilled Gene will be to help me if he knows he will then report to me."

"Don't worry about Gene. He is a good man and a company man. He will stay and help you get this thing going, and then we will move him to another site so he can hold his head up. We will give him a bigger job in a bigger plant, but I'm not ready to give him the Plant Manager's job, not just yet. But I am ready to give it to you."

"Does he know?"

"Yes, and he is right outside waiting to congratulate you.

That is if you happen to get around to accepting the offer."

"I'm sorry, of course I accept! I'm just stunned that's all. There is so much happening all at once, and it's happening so fast: first a horrible tragedy, now this wonderful opportunity. I'm not sure what my emotions are doing or what they should be doing."

"Well, I understand that, but you will have to compose yourself pretty quickly. I want to call a plant meeting to make the announcement before the end of the day, and then I am gone. You will need to present yourself as the "go-to-guy" right out of the gate. Do you think you can do that?"

"I'm ready and appreciate the opportunity....thank you very much"

With that he left the room, Gene came in, we said some niceties, the plant meeting was held, and the V.P. left town. That was two years ago, and I have been running things ever since. Gene left about nine months later and moved to a town somewhere in the Midwest. I never heard from him again, and never heard any updates about him from within the company. One day I'm working with two men whom I respect in very different ways and heading down a career path that might get me to the big job in five or so years. The next day, I'm sitting in the Plant Manager's office with my name on the door; my friend is dead, and my co-worker gone. It was a whirlwind of activity, and now I realize that it has already been two years. I feel a little guilty as I recognize that I have not thought about Joe for months...I have gotten so wrapped up in my life and my responsibilities that I have not thought of my friend and the horrible way he died for some time. I don't know what I'm supposed to do, but it seems that I should have been doing more: either something for his wife Abigail or something for their family.

Today, however, I have other thoughts. As soon as I hit the office, I made a call to Pastor Steve and left him a message. I really need to talk to him to get some guidance about this man that says he's in search of truth. I need some counsel. I need some advice. I know if Joe was here, he would help. But Joe is gone. Thankfully, Pastor Steve will be there for me.

I sit down and start going through my morning tasks: Check phone messages, open my email, and yell good morning to my assistant Beth. Then I spot it: an unopened email from "In Search of Truth" in my work email account. How did he know where I worked or what my email address was? Should I open it or wait to talk to Steve first? What does this guy want? How did he find me? After struggling over the decision I decide that it couldn't hurt to open it. I click on it twice to open the message.

"Good Morning, Jason. I hope you had a good night. The truth is often not easy to digest all at once, so I will give it to you in small bite size amounts until you crave it and want more. The truth can be painful at times, but you have proven you can endure. Do not fear and do not look to have anyone else talk to me. I came seeking you, and I shall open the door for you and you alone. Have a good day, Jason. I will look for you at our chat site when it is appropriate. Have Beth get you some morning coffee. You look like you need it."

A sudden chill ran down my spine. I jumped up and looked around and then half heartedly laughed at myself for thinking that he might be watching me. But he knew too much, and there was nothing funny about that. He knew I would seek out others to help. He knew that my assistant was named Beth. I collected myself in an attempt to calm my emotions. There seemed to be one, ever so slight, kink in this man's armor, however. I never drink coffee. I have never had a cup of coffee in my life, and Beth has never gotten me coffee or anything else of that nature. I wasn't sure what this little gaff meant, but I clung to the fact that he didn't know everything. He wasn't supernatural. He was trying to impress me and maybe scare me. He was definitely doing a lot of that, but he wasn't perfect.....He didn't know everything. I took comfort in that.

Chapter Three

Pastor Steve finally called me back at about two in the afternoon.

"Steve, where have you been?"

"Whoa, easy there, Jason. What's up? Your message didn't say it was an emergency. Is something wrong?"

"No. Oh, I don't know. I'm sorry, Steve. It's just that I've been sitting here on pins and needles waiting for you to call. I think I have gotten myself into something that is way over my head. I need your advice."

"Okay, Jason, I'm here for you. Do you want to talk on the phone or get together? I can drop what I'm doing and come over or meet you wherever you want."

"I don't know, Steve. Maybe I'm making something out of nothing, but I need to talk. I need to go over this with you. I need your perspective and your wisdom. I don't dare go any further until I get some advice from a stronger Christian."

"This sounds serious. Why don't I just come to your office? I could be there in fifteen minutes or so and I have the rest of the afternoon free. I'm sorry it took so long to get back to you, but I was meeting with a couple who are preparing for marriage. Your message didn't sound urgent. If I had known, I could have rescheduled the meeting because they aren't due to tie the knot for another three months anyway."

"I don't think it's that serious, Steve, or at least I hope it's not. I probably have just had too much time to dwell on it and have most likely gotten myself worked up over nothing. But, if you really don't mind coming by, I will lock up my calendar for the next hour so we can talk."

"I'm on my way. I'll see you soon."

"Bye, Steve... and thanks."

The phone went dead and I sat there staring at the office door for a minute. I just couldn't generate the power to move. This chat room character was beginning to unnerve me, and I didn't have the foggiest idea why. The outer office phone rang, and it brought me back into focus. I pulled up my calendar and saw that I had a two thirty production meeting planned in the conference room. I called out to Beth.

"Beth? You out there?"

"Where else would I be!" she shouted back.

"Beth, move the two-thirty meeting back to three-thirty will you? I want to keep the next hour open. Steve Kendal is coming by."

Beth walked to the door of my office. "Pastor Steve? Okay, I'll move things around, but you know you shouldn't just let him drop in and throw your whole schedule off like that."

"I called him, Beth. I asked him to come over. Can you just make sure everyone knows about the change?"

"I'm on it. Jason? You okay?"

"I'm good, Beth. Thanks. I just need to talk to Steve on a couple of issues, and he had an opening during this hour. I knew you could make it work for me."

"Okay, okay. Enough of the super woman stuff. I'll switch things around for you."

"Thanks, Beth."

Beth is a great assistant. Oh, she isn't the greatest in the sense that she knows all of the latest computer programs or the latest tools and software, but she really has a great attitude. That makes you forget about some of those technical shortcomings that pop up every once in a while. I'll wager she is about fifty five years old, if I was a betting man, and I'm not-especially when it comes to women's ages. She has a couple of young grandchildren and her kid's ages put her in that general vicinity. She had worked in payroll for years, and when I was promoted, I asked her to join me as my assistant. She had never been an assistant before, but she was willing and jumped in with the greatest attitude and willingness to learn. Since then, she has really made a difference. We don't socialize much, but occasionally Sarah and I will have dinner with Beth and her husband. I haven't had much luck getting her to come to church or visit any of our special programs throughout the year, but she is a lady that would be a natural Christian, if there ever was such a thing. She is always cheery and always thinking about others. She has no problem in jibing back at you, if appropriate, but it's always in fun and part of her personality, which I wouldn't change for a million dollars. Beth's husband, Jeffery, is a foreman at the local Coca-Cola bottling company. He has been there for almost twenty-five years. He has been talking about retiring for as long as I can remember, but I don't think they really are the type to sit around knitting and playing golf. They are both very active in their children's lives and, of course, their grandchildren's lives as well; but they both seem to love going to work. I don't see either of them giving in to retirement anytime soon. They fit together seamlessly and have done so for somewhere around thirty years.

Beth got the offer to be my assistant because Joe's assistant up and quit right after I was promoted. No notice, no reason why, she just said, "Thanks for the memories" and walked out. I'm sure it had to do with Joe's death and the fast turn around in my role. She had been with the company for several years and had worked for Joe and Gene the whole time. I'm sure that Joe's death and my promotion over Gene left her feeling cold about things. I couldn't sit around very long to ponder over it, though, because I didn't know my way around the office side of things and knew I would need help. I chose Beth because she had been around a while, knew the ropes, and had that great attitude. She was my first executive decision and my best. I never heard anymore about Jane Stuart, Joe's assistant. I have no idea if she stayed local or moved away. I never asked after she left. Isn't it funny how you think about things like that from time to time, but never really go out of your way to find out the details? Come to think of it, I have to say the same for Gene. With Joe's untimely death, the world changed quickly at Concord Manufacturing. We had to change with it if we were going to be able to keep the people employed and the doors open.

Most of the people jumped right into my camp and supported me from day one. Obviously, they were as shocked as I about Joe and Gene, but people like Beth just got right down to it and started delivering right from the first bell. It really made a big impression on me and certainly made my life easier through a tough transition. The death of Joe was a big deal in this town and certainly for the folks that worked at this factory. You add that to the changes in management, the exit of Jane and then Gene, and we could've had some real problems on our hands. But together we found our way, and people like Beth helped me develop into a pretty successful plant manager. Together we have created a real family here at Concord.

Steve was due any minute so I had to start getting my thoughts in order. If I didn't, I would just come off sounding like some crazy mad man, ranting about weird aliens on the net. I chuckled at the sound of that, but decided to take a minute or two and jot down a few notes so that I could hold my thoughts together. I realized that I was really keyed up and even a bit nervous about sharing this with Pastor Steve. I mean, maybe I was being silly, maybe he would laugh at me because I misunderstood the whole thing, maybe it was someone from the church and he knew all about it and would burst out laughing at me, or maybe he would wonder what I was doing surfing the net in the first place. This thought froze me in my tracks. I hadn't thought about that before, but I was on the internet surfing through the chat rooms. Most of them are very worldly. You can find almost anything to chat about and there is no doubt that sex and deviant behavior prevail in many rooms. It is a direct reflection of where the world's focus is right now. There are Christian sites and other real chats going on too, but maybe Steve would wonder why I was visiting the chat lines at all. I began to panic about this a little and felt my blood pressure go up a bit. Why was I there? What was I looking for? I hadn't visited any of the unsavory chat sites, but would he believe me and should I even try to explain that to him? What if he left thinking I was the problem? I mean after all, I'm happily married with two children, a great job, and a great walk with God. What was I doing on a chat site?

"Calm down Jason old boy," I finally told myself. "You're not a wayward Christian. You didn't go there because you were looking for anything other than a chance to chat with other Christians from around the world. Don't act guilty if you aren't guilty. Just because the world misuses the computer doesn't make the computer evil." I found myself sweating and had to sit back in my chair, take a deep breath, and calm myself down. These thoughts had popped out of nowhere, and my guess is it goes back to wanting to look good in front of the Church Minister. Man, I must have more of that old puritan upbringing inside of me than I thought. I finally regained control of my thoughts, put my fears at rest, and finished up my notes before Steve arrived. He was about five minutes late, and I was grateful. I don't know why I feel so full of anxiety and alarm, but it seems that I'm reacting strongly to everything. I know Steve will help me gather my wits so that we can sort this thing out.

"Hi there, Pastor."

"Hi, Beth. How are you?"

"I am fit as a fiddle and happy as a lark. You can go on in: he is waiting on you. You can only have him until three-thirty, though; and if you run a minute longer, you will have to deal with me."

Steve smiled back, gave a wave and a wink, and walked around Beth's desk and into my office. I had heard this little barbing from Beth, and it brought a smile to my face as Steve walked in.

"Okay, that's what I like to see, Jason, a smile on your face."

"Hi, Steve. Come in and sit down. I really appreciate you pulling yourself away from what you were doing to come over here so quickly. I am really beside myself on this thing I've gotten myself into."

"Well, let's kick it around, Jason. Beth only gave me until three-thirty, and you know I won't go past her time lines. Where do you want to start?"

I walked past Steve and gently closed the door. I turned back around and Steve saw my smile fade. I began to explain my chat room meeting and internet message from this man who said he was in search of truth.

It felt to me like I had talked for an hour, but when I looked at the clock, Steve had only been there about twenty minutes. I had shared the facts and my concerns. I explained my dilemma between my desire to help this individual, and my fear of what he knew and what he really wanted.

After I finished, I just kind of leaned back and looked at Steve.

"Well, what do you think? Am I worrying about nothing? Can we help this man?"

Steve also leaned back in his chair and rubbed his face in both his hands. He paused a minute or so before speaking.

He had listened intently, as I am sure Pastors are taught to do, and now he needed a minute or two in order to develop his thoughts.

"Jason, what you have shared with me is very interesting, and I don't believe that you are making a mountain out of molehill. If you thought I was going to get a laugh over this, you have misjudged the situation entirely. You want my advice? Run! Hide! Don't read another email, don't answer him again, and don't visit him in that chat room. I mean it Jason, RUN!"

I found myself shocked at Steve's reaction. It was so similar to my first thoughts. I knew that the man had frightened me with his words and his anger, but I hadn't expected Steve to react this way. I thought he would bring calmness to the issue and would help me sort out what was real and what was imaginary. Instead, he was telling me to stop sorting it out. Don't talk to him or answer his emails. Just run! That's his advice, to run?

"Steve, what do you think this is? Who do you think it is? Obviously, you are taking this very seriously. I hadn't anticipated that from you. Tell me what you are thinking."

"I told you what I'm thinking. This is dangerous. He knows you, your family, where you work. He wants to tease you about your faith and egg you on when he really has no interest in Christ or the truth. This could be very serious. I am advising you to stay off the computer and away from him as best you can. If he emails you, trash them without opening them. Do not give him dialogue to feed off of. If you're lucky, he'll get bored and go away."

"Steve, don't you think we should try to reach his soul? Don't you think that he may just seem to be challenging me, but down deep he wants to be convinced? You are much more rooted in God's word than I am and I respect your advice, but I am surprised by this. I guess I thought you would want to join me in this fight and help me behind the scenes."

"Jason, I am not trying to scare you, but I won't water this down either. This man is toying with you. He doesn't want to know more about God, he wants to know more about you! He loves your reaction when he drops names and facts that you don't think he should know. You don't know who this is. It could be someone from your work, or someone that you know casually, but I believe he is sick. I believe that he has no good intentions, and for your sake and the sake of your family I am going to tell you again, run and hide! Don't give him any more ammunition than he has now. Let him ramble on to himself. If you don't answer, he may just find something else to do. Let me give you one more piece of advice. If he contacts you again in any way: email, phone, or a visit, don't answer him, talk to him, or see him. Call the police."

Steve really had me scared now. Call the police? What would I say? "Officer, a guy keeps emailing me wanting to know about Christ. Can you make him stop?" Wow, that would go over big. Steve had also mentioned things I hadn't thought of. What if he phones or tries to visit me? He knew my last name. He had to if he emailed me here at my work. That means he not only knows my name, but my phone number and address, because our number is listed in the phone book. I hadn't thought about this thing escalating like that. I had resigned myself to thinking about a give and take of email chatter that couldn't harm anyone. What would I do if he did call or come by? Calling the police wasn't sounding so far-fetched. Steve had me scared, and he knew it. The worst of it was that he was scared too. I could see it in his eyes.

Chapter Four

The drive home seemed endless. The rest of the afternoon had been a total loss. I attended the production meeting as scheduled, but I don't know why. I added no value, and I could tell that everyone else knew it too. I couldn't think of anything but this mess I had gotten myself into. At four o'clock, I just packed up and decided it was time to get out. I know that Beth was both surprised and concerned, but I assured her that I just had to run some errands and that I would be back as good as new tomorrow. She smiled and acknowledged my lie, but it was clear to me that she knew it was a lie. The truth, that's what got me into this mess in the first place. Why did I go to the chat rooms last night? Why did I enter his site? It has turned my life upside down and got me thinking about nothing else. I needed to get home and figure out what I was going to do. I just couldn't sit and think at the office. Everyone seemed to be watching me. I have to get my arms around my next steps.

Next steps? What next steps? According to Steve, my next step should be nothing. Do nothing, say nothing, read nothing, and if anything happens or even looks funny, call the police. I wonder if he's right. Oh, I agree that I shouldn't encourage this guy. Look what he has done to me already after just one night of talking. I don't know about running away with my tail between my legs, though. Maybe I should tell him to leave me alone and not to contact me again.

Wouldn't that be a better approach if I do have to contact the police? I could show them a copy of the email that I sent him telling him to leave me alone. That would help my case wouldn't it? What case? What do I think is going to happen here? I'm already talking as though I'm building my evidence file and preparing for a show down. In all reality, the man hadn't done anything other than open a chat site, which I freely visited, asked me some tough questions, and challenged me on a few things I believe in. He told me things he knows-things about me and my family, and then sent me an innocent email at work. What do I really feel this is building up to? I just don't have to visit his site anymore. That takes care of that. If he emails me, I'll tell him to back off and leave me alone.

I pulled in the driveway and was surprised to see my wife's car already there. I left early to get some time to myself. What is she doing home already? I pulled in next to her car, gathered my briefcase, and climbed out. As soon as I shut my door, I heard Sarah. "Hi, Jason, I'm over here at Carol's!" I looked across the street to see Sarah standing at the front door of Carol and Ralph's house. She waved and then Carol waved as well. I gave them a smile and a wave and headed towards the front door.

"I'll be over in just a few minutes!"

I waved again acknowledging her call and went inside. What the heck was she doing home so early? She doesn't usually get off for another hour. Where are the kids? If she came home early, why didn't she pick the kids up? I knew instinctively that they weren't home. The house was silent. The house was never silent when the kids were home. In addition to that, Sarah was across the street visiting. She would never leave the children in the house and go outside, not even if she was standing in the neighbor's yard. Sarah loved the children, and she was very protective of them.

I threw my briefcase in the corner of my home office and

hung up my jacket in the hall. I wasn't really sure what my next move was supposed to be. I didn't come home expecting to find Sarah, and now that I had, I really didn't know why I thought it was important to be home before her anyway. I mean, I don't have an action plan. I don't have a list of "To-Do's" that I have to check off. No details that require my undivided attention. Why did I feel that it was important to get home before Sarah? Why am I feeling so edgy about everything? I do feel edgy though, irritated, and jumpy. I feel like I just want to get mad and yell at someone. I want someone to take this mess away, and yet the other side of me thinks I am acting like a big fool over a little computer horse play. Well, Steve was right. The way to handle this is to break off all ties. Don't give him any ammunition. I think Steve said that, and I think he was right. If you don't talk back, it makes for a very dull conversation.

Sarah came bounding in through the front door. "Hey, baby, glad you're home early!"

"Why are you home so early?" I asked.

"Well, thank you, sweet heart, it's good to see you too. I kind of thought you might be happy to see me. You know, like I am about you?"

"I'm sorry, honey. I didn't mean I wasn't happy. I was just surprised to see your car in the driveway when I got home. I thought I would be home at least an hour before you."

"Have a secret meeting planned that I interrupted?" She asked playfully.

"No, unfortunately, nothing anywhere near as exciting as that."

Sarah slugged me on the arm and I grabbed her and we both broke out in laughter while we hugged. It was a great relief. I know that I probably laughed harder and louder than the joke warranted, but Sarah didn't react to it and she just stayed in my arms hugging me back.

"Why are you home so early, Sarah? Nothing wrong at

work I hope."

"On the contrary, my little "glass half empty" husband. Something special happened to me at work today, and to celebrate, they let me go home early. The plan was that I would surprise you with a child free dinner out tonight, but you got home too soon and ruined everything."

I looked at her and found she was still smiling. "Okay, what did I ruin? Are you going to tell me what we're celebrating?"

"In due time, my sweet, in due time. Right now I have to go get the kids and drop them off across the street. Carol and Ralph are going to watch them for us. You need to clean up and get ready because we are going to that new restaurant that opened down by the water. You know Cherries, or Sherri's."

"Cheriz." I said

"Cheriz. Well, aren't you just the cat's meow. Whatever it's called, I heard the food was unbelievable, and we're going to get our chance to find out tonight."

"Okay, I'm game, but it better be special. I heard the prices were just as unbelievable."

"You are not going to ruin this for me no matter how hard you try, smart guy, so just get on upstairs and get ready cause your girl is taking you out tonight."

"I'm going. I'm going. I can't wait to hear what's up."

"I'm running to get the munchkins. Oh, by the way, why are you home early?"

That question suddenly jerked me back to the ugly reality of my dilemma. I had to think for a second. What should I say? I didn't want her to know about the whole chat mess. I had a feeling it was a dead issue so it wasn't worth worrying her. I'm not really sure why I came home early anyway. I could say that I just a bad day, but I didn't want to say that on a night that she wanted to make so special. How do I answer her question? MMMMMMM?

"I had a late meeting out of the office, and I didn't feel

like going back and getting entrenched with all of the day's problems. I took advantage of the opportunity and came home early."

I got no response, so I looked up and saw her looking at me with an obvious question on her lips. She didn't believe me either. Why can't I learn to be a better liar? Beth knows when I am fibbing, Sarah knows, the kids know.....what's the point?

"Well, I'm glad you're home anyway. It means we can get a jump start on that food at Sherriz or whatever it's. Okay, I'm off."

"Cheriz!" I shout at her as she runs out the door. A wave is all I get in return.

As I started toward the stairs I realized that for the last few minutes I hadn't thought at all about "Truth Searcher." Sarah had a way of making you forget about your little worries and problems. Her celebration, or whatever it was, couldn't have come at a better time. I bounded up the rest of the stairs and decided to get happy. Whatever she was happy about, I would be happy about. As far as I was concerned, the crazy mess that I had allowed to consume my day was a closed file. No more worries. Time to move on.

I washed up and picked out my sexiest shirt in the closet. Well, actually all of my shirts look pretty much the same, but I thought that my mood change might make it a special shirt for Sarah. I was looking forward to our night out together. No children, no worries, just Sarah and I and apparently something to celebrate. For this occasion I will even apply my little secret weapon. Cologne. Not just any cologne, but the cologne that drove her into my arms the very first time we met. Old Spice, the secret formula that no woman can resist. Or at least that was what my father had told me. I wore it faithfully, and landed Sarah. My father was a genius, and I will have to remember to share this hidden truth with my son when he gets older. I'm sure it had to be the cologne that won Sarah over. As I look in the mirror, I affirm that nothing else could have done it. I am no special catch: not exceptionally brilliant, not the best athlete in the world, and yet I won Sarah's heart. Had to be the cologne. No question about it! I only break it out on special occasions, and this sounds like a pretty good one. With no kids at the dinner table, I might even try some of my special love lines that work so well with Sarah. We usually get to laughing so hard when I try to be romantic, but I try and she likes that I do, no matter how silly I sound. I feel myself getting excited about being together, and the worries of the day seem to drift off as though they were never really worries at all. What could be more important than spending the evening with the girl you love?

About thirty minutes had gone by and Sarah hadn't come in yet. I headed downstairs taking two steps at a time, knowing she was standing around chatting across the street with Carol again. When she got a look at me dressed up like this, she would run across the street and throw herself into my arms. Once she smelled my secret weapon, she would be mine. She could not resist my powerful love, especially when I packaged it together like this. I threw open the door and marched down the walk to let her gaze upon me. When I got to the driveway, her car wasn't there. I looked across the street to see if she had parked in front, but no Sarah. Disappointed, I headed back inside. My big moment had been spoiled. My guess was that she had to stop at the store to pick up something for the kid's adventure at Ralph and Carol's house, or was it Ralph and Carol's big adventure? I hope she picks up a little something special for them too. My moment had been lost and I was a bit deflated, but I kept my spirits up and went back in the house to switch on the news until she got home.

An hour passed and I was sick with worry. No Sarah, no kids, no calls. What could have happened? Even Carol had come across the street to see what was going on. We were both getting more nervous by the minute. I called the school and found that Sarah hadn't picked the kids up yet. They were still waiting there. I immediately called the police department to check to see if an accident might have caused the delay, but no accident had been reported in the past hour or so. Panic began to set in again. The excitement turned to sickness as my stomach began to roll over. Carol had volunteered to go get the kids, but I wanted her to stay at the house while I picked them up. I wanted to retrace Sarah's drive towards the school so that I could see if she was broken down by the side of the road somewhere. She had a cell phone, but she seldom put it in the charger, and my guess is that she is sitting there waiting for me to come to the rescue. Ralph got home and Carol gave him an update. He came over and volunteered to go with me. I accepted his offer and we jumped in my car and headed off to find Sarah. Carol waved as we backed out of the drive, and I vaguely heard her yell, "Don't worry, I'm sure she is alright." She didn't sound convincing, and I could feel anxiety building in my head and stomach.

Ralph and I remained silent as we drove. We kept our eyes continually scanning the roadway and roadside.

"Come on Sarah, where are you?" I finally broke.

"Jason, she didn't just disappear. I know this is scary, but we'll find her and I'm sure there's a good explanation. A few months from now we'll look back and laugh about tonight."

I just looked at Ralph and made no comment. He made no further comments. His futile attempt at being reassuring was only that, futile. Where was she? Why hadn't she called? Didn't she know we would be worried? I found my fear evolving into anger. I started to get mad because she wasn't calling and because she probably hadn't charged her cell phone again. My Casanova mood was gone. My relaxed, enjoyable evening was shot. My "glass half empty" thoughts were back. She had to be hurt, in trouble, something. She wouldn't do this to me if she wasn't. She wouldn't do this to me? What's wrong with me? Am I so self-absorbed that I have already begun to focus on myself instead of my wife? Anger transformed to guilt. I began to feel desperate. I had to find her. I loved her. I would be lost without her.

Driving towards the children's school, my thoughts were not on the road or our children.

"Sarah!" I shout into the darkening sky, "Sarah, where are you?"

No answer came.

Chapter Five

Carol and Ralph took the kids home with them. The children didn't know that anything was wrong. In their minds they were on a special adventure at Ralph and Carol's, and they loved it. The police were on their way over to see me. Normally, they don't pursue adult missing reports without more time passing, but it was clear that they believed that there were some unusual circumstances in this case. Sarah Shepard had driven off to pick up her children and she never arrived. No trace, no car, no calls. Something was wrong, terribly wrong, and the police knew it.

I paced back and forth waiting for the police to arrive. I didn't know what to expect. I had watched some of those television movies; and they always made the police out to be rude, calloused, and often bumbling idiots. "God, please don't let that be the case here." God? I realized that I hadn't even thought about God through all of this. I hadn't asked his guidance, sought his blessing, or called out to him in prayer. I had just left him out of all of it. I dropped to my knees right there in my living room and began to cry out to God.

"God, bring her home. Bring her home safe. You know Sarah, how she loves you, and how she loves the kids. We need her God. We can't make it without her. Please find her and send her home. I know you have the power. I know you can do anything if it's your will. Forgive me for leaving you out until now, but please, God make your presence known."

The loud knock at the door startled me and interrupted my prayer. I jumped up believing that God had answered my prayer and that Sarah was at the door. I pulled it open to find two police officers standing there. No Sarah.

"Mr. Shepard? I'm Officer Devoy and this is Officer Lancing. We're here in response to your call."

Officer Devoy was a young officer; he couldn't have been more than twenty-three. Officer Lancing was in his mid fifties. I was surprised to see the young man doing the talking.

"I'm Jason Shepard. My wife, Sarah, is missing and I know something is terribly wrong. She hasn't called and she didn't pick up the kids from daycare. We were supposed to go out to celebrate tonight. I need your help to find her."

"Mr. Shepard, can we come in and go over all of this? Officer Lancing and I need to hear everything that has happened right from the beginning."

"Yes, of course. I'm sorry, please come in. Please forgive me. I'm not sure what's going on. I need to sit down. Let's go into the living room."

"That would be perfect. Don't apologize, Mr. Shepard. We just need some time to go over everything and see if we can start putting some of these pieces together. We are here to help. Together with your help, we'll see what we can do to get Mrs. Shepard back as quickly as possible."

We went into the living room and sat down. The questions began and I lost myself in the details, or what I could remember about the details. You don't pay as much attention to detail when you think everything is normal. Things have been far from normal since my wife drove off in her car.

An hour later the officers were winding down their initial investigation and they reassured me that they would begin the search immediately. Throughout the meeting Officer Devoy did most of the talking. Officer Lancing sat silently listening and watching me; watching me intently. I didn't feel like these were television cops, though. They seemed concerned, and they treated me with respect. They believed me, or at least I felt like they did, and I believe they will find my wife. Officer Devoy was young, but he wasn't youthful. He didn't ask silly questions, and he didn't try to act tough. At first I thought that he was in training, but it was clear he was seasoned and knew what he was doing. Officer Lancing was the puzzling one, though. When he spoke, he spoke with authority and intelligence, but he didn't speak often. He just listened; listened closely. Occasionally he would ask me to clarify something or elaborate on something else. He was an interesting man. He never relaxed for a minute, never seemed to let his radar down. He kept looking around the house as though he was sizing us up as a family, sizing up our marriage. He never did it in a way that offended me. I knew he was doing his job. These guys were professional, and I have to admit that I felt relieved about that when they left.

We said our goodbyes as they walked across the street to talk to Ralph and Carol. They knew that our children were over there, so they told me they would be very careful. I never doubted it. They seemed to care about our family, about getting Sarah back, and about finding the person responsible. I really felt like they could do it.

When they left, I went in and stood around for a few minutes trying to determine what I was supposed to do next. I dropped back down on my knees, tears in my eyes, and called out to God. "God in Heaven, you know all things and you are in control of all things. Please, God, help these men find my Sarah. Help them bring her home safe. Lord, I have faith that you hear my prayer and will answer it. I know that the world is Satan's playground, but I know that you can be victorious over Satan. We are not immune from the pain and anguish of this world, but I come to you asking you to lift this burden from my heart. I love you, Lord, I trust you. Through your Son, Jesus Christ, I cry out to you, Amen."

I remained on my knees for some time crying and trying to make sense of all of this. There was no sense to be made, though. Nothing seemed right; nothing seemed sensible. One minute I felt confidence and trust in God and the police, and the next I was crawling out of my skin not knowing where my wife was or what she might be going through. Finally, after several minutes I regained control and pulled myself up to the sofa. I reached over and grabbed the phone. I needed to talk to Pastor Steve.

Pastor Steve must have set a new land speed record getting to my house. He lives on the other side of town, but it didn't seem like I had even hung up the phone before I was answering the door with him there. It must have taken longer than I thought because I saw that the Police were gone from across the street. They must have finished with Ralph and Carol and had set out to find my wife. I hoped.

I gave Steve the run down of what I knew. He was, as he always is, supportive and compassionate. We prayed together and he made some calls to some of the Deacons and Elders. I'm sure that he was setting up a support group to help throughout this crisis. About two hours after Steve arrived, he prepared to leave. As he made his way to the door, he asked me a question that startled me.

"Jason, did you tell the police about the man that you were talking with on your computer? Did they think anything of it?"

I hadn't even connected the dots. I hadn't put the two together until Steve asked that question. "No." I responded. It was all I could think of to say.

"No? But Jason, these two incidents could be connected. All of a sudden this man emails you and says strange things, tells you he knows all about you and your family, and within twenty-four hours your wife is missing? This might not be a coincidence, Jason. You have to tell the police. You have to give them a fighting chance. Maybe this is a standard method used by some weirdo that the police know. You have to tell them."

"You're right Steve. I didn't put the two together until you just mentioned it. I never even thought about that guy on the net. Oh God, Steve, you don't think this guy is some kind of sicko do you?"

"Jason, don't panic. We are going to find Sarah. We will bring her home. Well, more specifically, God will; but you have to give the police all the ammunition possible. Don't tie one arm behind their backs, Jason. It may be nothing. The two things may not be connected, but they should know. If they are not connected, no harm no foul; but if they are, it could make the difference. It could give them the lead they need to ensure that Sarah gets home safe and sound."

"I'll call them as soon as you leave, Steve. Thanks so much for coming over and helping me think this thing through. I might have put these two things together at some point, but I'm just so upset. I'm not thinking straight. I appreciate your helping me get back on track. I will call the police right away. I'll let you know what I have heard first thing in the morning."

"Okay, Jason. Don't be afraid to call at anytime, day or night, if you need anything. You know, like someone to watch the kids or just someone to talk to. Don't worry about fixing any meals right now either. A few of the church leaders are calling some of the families to help meet those needs too. Try not to worry about a thing. Just stay close to God, and he will stay close to you. I know we will find her. I know she is okay, Jason. You keep that faith too."

"I will, Steve. I will. God is all I have right now. Tell everyone that I appreciate their efforts, and I'll keep you posted on any progress. Good night, Steve."

"Night, Jason. We'll all be praying for you and Sarah."

With that he left. I was alone again. The house was quiet. What do I do now? My mind began to race. Could the guy on the computer be behind this? Could he be hurting Sarah? I found myself getting tense and welling up with tears again. The guy on the computer! I've got to see if he's there now. I have to find out if he knows anything. I practically ran down the hall to my office and hit the on power button on my computer. "God, let her be okay. Help me find her," I mouth as I waited for the computer to boot up. To the chat rooms I go, in search of "Truth."

Chapter Six

S arah was cold and shivering. She knew she was in the trunk of a car, but the car wasn't moving. She had no idea how long she had been there or if the car had ever moved. Sarah was alone and scared. She had been on her way to get her children, to celebrate her promotion at work, and to take Jason to dinner. "Jason, where are you?" She cried silently.

"Everything is so fuzzy," she thought. She needed to regain her focus, to get her wits back, and to figure out where she was and how she could get out of here. "What happened? How did I get here? Am I hurt? Who is doing this to me and why?" Sarah remained very quiet, trying hard not to make a sound. She still felt very groggy. She realized that they must have given her some kind of drug to reduce or eliminate any resistance. She didn't want them to know she was awake. Who knows what they would do then. She needed time to think; time to gain control of her thoughts and control of her body.

Sarah had no idea what time it was or where she was. It was very dark and quiet. No traffic sounds at all. She couldn't hear or see anything to help her determine where she was. "If I can't figure out where I am, I should try and remember how I got here," she thought. "Let's see. I left Jason and drove down Sycamore like I always do. I pulled up to the light at Kennedy Blvd. and noticed the man in the red SUV staring at me in the next lane. I smiled at him and pulled away from the light when it turned green. The popping sound of my tire came immediately and I pulled over to the side to see what was wrong. I already knew it was a blown tire, but I went through the motions of getting out and looking anyway. That's right!" She thought, "I got out of my car and walked back to look at the rear tire on the driver's side. It was flat. I turned to walk back to the car to get my phone when I was grabbed from behind and someone put something over my face." She remembered fighting and struggling a little, but she couldn't see and had been totally surprised. She was being held from behind and her face had been covered with some type of mask or shroud. She remembered beginning to lose consciousness, fighting to keep her eyes open. She recalled the feeling of panic yet at the same time an over-whelming desire to lie down. "They drugged me. I know they had to of drugged me. But who? Why? What did they want? Was it the man in the red SUV? I never saw him drive by after I stopped, but I couldn't swear he hadn't either." It was more than one person though. She knew that. She remem-bered hearing multiple footsteps as she struggled. She remembered growing weak and limp in their arms. "How could they have done all of that right there on Sycamore in full daylight? Why didn't anyone see them; stop them? What were they going to do? Would they hurt me? Ransom me? Rape me? Kill me?" Sarah felt panic raising up in her as she thought through the details of her kidnapping, but it shed lit-tle light on who did this to her and why.

"Jason, where are you?" She whispered. "Come find me, save me, take me home."

"I have to think about every sight, smell, and sound: every detail I can think of. What did the guy in the SUV look like anyway? He was about thirty, brown hair, brown mus-tache, no glasses. There was no one in the passenger side. Where did the second person come from? Was the man in the SUV even involved, or did he drive by when I was pre-occupied with my flat tire? Maybe the SUV wasn't even involved? Oh, God, I don't know anything. Maybe, I'm just going to lay here and freeze to death. Maybe the car is abandoned somewhere and I should try to get out. Why me? Who am I? I'm no spy. We don't have a lot of money or influence. What could they possibly want with me?" Sarah got scared and started to think that maybe they had already hurt her or done something to her. Could they have just abandoned her in the trunk of her own car? She tried to sense her body with her mind, as she was unable to move to determine if any injuries existed. Sarah wanted to find out if she was alright. Her hands were tied behind her back, but her feet were free. She didn't seem to have any pain, except for aches associated with lying tied up in the trunk of a car. Her clothes felt like they were on, although she couldn't see. She realized that she still had the shroud or mask over her head. "How long had I been out? Was it daylight outside, or night?" She realized that the mask she had over her head was distorting her ability to determine much of anything. She didn't feel like she had been abused or mistreated. Not yet anyway. "So why? Why put a hood over my head and throw me in the trunk of a car and then leave me out here to die?"

Dread suddenly engulfed her. Sarah started to cry again. She was alone and cold. She had never felt so alone. She was afraid of what had happened, of what was going to happen. Totally disoriented, she felt abandoned. No one knew where she was. "Was anyone searching for her? Was Jason looking, trying to find me?" she wondered. "No one knows where I am or where to look. Oh, God, help me!" With that her crying became sobs. She began to pray through her sobs. "Oh, God, I don't understand this, but you do. Please help me get out of here and back home to my family. Help me escape my captors, Lord. Help me destroy their plot whatever it is." She continued crying and praying until she heard someone near the back end of the car. Should she make noise and call for help, or lie silently and pretend she is still sleeping? What if it were her captors? What if it was a possible rescuer? Before she could come to grips with her next move, she heard a key go in the lock and the trunk lid popped open.

No light rushed in but the cold did. Sarah believed that it was still night and that two people were standing there, but nothing was spoken. She could feel it more than hear it. Someone scooped her up in their arms and pulled her from the trunk as though she were weightless. Was he the rescuer, the Angel sent from God? As she lay motionless in the stranger's arms, she could hear him walking over gravel as he plodded on. She heard the car's trunk close behind them. "I knew there were two of you." she thought quietly.

Sarah grew more and more concerned as they walked. They seemed to walk for a long time. No words were spoken. This man didn't try to revive her or make sure she was okay. He didn't call out for an ambulance or try to resuscitate her. This wasn't the behavior of a rescuer. He knew her condition. He knew what was wrong with her. He wasn't carrying her to a nearby house or safe place either, only the sound of gravel under his feet. It seemed to be getting cooler, and the smell of pine made her think that they were going into the woods. "Oh, Lord, are they going to kill me and bury me out here?"

Sarah felt she had been quiet long enough. There seemed no point in continuing this charade. If they were going to kill her or hurt her, they would have to do it knowing she was awake. She began to move, but his iron vise grip tightened and held her. He walked on. No words, nothing, just gravel.

"Who are you? Why are you doing this to me?"

Nothing. Only silence and walking on gravel....

"I don't have any money. Please don't hurt me. Will you please tell me who you are? Why you are doing this?"

Silence was the only response.

Sarah didn't have the strength to fight or to force him to put her down. He would not talk to her and seemed tireless in his efforts to carry her wherever they were going. He couldn't go forever though. "I'm not heavy," she thought, "but I do weigh enough that he will grow weary before too long. He will have to put me down, and when he does, I will run, run with all my strength, run for my life!"

"Jason, Oh God, Jason, save me......Take me home!"

Chapter Seven

The computer seemed slow in booting up. It always seems slow when you're in a hurry. I finally get on and head right to the chat rooms where I originally found "In Search of Truth." I started looking where I thought his site was located, but I really couldn't remember exactly. I was just surfing when I originally found it, so I had to surf all of the sites all over again to try and find it. It seemed to take an excruciating amount of time before I finally spotted his chat room. There it was, "Looking for Christians." I could see that the site only showed one person in the room, so it had to be him. I clicked on the link and it took me to the chat room. When I got there, the screen said that the host was away. "What did that mean? Where was he? When would he be back? How long should I sit around waiting?" I typed in a note anyway. "Where are you? I need to talk to you!" I waited for a response. None came. I sat and waited for almost thirty minutes. No response.

The phone rang and I jumped about two feet in the air. I hadn't realized it, but I had been pacing back and forth in front of the computer watching the screen. The phone rang again and I grabbed it. "Hello?"

"Mr. Shepard? This is Officer Lancing."

"Do you know something? Have you found her?"

"No, not yet, Mr. Shepard. I need to talk to you."

"Officer Lancing, I'm here, you can talk to me anytime

you want."

"Well, I know it's late but it is important."

"Do you really think I'm going to sleep anyway? Nothing is more important than finding my wife. If talking to me again will help you accomplish that, then let's talk."

"I need to talk to you in person. I can be there in about ten minutes if it's okay with you."

"I'll be waiting."

The line went dead and I just stood there wondering what was going on. What did he need to talk to me about that was so important or secretive that he couldn't ask me over the phone? Was he coming with Officer Devoy or was this a solo visit? I hoped this wasn't where the television movies began to be more accurate: the good cop, bad cop scenario. God, I miss Sarah. Where could she be? The possible answers to that question are too diverse and scare me. I don't have any idea of what to do while I sit here waiting. I glance back down at the computer screen and realize that I have received an answer from "Truth."

"I expected you here tonight," was all it said.

I typed back in another note. "Are you there now? I need to talk to you."

"I know you do," came his response.

"Where is my wife? What have you done with her?"

"Jason, you're jumping to wild conclusions. I'm afraid I don't know what you're talking about."

"You lie!"

"I hear the emotion in your voice, Jason. It is good to get emotional sometimes. I am glad I have stirred you a little."

"I don't want to hear your philosophical crap! I just want my wife back. I know you are connected to this somehow. Where is she?"

"Now, Jason, a little emotion is good, but you actually used a swear word. Did you know that? Would Jesus be happy with you now?"

"Stop toying with me. I want to know if she is alright."

"She is safe."

She is safe? That's all he said, but it showed me that this person did know where my wife was and that he was involved somehow. I wasn't sure what my next move should be. What should I say? How should I deal with him?

"Why have you done this? What do you want?"

"Oh, Jason, again you jump to conclusions. I didn't say I had anything to do with it. I just said that she was safe. She is in good health and safe. You need not worry."

"How do you know, if you aren't involved? Why would anyone take my wife? What is this all about? How can you tell me not to worry? She's not your wife!"

"I just know things......I am who I am. As for why, she is a lovely lady, Jason. Maybe the reasons are just pure animal instinct. Maybe this happened for just the basic barbaric needs. She is lovely, Jason."

"You touch her or let anyone else touch her and I will kill you. I hope you understand that."

"I was kind of waiting for that emotional threat. It had to come sooner or later. Do not threaten me, Jason. Fear me. Fear me if you know what is good for you. If you want your wife back safe and intact, fear me. Don't tell me what to do or threaten me, Jason. I will accept it this time because you are in shock, but future outbursts of this type will cost you. Let us have a clear understanding of our relationship."

I was stunned by his message. I did fear him. I didn't know who or what he was, but he had entered my life about twenty-four hours ago and turned it upside down. Now he had my wife and I had no power. I had no answer. I just sat and stared at the screen.

"That's better, Jason. Calm down. Your emotions will get the best of you if you let them, and no battle was ever won using emotion. I am emotionless, Jason. I understand your emotion, but I do not respect it. I do not like it. I control all things including emotion."

I just sat deflated. No response at the tip of my tongue. Nothing to say. How do I respond to this madman?

"Why? Why did you take my wife? What do you want? How do I get her back?"

"All good questions and I will have answers to all of them in due time. Right now, however, I have a task for you. This is very important, Jason, so don't drift off. Don't get distracted. Listen to what I am telling you."

"Distracted? You have my wife. How could I let anything distract me from that?"

"Yes, good point. You have already called the police and reported Sarah missing. This was a wise and prudent thing to do. I also know that officers are coming back to your house right now. DO NOT, I say again, DO NOT tell them about me or our conversations. If you do, it will cost Sarah her life."

I read this over two or three times. He was so calm about taking her life. He just simply said, if I do A, he will do B. If I tell them, he will kill her. That was the gist of his threat. There was nothing flowery or showy just matter-of-fact. He was straight forward and to the point.

"I don't know why they are coming back here. The officer said he wanted to talk to me."

"They always want to talk more, but this topic is off limits. Do you understand that?"

"Yes." I typed, I couldn't think of anything else to say.

"Jason, remember who I am. I will know. I knew they were coming over didn't I? I am everywhere! You cannot hide things from me! You have a decision to make. It is yours to make and to live with. May your Jesus help you make the right one."

"What should I say to them?"

"Tell them anything you want but nothing about our chats or about me. That would result in a death sentence, which is totally unnecessary, Jason. Sarah can come back to you unharmed and your life can go on as normal; or you can make some bad decisions, and your whole world will come apart. Your choice."

"I won't say anything, but what do I do to get her back?"

"Be patient, Jason. I know you won't go to work tomorrow. Who would under these circumstances? Be here tomorrow at 9am sharp for further updates. By then I will know what you told the police, and we can talk about your next steps. We must stop now, Jason. Your visitor is almost there. Handle it right and you will be rewarded."

"I just want my wife back."

"I know, Jason. I know. We will get there. For now, know she is safe and unharmed. No one will hurt her or touch her. I can control destiny, Jason. I can get your wife back, but you must follow my directions explicitly. No wiggle room. No room for error."

"I will do as you say. I will be here tomorrow at nine."

"Good boy. Now go to your door. The police should be there any second. We will talk tomorrow."

With that the host was gone from the conversation. He signed off and was gone. I had a thousand questions and no one to talk to. I was scared, mad, and helpless. I didn't know what to do.

The doorbell rang and again I jumped. He even knew the time that the police would arrive. How could he know so much? Who is he? Does he control everything that he says he does? He did fear the police though. If he didn't, why would he be afraid that I would tell them about him? If he feared the police, he couldn't be more than just an ordinary man. Or maybe it isn't fear. Maybe it is a test for me. I don't know who "Truth" is, but I am determined to find out and to save my wife. I have no idea why I was chosen for this, but God promises to only allow all of us to be tempted to a point that we can bear. "I think I am at my limit, God!" I think I have reached a point that God will have to help me. I want my wife back, and I know that I will do anything to bring her home. "God," I pray out loud. "Give me strength, Lord, and forgive me for my thoughts and anger. I need Sarah, Lord, and I will do anything I can to find her. Please, help me. Guide my steps."

With that the doorbell rang again and I jumped up and went to the door. I didn't know what I would say or what the police wanted, but I knew I couldn't tell them about "Truth." I knew that I was not ready to confide in the police about this man even though I knew he was behind her disappearance. He had my wife, and he had threatened to kill her. I had to fight this battle alone. Well, God and I had to fight this battle. "God and I," I thought. "Who can stand against us? Together Jesus and I will find my wife. Together we can defeat this evil. Together we can accomplish anything. We will find out who is behind this." I mouthed these words of confidence as I opened the door.

"Officer Lancing, come in."

Chapter Eight

Officer Lancing walked through the door without a hello and no acknowledgement of any kind. It seemed obvious to me that he had something on his mind and his thoughts were not allowing the normal courtesies to get in the way.

"Do you want to sit down?" I offered.

"No thank you, Mr. Shepard. I'm here with a couple of very specific questions, and I don't know any other way to approach them than to be direct and forthright about it. I hope you don't mind, but I need some information and I need it fast."

"I will share anything I can with you. What do you need to know? You don't have to beat around the bush with me. I want to do anything that will help you find Sarah."

"Mr. Shepard, have you been contacted by anyone recently? Contacted by someone that asks you unusual questions or challenges your religious beliefs? It could be someone who would most certainly remain anonymous and who may have made unusual requests of you?"

My mind went into a panic. It was as though this officer knew about everything. He described my conversations with "Truth" exactly. Well, almost exactly. "Truth" hadn't made any unusual requests of me, yet. He did order me not to talk about him to the police, but that request wasn't all that unusual. The kidnapping suspect doesn't want me to tell the police about him. That doesn't seem so unusual to me.

"No, nothing like that has happened that I can think of. Why?"

It was obvious that he didn't believe me. He had been watching me intently and my delay in answering and my inability to look him straight in the eye had given me away. Maybe it had, but I will not jeopardize my wife's safety by admitting anything now.

"Think harder, Mr. Shepard. Take your time. This person might have contacted you by phone or email or fax. You won't know who it is, but the questions or requests will be unusual enough that you will know who I am talking about. Try to think for a minute."

"I don't have to think about it! Nobody has contacted me by any of those methods. No one has asked me any unusual questions or requested me to do anything unusual. What does any of this have to do with my wife? Why are you here alone, Officer Lancing? Where is Officer Devoy? What is this all about?"

I could feel my blood pressure building, and I'm sure it was obvious to him too. It continued to climb because I knew he knew I was lying. Officer Lancing never took his eyes off me. I had no idea what he was thinking, but it is clear that he did not believe me and he was sizing up his next step.

"Mr. Shepard, I am here alone because I am working a separate case that is top secret. Officer Devoy doesn't even know about this other case. I am trying to determine if these two cases could be related, or interconnected somehow. I don't mean to offend or challenge you unnecessarily, but this is very important. It is very important to Sarah, and very important to others that may be impacted by this individual in the future. I don't want you to get upset, and I don't mean to make this night any worse for you than it already is, but I had to ask. I have to turn over every stone to try and find the truth."

The Truth! He even used his name. Did he know that?

Was that a trick to see if it got a reaction out of me? How do I know whether this officer is, in fact, closing in on the man who took my Sarah, or could he be working with "Truth?" What I say tonight may come back to haunt me and be used against me tomorrow when I talk to him on line again. I don't know who to trust. I don't know what truth is anymore. I can't do anything but stick to my story.

"Officer Lancing, I would do anything, give anything to help you find my wife. I don't think I will be able to sleep or eat until I can bring her home and bring her home safe. I just don't know what you are talking about, and I have no information that I can share that relates to what you have told me. I just don't understand, and, frankly, your questions are scaring me. What is this top secret case? How does it relate to me and my family, and what does it mean to the safety of my wife?"

"Mr. Shepard, I can't tell you anything about the case I am working, and I don't know if they are at all related. You have to understand that this is not a large community. A kidnapping or missing person is a big crime here, and I am working a separate crime of equal importance at the same time. It would be a big mistake not to take the time to see if there is any correlation. I don't mean to scare you, and I am sorry for coming over here so late, but I felt it was important enough to justify the inconvenience."

"Quit apologizing. I don't care if it's late or how often you think of things you want to talk to me about. I just want to find Sarah. I just want to bring her home. I can't help you tonight. I don't know anything about what you are asking. I have no information to give you. Something is wrong, and my wife is in the middle of it. I want to know what is going on as much as you, but you have an advantage. You know about this other case and I don't. I will have to defer to your expertise to determine if they are connected, because I have nothing I can add."

Officer Lancing was watching me again. He just stared at me. He was communicating without words that he did not believe me and that he would not give up his quest. He had to have seen the fear in my eyes. We were too close to information that I couldn't share. He knew I had something to tell him, but I think he also knew that I was not going to share anything tonight. He finally dropped his eyes and looked around the room. I followed his eyes, and realized that he could see the glow of my computer on in the other room as the lights in most of the house were dimmed.

"Were you on your computer, Mr. Shepard?"

"Yes, I just got on to check my email. I don't know. It probably sounds stupid, but I thought maybe she might email me something."

"It doesn't sound stupid at all. Was anything there?"

"No, of course not! Don't you think that I would have shared it with you if there was?"

I realized that I had raised my voice and probably came off sounding angry to Officer Lancing.

"Of course you would. I'm sorry if I upset you. I know you want to help your wife, and I know you want to get her home. You and I have the same goal there. Mr. Shepard, I believe that there may be some connection in all of this. I believe that your wife was taken and is being held because they want something from you. I can't prove that yet, and I can't identify who they are or what they want, but I believe it in my bones. If you haven't heard from them, I believe you will. I want you to contact me if and when you do. Is that clear, Mr. Shepard? Contact me directly."

He handed me a card with his name and number on it. On the back his home number was written down as well.

"Mr. Shepard, I have one other request that is of equal importance."

"Yes?"

"I don't want you to talk to anyone about my visit. Do

you understand what I mean when I say anyone? I mean not your friends or police. Not even Officer Devoy."

"I don't get it. I'm not supposed to talk about this with the police either? What if I can't find you? Who do I call? This all seems so cloak and dagger to me. Please, tell me what is going on."

"Mr. Shepard, you will be contacted by other officers about your wife. Detectives, maybe even the FBI. You should share everything you can with them. You need to help them as well. There is another investigation that I am conducting that they are not on, however. If I find that it is connected with your wife's case, then I will call in the cavalry; but I do not want them running around mixing up these two cases until I am sure that they are, in fact, related. If they are not, it would take valuable time off the right track in finding Sarah. If they are somehow related, I will find the connection and we will use what I find to get her back. I know this is unusual and I know it is a bit scary, but I have to ask you to keep this visit to yourself. If you think of someone or something that might be of interest to me, call me. Don't be afraid to call me day or night. If you get contacted by anyone after my visit that you think is unusual or odd, call me. Even if the contact doesn't appear related to your missing wife, call me. I would prefer more information than less right now. Let me decipher what is important and what isn't. Do you understand, Mr. Shepard? I know this is unusual, but it is important. I can't tell you how important."

"I understand." That was about all I could say. I was between a rock and a hard place and both ends were moving towards me. I had "Truth" on one side with strange questions and secrets, and it was obvious he wanted something. Most importantly, he had my wife. On the other, I now had Officer Lancing, who had his own secrets and seemed intent on finding my wife and finding the "Truth" at all costs. I wasn't supposed to talk to anyone, and I couldn't trust anyone. I felt like

I was melting under the pressure. I was growing so tired.

"Good night Mr. Shepard," I heard Officer Lancing say from a distance. I looked up and realized that he had walked off and made his way to the front door. I had just stood there with my head down, and didn't even know he had moved.

"Good night, sir. Please find her. Please bring her back. She is everything to me. She's my life."

"I promise to do everything in my power. The more information I can gather, the better chance I'll have. Time is of the essence, Mr. Shepard. Call me the minute anything pops into your head."

With that he just walked down the steps and to his car. He didn't wait for a response, and apparently did not expect one. "Time is of the essence," was all he said. He knows I know something, and he is trying to tell me that the longer I hold back, the more dangerous it becomes. What am I supposed to do? Do I trust him? Is "Truth" more than a man therefore knows the minute I tell anybody? Will he really kill Sarah? Are my children in danger? What should I do? I feel empty of all strength. All these questions run around in my head, but only one answer to any of them is clear. He would kill Sarah. He could do it with no emotion. He would do it just to prove a point. He wanted something, but I had no idea what. I couldn't risk my wife's life. I would have to keep this to myself for now, but I knew that I could not stand the pressure long. I was on pins and needles and yet I was exhausted. I could hardly keep my eyes open, yet thousands of questions filled my brain.

I watched as Lancing drove away and then began to shut the door to lock up. Before I closed it all the way, I looked across the street at Ralph and Carol's. It looked peaceful and quiet. The kids must be deep in sleep by now. It was great to have friends like that to help you through the tough times. The kids probably didn't even know that anything was wrong. I began to fully close the door when I spotted movement across the street. I watched intently. Yes, there it was again in the shadows along the fence! There was someone hiding near Ralph's backyard fence. I shut the door and ran to the living room window to see if I could spot them again to track their movement. Were my children in danger? Could these people be coming for them? I grabbed the cordless phone and opened the corner of the drapes to peek across the street. I was dialing the police when the shadow moved again.

The shadow moved slowly towards the front yard and into the light. Ralph came out of the shadows and stood by his driveway. He was the shadow I saw. He was the man hiding and watching. What was he doing? What was he watching my house for? Could he have been worried and just keeping an eye out for me? Was he worried about the children? I watched him for only a few more seconds as he slowly drifted back into the shadows. I watched as he went into his backyard through the side gate. He was gone. I hung up the phone.

What is going on? Who can I trust? Am I just being paranoid? I need sleep, but I cannot close my eyes. I fall back on the sofa. I will stay here near the door, near the phone, near the children. I have nowhere else to go. Sleep came fast and furious. I wouldn't have believed I could sleep at all, but the stress forced it over me. I had no choice. There was no fighting it. I was down for the count.

Chapter Nine

Sarah lay on a hard mattress that felt like a cot or makeshift bed. She remained with her face covered and her hands tied. No one tried to hurt her, but no one talked to her either. She could hear others, but she heard no words spoken, just the rustle of movement from time to time. Sarah didn't know how many people there were, but it was definitely more than one. She was quite sure of that. What did they want with her? They didn't talk to her, they didn't ask any questions, but they weren't mean either. No pain. No abuse. They just seemed to move her around and handle her like a sack of flour. No emotion, no discussions, just matter of fact.

Sarah's mood changed constantly. Sometimes she felt angry and wanted to yell and scream at her capturers, whoever they were. Then she would just break down in tears, sobbing uncontrollably. That in itself would make her mad, as she hated letting these people know she was terrified. The fact is, however, she was terrified. She had no idea why she was here, no one to ask, no verbal contact at all. Sarah was exhausted but couldn't relax enough to fall asleep. Her hands ached from being tied behind her back for so long. She felt numb. Claustrophobia was another emotion that she was fighting. The hood over her face, her hands tied, having no idea where she was or who was handling her. It added to the terror, and she thought they knew it. She somehow felt these people were doing exactly what they wanted to do with her. She didn't believe that they intended to hurt her, at least not yet, and not in the way that many women fear. She felt that they were after something, and she was a pawn in a much bigger game. A serious and deadly game. She wasn't sure how she knew that, but Sarah felt it in her deep inside.

Listening intently she thought she heard a car pull up outside. Was it really a car? It sounded to her like a car that was driving across gravel; but if the driveway came all the way up to the house, why did they carry her on foot for so long when they first arrived? She heard it for sure that time! A car door closing and then another one! Footsteps walked in the gravel and then silence. Where did they go? She didn't hear the door open or any movement from inside the house. Where did the noise come from and where did the people go? Suddenly she heard another car. What was going on? Maybe she wasn't in a house. Maybe she was someplace more public. Someplace where people came and went. It had to be in the woods somewhere. She recognized the smell of pine when she was being carried up to the house. She knew they walked on gravel when they carried her up here, and she knew that the cars she was hearing tonight were driving on gravel as well. Where could she be? Is it possible that this could be a motel in the mountains or a room or apartment above some type of business? She listened more. Listening gave her a mission, and it diverted her thoughts away from her dilemma and her pain.

Sarah was able to determine that she was on the ground floor and not above a business. The cars that drove up were close. She could hear the tires press into the gravel, throwing rocks up against the fender wells. She was confident that she would not have been able to hear this if she was on the second floor. Well, now that she knew this fact, what good did it do her? What would she use this choice piece of evidence for? Sarah broke down in tears again and cried. She cried softly, whispering Jason's name.

Sarah felt someone tugging on her and pulling her over on the mattress. It startled her and she realized that she must have cried herself to sleep. She didn't feel as though she had drifted off for too long, however, but her focus now was on the person that was moving her around.

"Please, won't you talk to me? I just want to know what's going on. Why am I here?"

No answer just silence. This was maddening! The man was right here. She could feel the strength of his grip. He did not manhandle her, but he was firm with her. He left no question in her mind as to who was in charge. He checked her hands and hood to make sure that she was still intact.

"Please, I don't have much money, but you can have it all. Please let me go. Let me go home."

"You will go home soon enough if your husband does what he is told, exactly what he is told!"

This voice came from across the room. It did not come from the man that was checking her hands and rolling her over on the bed. Hearing the voice almost startled her as it had been hours since she had heard the sound of human conversation, and this person was actually addressing her. The voice was deep. Sarah didn't know what she was hoping for, but she was trying to grapple with a description of the voice. There was no accent. It was not peculiar. It was deep, forceful, and it scared her.

"Oh please, can you untie my hands? My arms are going numb. I will be quiet. I promise. I won't do anything. Please, I just can't keep them behind my back much longer. Please?"

Nothing was said. More silence. Something was happening though. Apparently some silent order was given, as the man that had been near her began to untie her hands. Sarah began to feel excitement, and the anticipation of having her hands free seemed to make the minutes and seconds click by more slowly. She felt the pain more. The aching in her joints became more intense. She felt like she would burst out crying any minute. She knew her emotions were running out of control.

"Thank you. Thank you! I will be good." That was about all Sarah could think to say. She felt like a little child talking to her parents. She knew in the back of her mind that this was their intent. This is exactly the way they wanted her to feel. She wouldn't let them down. If they wanted her to beg, plead, and act submissive; they would get it. All Sarah wanted right now was for her hands to be free.

Before the man let go of her wrists, the voice near the door came again.

"Do not move off your bed. Do not touch the mask on your face. Do not cry out. Be a good girl and you can keep your hands untied. Be a bad girl, and you will suffer far more painful things. They are not necessary, but they will happen if you do not keep your word. Do you understand?"

"Yes, yes I understand. I will be good. Please let my hands go."

With that the man on the bed released her hands. He stayed right there next to her. Sarah assumed that he was standing ready to see if she would try something, anything that would force him to have to become physical with her. She wasn't going to do anything. Her hands were free, and Sarah was rejoicing in that milestone right now. She rubbed her hands and shoulders, but she was careful not to get her hands close to her face or to move them in anyway that these men might interpret incorrectly. Right now she was happy. She had a victory, and down deep inside she was celebrating.

Silence filled the room again. She knew that three grown adults were all sitting or standing within four or five feet of each other, but no words were spoken. She sat silently for a few minutes enjoying the return of blood flow to her hands and arms, but she couldn't remain silent.

"Would it be possible to take this hood off my face? I would love to be able to breathe more comfortably. I will be good, I promise."

"That is the problem. When you give children an inch, they want a foot and so on and so on." These words of wisdom came from the man near the bed. He had a higher pitched voice. Sarah believed he had to be younger than the first man? He was not uneducated, but he was no philosopher either.

"Enjoy what you have been given and do not ask for more." This came from the dominant man across the room. He was dominant alright, and the second man near her was subservient to him. She could hear it in their voices, and she could sense it in the room. There was no doubt about who was in control, and she felt that the younger man was probably in a bit of trouble for speaking out at all, especially with her in the room.

"I'm sorry, I just wanted to breathe. Can you tell me why I am here? Why you are holding me?"

"All things will be told to you in due time. Not now. You should do your best to lie down and try to get some rest. Daylight will be here in a few hours, and we will have a very busy day ahead of us. You would be better suited if you were rested."

"Thank you. I will do my best, but I'm sure you understand that my head is full of questions, and my nerves are shot. Sleep, albeit an exciting vision seems unlikely at this point."

"Do as you see fit. But remember, not a foot off that bed, not one hand to your mask, and no sound from you at all. We will know, we will hear you, and you will never be able to fix the mask back to how we have it. We will know. Just as we have been kind to you now, we can be equally harsh. You are in control of that. I will tell you that when we are given orders to move, we will move fast. Sleep would be helpful if

71

you can achieve it. If you cannot, we will move fast anyway."

This was the longest dialogue that Sarah had gotten out of anyone to this point. Sarah knew that it was still early morning. The man had said that daylight would come in a "few hours." She also was able to determine that this man, although dominant here, he was not the man in charge. He was given orders, and he carried them out. Something was going to be happening soon too. She was probably going to be moved around a lot. They were on the run, and they would not stay in one place very long.

The man moved away from the bed and seemed to move towards the voice across the room. Sarah lay down on the bed and enjoyed the freedom of her untied hands. She heard them both leave, but she assumed that the door was left open, if there was a door. She heard no sound of wood or metal latches that might indicate she was being locked in. She was exhausted, but right now she found happiness because her hands were free and she felt like she was safe. She was confident that for right now neither of these men had the authority to hurt her, and they seemed disciplined. They knew where their orders came from, and she didn't believe that she needed to fear any rogue intentions from these two.

One last thought came into Sarah's mind as the new found freedom and the realization of safety brought sleep. She couldn't be far from home. She had been taken right after leaving her house to pick up the kids. Taken? Captured? Stolen? What was the right thing to call it? She was driven directly to this location: she knew of no other stops along the way. She had been carried up here and put into this room several hours ago. The voice had said that it was a few hours until daylight, so it must be around three or four in the morning. Where could she be? Where could she find pine trees and mountain smells only hours from her home?

Sarah could fight exhaustion no more. She drifted off to

sleep with a new found hope that she could get out of this alive. She was not sure why she felt that way, but she wasn't going to analyze it. She was just going to go with it........Sleep stole her away. She had no strength left to resist.

Chapter Ten

Officer Lancing sat at his desk. He should have been home hours ago, but he had to stay and think through this new chain of events. He knew that this Shepard case was related to the other file that he still had open. He didn't have anything tangible yet, but he knew they were tied together somehow. It was very late, and the department was only maintained by a skeleton graveyard crew. He knew they were probably all wondering what he was doing here, and it would be better right now if he didn't attract any undue attention. He knew he should go home, but he just couldn't seem to push back from the desk. Jason Shepard was lying. There was no question about that. His tone of voice, body language and inappropriate pauses said so. He had been contacted by someone. Officer Lancing knew this like he knew his own name. He didn't need evidence. He just needed the intuition that he had built up after serving twenty five years as a Police Officer: fifteen years in Los Angeles and ten more here. He had come up here to escape the politics and the big city blues. Shortly after he arrived, he found that L.A. had nothing on this little resort town, and politics were alive and well here too.

"Something I can help you with, Ed?"

Lancing looked up to see Laura Brown the graveyard communications supervisor. She was in charge of the dispatch center and, in fact, ran the whole place after hours. Oh, there were officers around and a Watch Commander, but Laura kept everything running smoothly. She had been on the department for a long time: longer than Lancing knew. Many years ago she had been married to an officer who had been killed by a hit and run driver while on a traffic stop. She was never the same. She buried herself in her work and became everyone's mother. She worried about all of us, and she kept us all in line as well. "Keep the office clean, turn out the lights when you are done, put the toilet seat down." She was on top of everything.

"Hi, Laura. How are you tonight?"

"Well, I'm doing fine, but what's up with you? Your shift ended about four hours ago, but you're still here? Working on something exciting? Need to bounce something off me? Did you have a fight with Marion, and now you don't want to go home? What's up?"

"Yeah, I know. I need to get out of here. Just got a new case today and I can't seem to let it go. I know the detectives will pick it up in the morning, but I just keep thinking I should be doing something more tonight." You're right, though. I'm beat and I need to get home."

"Ed, you have been working at an unbelievable pace since you got busted back to patrol. Sorry, maybe I should have said transferred. Anyway, you have just never let up. You work every case like it's the most important one in the world, and you go way beyond a patrolman's responsibilities. You chase these cases way beyond your scope, and you do most of the detective work too. I hope you don't mind me saying so, but everybody sees it. Everybody talks about it. What drives you? What are you looking for?"

"Laura, it's late, and I should get out of here. When I'm tired, I say things I shouldn't." Lancing paused and then decided to continue. "I'm looking for justice, Laura. I was busted back to patrol just as you said. I didn't like the way they were working a case, and they didn't like the way I wanted to work it, so they put me back in patrol. Well, I decided right then and there that I just needed to work hard in search of what I call justice. I couldn't assume that anybody else was going to button up a good case or turn over that extra rock on a bad one. I just needed to stay on top of all of them. If that's the wrong way to look at it, then so be it. It's my way."

"You're preaching to the choir, Ed. I'm not busting your chops here. I'm just talking to you as a friend. I'm worried that you will burn out and that I won't have you to kick around anymore. Don't read into what I'm saying. I just worry about you. I can tell that you aren't going to get much sleep tonight either."

"Well, I won't if I stay here yammering with you. I'm out of here, Laura. I appreciate you coming in here to check on me. I would also appreciate it if you didn't spread it around that I was here all night either. I don't want the execs to think I'm losing it."

"Your secret is safe with me. I hope you get some rest. You know you can count on me if there is anything I can do to help you find any of that justice you are in search of. Call me if you need me."

Lancing wasn't sure what Laura meant by that. Was that an offer to do some behind the scenes record checks and suspect searches for him? Was she being flirtatious and offering him a reason to call her at home? Was she just trying to drag more out of him on what he was working on? He knew he was tired, and he knew his questions proved it. Laura was a straight shooter and a good friend. The fact that he was having these kinds of questions popping up because of a simple remark told him that he was delusional and badly in need of sleep.

"Thanks, Laura. You know I appreciate you and all you do. If I need you or can think of a way you can help me, I won't hesitate to call. Right now I think you pegged it. I'm beat and in serious need of sleep. Marion may be calling you soon to find out where I'm at so I may need your help with some marriage counseling before the night's done."

Both Laura and Ed chuckled as he picked up his gear and began shutting down the computer and lights. She walked with him to the dispatch center where she turned and went in without further conversation. He turned and walked the other way to get out to the parking lot and then he headed for home.

Something was going on in this sleepy little town that wasn't so sleepy. People had been murdered, people had been kidnapped, people were lying; and what ever it was, it was being over looked by many in the know. Lancing had lost his detective's badge over a case like this. He believed that the case he was holding open, when everyone else wanted it closed, was related to the Shepard family kidnapping. Lancing felt that if he didn't do more, if he didn't figure this out, this case would end like the one he was still holding on to. A murder would occur, the evidence would disappear, the witnesses would drift away, and it would go unsolved. There was something horribly wrong: something that connected these two cases. Lancing had to discover the connection. He had to find out what was going on or go crazy trying.

He reached his car, inserted his key in the door. He found it was already unlocked. This was wrong. Lancing never left his door unlocked. He was a creature of habit. There is no way he left this car here with the door unlocked. He slowly backed away and pulled his S/W 9 millimeter from his hip holster. This parking lot was for police personnel only, but it was not a secure lot. Anyone could come on to the lot; and if they went unseen, they could do anything they wanted to these cars. We have even had cars stolen from this same lot. Although the Police Union had put it in our recent contract negotiations to secure the lot, it eventually got dropped for more money or better benefits. Lancing scanned the car inside and out and saw nothing amiss at first glance. It was clear that no one was currently in the car. He then scanned the parking lot to make sure that he was not being watched and that no one was going to try and attack him when he returned his focus to the car. No one was in the parking lot that he could see; and because his car had been there most of the day, many of the other cars were spread around the parking lot leaving his car almost alone in this section. Not many cars were in the lot anyway at this time of the night. He looked in the car and saw the glove box open. He never stored anything in there of any value. If this was just a typical theft, the thief would have been disappointed. Lancing walked around the car to see if the hood was open or the trunk ajar. Nothing. Then he spotted a note on the window. He walked over cautiously and plucked it from under the driver's side wiper blade. It was folded in two. Lancing opened it slowly. Not because he thought it contained anything harmful, but because he was still trying to put this all together in his head. Car's open, no signs of force. Glove box is open, no signs of theft. Just this note............

Some things are best left buried. Some things are best left alone. Your fate remains in your hands, Officer Lancing; but as you can see, you are not "untouchable."

Someone already knew that he had connected these two cases, and they were sending him a message. Not even twenty-four hours had gone by since the Shepard woman was taken, and Lancing had just started putting things together. They already knew and wanted to scare him away. They wanted to send him a message. They had accomplished that.

"You scared me. You scare the hell out of me, but you won't scare me away." Lancing whispered under his breath.

He grabbed the note, jumped in the car, shoved his key in the ignition and turned it over. He had no fear of a bomb or any more reprisals. They wouldn't send him a warning note and then hurt him all in the same move. If they wanted to hurt him, they would have just done it with no note, no ceremony. They were sending him a message, a very specific and pointed message. Lancing got it. He understood the message, but he wouldn't just walk away from this case. He left Joe Deener's case unsolved when he was thrown out of the detective bureau, but he had never let it die. He kept copies of all the files and all the evidence. He was tracking the killer, and now he knew they knew it. They had the power to get him tossed from the detective bureau, and as a result the case floundered and died when he left. These people were flexing their muscle again and showing that they could do pretty much whatever they wanted to do, even if that meant threatening a police officer with a note like this. They had no fear. They didn't pretend to care. Who were they?

Lancing drove off but watched in his rear view mirror as he went. He knew somewhere back there someone was watching him. He knew that someone had created this computer generated note and put it on his car. They broke into the car just to show that they could. They wanted to show that they could get in the car without a key, and if they could get into the car, they could get into the trunk and the engine compartment as well. They could do all of that, and if they didn't want him to know, he never would. Lancing pulled his car to the side of the road, popped his trunk, and jumped out to make sure nothing was in his trunk. He didn't expect anything to be there and wasn't surprised when everything was normal, but he had to check. His imagination was now running full speed.

"I need to get to Shepard," he whispered to himself. "I need to know what he knows. I will fight back this time. I will not let Sarah Shepard be another Joe Deener." Ed

Lancing would not walk away from this case no matter how dangerous it got. He would not leave Mrs. Shepard out there to suffer as Joe had suffered. He would not let whoever was responsible for these horrible nightmares go unpunished without a fight.

Ed Lancing headed home to check on his wife and to get some rest. He had a lot to do and very little time. He knew his activities would be watched, and right now he couldn't trust anyone. He had to try and do something. He couldn't live with himself if he didn't.

Chapter Eleven

I woke up with a startled feeling. At first I felt like the whole thing had to have been a bad dream, but then I found myself on the couch and realized that it wasn't a dream at all. It was a nightmare. When I first opened my eyes and realized that the nightmare was real, I began to feel guilty that I had fallen asleep at all. I felt like I had let Sarah down. She was out there somewhere with God knows who, and here I was safe and sound in our house sleeping on our sofa. I pulled myself up and looked outside. It was daylight. How long had I slept? I looked across the street to Ralph and Carol's. I saw nothing out of the ordinary this time, but my memory of Ralph's behavior was crystal clear. The questions surfaced again: Was he on my side? Was he one of them? Were my children safe? As I thought through those terrible questions, I again drifted to the question of who "them" was. I mean, why were they interested in my family? How did they seem to know everything about us? Everyone likes to think of themselves as special and important, but in all honesty, I don't know of anything that I have that anyone else might want-except for Sarah and the kids that is. That thought sent a chill down my spine and I convulsed in a sudden shiver.

I got up and went into the kitchen to check the time. It was eight o'clock in the morning. I couldn't believe I had slept that late. I had requested an extended leave from work so I had no meetings to attend and no calls to make, but I never expected to sleep this late. I had to get my thoughts together before I talk with "Truth" at nine. I needed a shower to help clear my head. Before I got to the top of the stairs, I felt a driving urge to seek the Lord's guidance. I reached the landing and went to my knees.

"Lord, I don't understand what lies before me. I don't understand the wickedness of men. Lord, I know that I can overcome this evil with your help. God, be with my wife. Be with her right now, God, and let her know I am praying for her and that I will come and get her. God, give me your help. Give me your guidance. Tell me what to do, Lord. Lead and I will follow. I have no one to trust except you. Please, Father, show me the way."

I rose up waiting to see if the Lord would send a lightening bolt my way, but nothing happened. Pastor Steve always told me that I needed to listen for the "whisper" of God. I was listening. I was listening hard, but I really needed a trumpet blast right now. I needed God to boldly and clearly speak out. I didn't know how to go on without Him.

Feeling rejected and alone, I walked up the remainder of the steps and headed to the master bath. A shower was the only way I knew to clear the fog in my head. I climbed in the shower and began to lose myself in the hot water. My mind kept drifting to Officer Lancing. He was the only one that I had met thus far that seemed to have a clue. He seemed bothered by this case on multiple levels, and he seemed to know what was going on. The question is, did he know what was going on because he was a part of the game, or was he telling the truth? I was so conflicted, so torn! I had no way of knowing which it was, and it was a terrible chance to take with dire consequences if I was wrong. My mind kept drifting to him, though. I would force my thoughts to something else like preparing for my nine o'clock meeting with "Truth." I wouldn't get far into those preparations before

Officer Lancing would force his way back into my mind. Was this a message from God? Was this His "whisper?" Was He trying to tell me that Officer Lancing could help and that I should trust him? What if I was wrong and it wasn't God? What if I was wrong to trust him, and in doing so, I sacrifice Sarah to these crazy fools? "God, you are going to have to be clearer. You are going to have to hit me with a two by four or send an Angel down to tell me what you want me to do. I can't decipher what is coming from you and what is being generated by my own mind. Please, God, reveal yourself to me!"

I finished my shower. Feeling no clearer than I had before, I threw on some clothes and hurried to my computer. I sat staring at it, waiting for a revelation, twenty minutes ahead of schedule. I logged on and went looking for his site. I found it and joined the room. Again the site told me that the host was out. Somehow I knew he would be. I knew he would make me wait. He wanted to exercise his power over me and he probably wanted to show me how disciplined he was. He wanted to show me that he was in control, he was in charge, and that he would communicate with me on his terms. I'm sure he knew I would be early, and if he can see the site from where he is, he is probably taking great delight in knowing I am here. He won't sign on early. He wants me to simmer in my insecurity for a while. I will wait as long as it takes.

I did type in "I'M HERE" just to see if I could initiate a response. Of course, I got none.

At precisely nine the room came alive.

"Good morning, Jason. Were you able to sleep?"

"Can we skip with the phony personal interest questions and jump to why you took my wife?"

"That's what I love about you, Jason; you just go after what you want. We are the same in many ways."

"We are not the same at all! I live to serve others, and I

live for my Lord Jesus Christ! I don't know what you live for, but it's evil. I feel pretty sure about that."

"Well, Jason, if you live to serve, then serving me will come easy. As for your Lord, has he sent you any messages on how to resolve this? Has he enlightened you on why you were chosen and why Sarah is where she is? For that matter, has he shared with you where she is? No? Well then, maybe he doesn't know. Maybe he is not the God you think he is." There was a short pause and then he continued.

"As for evil, Jason, I too serve a higher being: one who does know the truth and power of the one you call God. He knows this God and does not fear him. He is called evil by some, but that is because you have allowed yourself to restrict your thinking to the puritan ways that were handed down to you by your family and their family. My family didn't hand me anything. I took. I found a higher being that allowed me to be who I wanted to be. Are you who you want to be, Jason? Are you happy in your little church going puritan way? Is Sarah really enough for you? There is so much more you know. So much you have not even grasped yet, but I can show you those truths."

"Your truth is evil. It is in conflict with God. If you wanted to teach me your ways, you would not have had to steal my wife to get my attention. You aren't here to be my teacher. You don't care whether I buy into your way of life or even accept who you worship. You want something else. For the life of me, I can't figure out what it is, but I would prefer it if you got to the point of why you sought me and my family out. What do you want and what do I have to do to get my wife back?"

"You are wrong on many counts, Jason, but so be it. You are naïve and you do not understand the higher truth, at least not yet. Maybe through this little ordeal I will be able to prove that I do care about teaching you a new way, and that my leader is far more powerful and honest than your God.

But I understand your concern for your wife, so let me tell you what I can. She rested well last night. She is safe and unharmed. She can stay that way if you do what you are told. I do know that the police visited you again last night and that you were a good boy. You didn't tell them about me. That was smart."

There was another short pause, and then he continued his diatribe. It is as though he was waiting to see if I would interrupt with questions.

"I should go on to tell you that I am privy to more than you can know about the police and what they are up to. They are a funny group. They don't realize that they are chasing a supreme being and that they cannot find what HE chooses to hide. I know Officer Lancing and Devoy are assigned to your case and I also know that they are clueless. I know they want to solve this case, but they don't know where to start. You were very smart not to tell them about me last night. That shows me you can be trusted. I will do my best to resolve this little issue and get you back your little Sarah."

I felt I needed to throw something into the conversation just to break up his monologue, so I asked him a question. "What do I call you? I mean your chat name says "Truth," but since I find that absolutely distasteful, what is your real name? Who are you?"

"You find my name distasteful? I think you find it distasteful because you like to refer to your Christ as "the Way and the Truth." Well, Jason, I don't care what you find distasteful. I am Truth. You will learn to understand it and respect it before we are through. You will learn that I am in control, not your God. I pull the strings, not your Christ. I have the power over life and death. Do you think your Holy Spirit has that power? I will prove that I have more and that I, only I, can lift you from your burden. I, only I, can set your wife free. I, only I, can answer your prayers. Go ahead, Jason. I know you are praying to your God. I encourage you to continue. He won't listen. He won't answer. He is but a false God. I will prove that to you. Once I prove that to you, you will serve me. You will worship me. I can bring your precious little Sarah home. Are you prepared to follow my instructions now, Jason?"

I sat waiting patiently between his responses. His typing took time, and I knew that he was not quick on the key board. I thought he was getting angry with me, and I had to be careful of that. I felt that he might give me something to grab on to if I could keep him chatting, especially if I could keep him bragging about himself. One piece of news that he shared proved to me that he did not know everything that he pretended to know. He was obviously correct about the police coming out last night, but the way he worded his note said to me that he thought Devoy came out with Lancing. I might be wrong, but this was a pretty big mistake. That is if I am right. If Lancing was an insider for this guy, he would have surely shared with him that he had come alone and that I had not shared anything with him about "Truth." I don't think so, though. I think this guy has someone on the inside of the police department alright, but I don't think it's Lancing. Was this God's two by four? Was this His trumpet blast or His whisper? Was He telling me to trust Lancing? The tug of war in my soul raged on. I'm scared that I will make the wrong decision and my wife will suffer for it. If I don't trust Lancing, I may ignore God's whisper and miss His help in getting Sarah back. If I share with Lancing, it could result in Sarah's death.

I shook myself back to the task at hand. "I'm ready for your instructions. I was ready last night, again early this morning, and I'm still ready now. I just want to get my wife back. Nothing else matters."

"Good boy, Jason. Your wife is safe and has not been touched by anyone. I will do my best to keep things that way for you. She must behave though, Jason. If she does not, she will be punished. Her punishment may not please you, but it will definitely please the men watching her. Do you understand, Jason?"

Even though I knew he was trying to push my buttons, I could not control my emotions. "Why are you telling me this? Are you trying to make me mad? Scare me? How can I do anything to control whether my wife does what she is supposed to? I am having a hard enough time controlling myself, much less a wife I have no contact with."

"Good point, Jason. You can't control her, but I want you to know that we can. You know what makes her tick, Jason. If you do anything to cause her to misbehave, her penalty will be unpleasant. Yes, you should be scared. Anger will not benefit you. Know my power, Jason. Not just over your wife and her sexual purity, but over you, your children, and your whole life. I am in control now. I am in control of it all."

I was almost frantic as my mind raced to it's own conclusions. He knew how to use sexual innuendos to force my mind where I didn't want it to go. He wanted to show me humiliation, and that he was in control. Right now he said Sarah was safe. I needed to keep things in that condition for as long as I could. He expanded my fears by bringing up my children. He only referred to them in passing, but he knew how I would react. I needed to get them home; and, if possible, secretly send them off somewhere safe. I didn't know who my friends or enemies were right now. I had to do something quickly to make sure my children were not drawn into this.

"I understand your power. I understand you have my wife and that you can hurt her. I am asking you not to. I am telling you that I will give you whatever you ask so there is no need to hurt her. I just don't know what you want. I don't understand what it is you want me to do.

"Very good, Jason. I am happy that we have an understanding and are communicating so well. You know, Jason, half of the failed marriages and collapsed business deals are a result of poor communication. If we can communicate well, I am confident that this can proceed to a satisfactory conclusion. I will get what I want, you will be enlightened, and Sarah will have found a new peace. You will have her back, Jason. I promise you that."

A coldness crept over me and I knew right then that he had no intention of leaving her unharmed. I didn't know exactly why I knew it, but it was clear in my mind that he would kill her. He might give her back to me but not alive. He intended to get what he wanted from me, enlighten me somehow as he called it, and ultimately kill my wife to prove his power. What he would put her through before that was a horror movie playing over and over in my mind. If I am to beat him and get Sarah back I need to keep playing this game, but I know that I have to cheat. If I do cheat and get caught, he will kill my wife. If I don't try to fix the ending and let this thing run its course, he is going to kill my wife anyway. God help me! I am in a no win situation with a lunatic as my competitor. Sarah would find a "new peace" he called it. Was he referring to death? What else could it mean? Well, he doesn't know me very well. He was leaving me no choice but to fight back. I would do all I could for Sarah. I just knew it wouldn't be enough unless God was by my side. He had to take this yoke from me. He had to take over. I knew I would blow it on my own. I knew I was no match for a man that could think up something like this and execute it flawlessly thus far.

"Okay, Jason, pay attention. This is very important as it is the first step to fulfilling your requirements. Go to the library, the big one downtown, and check out a book entitled "Satan, To Know Him Is To Fear Him.""

"That's it? Go check out a book? You have got to be kidding right? Check out a book?"

"Yes, check out the book. Check it out from the branch

I told you. I want you there before noon. It is nine-thirty now. Check it out, Jason, and read the first three chapters. You will learn the truth. You have a choice, Jason. Stay ignorant, and your wife dies; or enlighten yourself, broaden your knowledge, and your world will expand."

I'll play his game. I have to make him think that he has me right where he wants me. He wants me at the library before noon, so I'll go. He will probably have someone contact me there. He just wants to get me to that library. If he wants to put me through the paces, I'll play along. He never did say that my wife will live. He only said that if I don't do what he wants, she will die. If I do as he asks, I will "expand my world." It would have been a lot easier for him to just say your wife will live, but I know he has no intention of letting that happen. I can sense that it's not part of the plan to let her live, and I don't understand why-yet.

"I will do as you say. I will check out the book and read it. I need to know my wife is alive though. I need to know she is safe. I need to talk to her and hear her voice."

"You are so predictable, Jason. I knew this was coming. I don't really understand this worldly love that shackles you together with another human like this, but it is the way it is. I expected you to ask this, and I am prepared to let you talk to your wife. I want you to read the first three chapters of the book Jason. I want you to have it done by two this afternoon. If you complete the task, I will have your wife call you at two-thirty. You won't talk long, but you will know she is alive and safe just as I have promised. Understand, Jason, hearing her voice is not a given, you must get to the library on time, get the book, get home and read it. I will know whether you have done your assignment and whether you have completed it on time. If you prove yourself, when the phone rings at two thirty, it will be her. If you fail on your assignment for any reason, the call will be from someone else. You won't want that call, Jason. Do what you need to do!"

"I will do as you say. I will read it. I want to talk to my wife."

"Call me "Truth," Jason. You have not referred to me by name since we got on line. Call me "The Truth." You may not believe it now, but you will. You will believe it. You will worship it, Jason. I want to hear you call me by my name."

I felt the bile rise in my throat. I had no choice, but I prayed before I typed. "God, know that these are only empty words that I type. I do not refer to him as truth by title. I do not worship him. I renounce him. I reject him. Forgive me Father."

"You are the truth."

"That is a start, Jason. I notice when you refer to your God or Christ, you capitalize the name. I will expect the same in the future. For now, it is a start. We must go. You have an assignment. Go to it."

With that he was gone. I quickly pushed the print button and my laser printer began spitting out the whole chat dialogue. I wanted it all. I wanted to read it again to see what I could find. He has made small mistakes so far and I must search for more; for some weakness. There has to be some way out-some way for me to find Sarah.

Chapter Twelve

Five minutes after our chat ended, my phone rang. It made my heart race, and I was getting tired of that. Everything startled me now, and everything seemed to make me jump out of my skin. I had finished printing the cyber conversation and stacked the papers neatly up on my desk to review later. The phone rang for the third time and I picked it up.

"Hello?"

"Mr. Shepard, Officer Ed Lancing here."

I was silent for a second or two, and I'm sure it felt awkward for both of us. I had to decide which way I was going to go. Were the messages I thought I was getting coming from God? Were they a product of my own imagination or subconscious? I decided that this was a "God thing" and I had to trust God. I had to go with what "I thought" he was telling me. I would take the risk and confide in Officer Lancing. I would share it all with him.

"Hello, Officer Lancing."

"I just thought I would call to see if anything came to mind last night, or if you had any contacts thus far about your wife?"

"I want to tell you that I feel very vulnerable here. I fear if we make a mistake, my wife could die. I am having a terrible time trying to understand how to handle this and who to trust. Are you a God fearing man Officer Lancing?"

"Well, I believe there is a God, yes. I guess I'm not too good at getting to church on a regular basis, though. I only go on special occasions, but I do go."

That was good enough for me. I obviously couldn't tell if he was lying, but clearly I had to believe that a follower of this man calling himself "Truth," would never go to Church. I had to go with my gut. I had to tell him what I knew. It dawned on me though that my phone lines might be tampered with. Had I already said anything that might cost me if someone was listening? Fear struck me once again.

"Officer Lancing, I can't talk right now. Can we meet somewhere to talk about my wife's case? Do you know of a place we can meet? Soon?"

"Yes, yes, of course, Mr. Shepard. I'm in need of some caffeine so why don't we meet in about twenty minutes at the Café Mocha on 12th and Elm. Do you know where that is?"

"Yes, I know where it is. My name is Jason, Officer Lancing. I would prefer that you call me by that name. Mr. Shepard feels too formal."

"Alright, Jason. I will be at the Café in twenty minutes. We can have a cup of coffee and go over what we know about the case. I will give you an update on what I have thus far."

I thought that Officer Lancing caught on very fast. He was obviously playing on the chance that someone might be listening. He was playing up the part about bringing me up to speed on the case, and playing down what I might be able to bring to the table. I would play along as well. I had no idea if anyone else was listening, but we couldn't afford any mistakes now........ever.

"I hope you have something. I feel like the more time that goes by the less chance there is of getting my wife back unharmed. I hope you guys are getting somewhere."

"See you in twenty, Jason."

"Bye." It was all I could seem to get out of my mouth. The phone went dead, and I knew that I would have to hustle to think through all of the things I needed to do. I really didn't want to take any action until I talked to Officer Lancing. I'm sure he has had more experience with these types of things than I, and although I had a few ideas, they might be big mistakes if I am wrong.

I did make a few calls to family and found some safe havens for the children. I would split them up and put them with family members out of state. I didn't explain why to my sisters, but I told them it was important and that I needed their help. Both of them jumped in with no questions asked. I told them that I would call them again later in the day when I had developed some plans, but for right now they should expect that the children would arrive tonight.

After I finished that task, I realized that I had done the whole thing on my phone. I was so clever with Officer Lancing. I had told him I couldn't talk about things on the phone and we were so good at not giving anything away while we talked. Minutes later I was using the same contaminated phone to call my sisters and set up living arrangements for my children. If they had a trace on the phone, or if it was being recorded, they would be able to tell where my children were. If they knew that, then what good would the whole move be? Well, I didn't know that the phone was tapped, I was just afraid it might be. I would have to ask Officer Lancing what he thought before I went through with this plan. I may have already jeopardized the security of my children.

I had to think better than this. I had to be smarter. These people were assuming that Sarah and I would be emotionally exhausted, and that we would not be very smart. I had to convince them of that if we were going to try anything. I had to play along. I had to make them believe that I was in the exact condition that they thought I should be in, and I had to out smart them. One mistake could cost me a lot. One mistake could cost Sarah her life.

It was almost ten, and I felt I needed to call over to Ralph and Carol's to see how the kids were. I dreaded the call because I didn't know whether to trust them or not. I couldn't divulge anything to them, and this hurt as they were not only friends and neighbors, but they were members of the community church we attended as well. I had always assumed they were Christians. If they were involved in this horrific plan, then they were not Christians, they were Satanists! Or at least that's what I assumed my enemy to be. Was that possible? Could there be such a thing as Satanists who attend a Christian Church? I wasn't sure, but it didn't sound right to me. I hated talking to them as I was afraid they would notice something in my voice-maybe a change in the way I felt about them. I had to believe that with all that had happened to me in the last few hours, they would write off any changes they might notice to the stress I was under. With that thought I dialed their number. Carol picked up the call on the first ring.

"Hi, Jason. Have you heard anything this morning?"

"How did you know it was me, Carol?" Right away I assumed the worst. I assumed that they knew what I was doing, who I was talking to on the phone, and even my own thoughts.

"Caller ID, Jason."

"Oh, of course. No, nothing yet. I did get a call from the officer that was out here yesterday wanting to know if I had heard anything. I'm going to meet him to see what he knows and to see how the police are approaching this case. I'm afraid I have nothing to offer from my side." I had to cover my tracks on my meeting with Officer Lancing. I didn't know if these two were really my friends or not, but for Sarah's sake, I had to assume everyone was the enemy, almost everyone anyway. Was I being too obvious? Would she read through my lame attempt to discredit my value in the case? All I could do was to keep going.

"How are the children, Carol?"

"Oh, they are fine. Don't worry about them. They are busy watching something on T.V., and we are going to bake cookies later today. They are just fine, Jason."

"Well, I really appreciate you watching over them for me. I need to run out for a little while, but when I get back, I would like them to come home this afternoon."

"Jason, do you think that is wise? Why don't you let Ralph and I watch over them for you? There is no hurry, and with all that is on your mind, I'm sure having them out of your hair would be a good thing."

Again, I didn't know how to read this. Were they being loving friends or were they trying to keep their hands on my children. I couldn't afford to offend them now, so I just played along.

"I appreciate your help, Carol. You will never know how much. I just need to have the kids home to give some kind of normalcy to this house. I will have to talk to them about this whole thing. They will hear something on the news or through friends. I may send them back your way later, but I want to have them home this afternoon, at least for a little while."

"I understand, Jason. You decide what's best, and we will help you where we can. Just know that we are here and that Ralph is taking some time off work to be here for you. Don't worry about a thing and especially about your lovely children. They are in safe hands with us."

That was my big question. I wish I knew that they were in safe hands. If it was true, it would take a load off my mind. Right now, though, whose hands were safe and whose were not was unclear. Ralph's behavior last night outside of the house was a big question mark for me, and I needed to make sure my children were completely safe miles away from here-out of the reach of those who could do them harm.

"Jason, do you want to talk to Ralph? He's right here."

"No, not right now, Carol. I have to run. I will be back soon, though. Tell Ralph I'll check in with him then. Thanks for all of your help, both of you, and tell the kids hi from dad."

"I will, Jason, but, well, where are you going? Do you want me to run an errand for you? Is it something we can handle for you?"

Again, I felt the pangs of suspicion creep in my heart and mind. "No thanks, Carol. Something I have to do for myself. I'll see you later, though. Bye."

With that I hung up the phone. I didn't want to wait for any further responses from Carol. I was going to have to hurry if I was going to even come close to meeting Officer Lancing on time. I knew where the café was, but when I looked at my watch, I knew I would be late. "Well, let him wait." I thought. Then I realized that Officer Lancing was my big hope. I was placing all my bets on his help. I needed to adjust my frame of mind. I had already decided to take a chance on him, so I needed to play it out all the way. If I was wrong, Sarah was dead either way. I had to give Officer Lancing everything I had, including my respect. Together with God's help we might be able to win. Alone I had no chance. More importantly, I believed that God had connected me with Lancing. If that was true, I couldn't go into this halfway. I had to trust him 100%. "I trust you God, and if you trust Lancing, then so do I." I mouthed these words as I grabbed my car keys off the table by the front door and headed out to the car.

I saw Ralph come out of his house as soon as I locked my front door, and I knew that he intended to come over and talk. I kept my head down and went straight to the car. I knew he couldn't reach me before I reached the car unless he ran, and that would be totally out of character. When he saw that I was at my car and planning to climb in, he called out to me in mid stride as he continued across the street.

"Jason, hold up a minute."

"Can't Ralph. Got to go. I'm already late. I'll check in with you when I get back. See you soon."

With that I climbed in and started the car. I noticed he was continuing to approach the car, so I put it in reverse and started to move. He walked along side and watched me. I looked back at him and gave him a half smile. He didn't return it.

"Be careful, Jason."

I looked back at him and he was dead-pan. No smile. No friendly wave. Chills went down my spine as I pulled away. I gave a little wave as I drove away, but nothing came in return. What did he mean by "Be careful?" Was that a warning or a threat? Was I reading more into it than I should? We always tell our friends to be careful when they are going away, and he could have meant that as a friendly reminder knowing I was under stress and driving a car at the same time. Or, he could have meant something totally different. All I know right now is that I'm scared. I know that because of what has happened I don't feel the same about Ralph and Carol, but were my feelings justified or the result of paranoid delusions? Well, right now I can't sort that out. They were not on the "trusted people list," so I had to get back soon and get my kids. The "trusted people list" consisted of only one person right now, and that was the man I was going to see. Even Pastor Steve is only on the "need to know" list. I trust him, but I can't share what I know with him. It was too big a risk. I pray that I am placing my trust wisely.

Officer Lancing arrived at the café several minutes early. This was his custom. He didn't like to walk in and find people already in place and waiting for him. He wanted time to scope out the place and to see who was there, who was coming and going, and to find just the right spot to watch the door. Café Mocha used to be an old favorite of Lancing's, but it had been a while since he had been there. He didn't recognize the girl behind the counter. Not that it mattered, but he realized that it had been longer than he thought since he was last here. Why did he stop coming in? What makes you comfortable and at home with a place one day and then you quit coming all together the next? "Who cares," thought Lancing. "Get your mind in the game, boy!" Lancing found a vacant booth and took the seat facing the door. This action was more by nature than thought anymore. He could not stand having his back to the door. If he was forced to take that seat, even in social outings, he would be uncomfortable the whole night. The booth he had chosen was a good spot for the meeting today. He could see the parking lot from the window and the front door. He could easily watch who came and went. The only thing behind him was the bathroom. He ordered a cup of regular coffee, black, and got up to check the restroom. There was no one in it. Since this restroom was shared by both men and women, it meant that the only people in the place were in front of him. That made him comfortable. It allowed him to relax just a little.

Lancing returned to his seat and surveyed the clients in the café. Not too many customers today. Not a surprise really. After all, it was 10 a.m. It was a little late for the breakfast crowd on a work day and a little early for the lunch group. Nobody seemed out of place here. A couple of older ladies were having a late breakfast, and a guy at the counter was having coffee and reading the paper. It looked like he was reading the classifieds. He was probably looking for work. Lancing would keep his eyes on him, but he was far enough away to make it impossible to hear any of he and Shepard's conversation, and his distance would give Lancing time to react if he made any questionable moves. Two other men sat in a booth near the door and looked to be truckers. A quick survey of the parking lot proved his assumption to be correct. Two logging trucks loaded down with timber sat in the lot. These guys were just taking a quick java break. No problem there. He then surveyed the employees. The girl at the counter couldn't have been older than twenty-two. She was pretty in a simple way. It was obvious from her work and behavior that she was not new here. She knew her way around and seemed to chat easily with the customers and the cook behind the wall. Who was in the kitchen? That was important to know. Lancing got up again and walked over to the counter. The girl, who wore a name tag that read 'Amanda,' greeted him and told him she was just coming over with his coffee. Lancing just smiled and looked in the back where he spotted the cook. He knew this man. It was Larry, the owner. Larry looked up and spotted Lancing.

"Hey, stranger, where the hell you been?"

"Hi, Larry, just been running like crazy. They don't give me much time for coffee anymore. How are you?"

"Oh, we're okay here. Business is a little down, but what do you expect with this weather? Nobody wants to come out. They just use those coffee drive-thru joints and grab a packaged pastry while they are there. No respect for good brewing and good eats anymore."

"Does seem a little slow, but I assumed it was just the time of day."

"Yeah, it will pick up soon for lunch, but it's not like it used to be. I hope it wasn't anything I said that kept you away."

"Me? No way, Larry. I've just been working like a dog. I'm going to sip on some of your good coffee and meet with someone here this morning. Maybe I can get back into the swing of things and get in here more often."

"Well, I hope so, Ed. We miss your ugly mug around here. Amanda, this guy's coffee is on the house."

"Thanks, Larry. You working by yourself today: just you and Amanda?"

"Yep, just the two of us this morning. Shelly comes in at around eleven for the lunch rush. You remember Shelly don't you, Ed?"

Lancing smiled. He remembered Shelly. She was about thirty, great looker, and she knew it. She always wore her skirts shorter than everyone else and her tops tighter. She had a great heart though. She was always helping out some old stray around the neighborhood, both the animal and human kind. It would be good to see her again, but Lancing didn't really expect to be there that long. He was just happy to know that some of the fixtures hadn't changed. He knew the world was turning, but it just seemed to be turning too fast for him lately.

Lancing wandered back to his booth with his coffee and checked his watch. Shepard was about ten minutes late. He didn't know what to think of that. He didn't know this Shepard guy yet. Seemed like a straight shooter, but who really knows? Maybe he's just late to everything he does. Maybe he's in some kind of trouble. Maybe he deserves a little slack since his wife was just kidnapped a few hours ago. Lancing sat quietly waiting and watching the goings on at the Café Mocha.

Jason pulled up fifteen minutes late. Lancing saw him in the parking lot and watched to see if anyone had followed him as he walked to the door. He was a bit disheveled, but he was not unkempt. It looked to Lancing like he had gotten some sleep and had taken a shower. That was pretty impressive since his wife had been kidnapped just yesterday. A lot of guys that Lancing dealt with during his career would have been a giant mess right about now. Lancing wondered how he would react if such a thing ever happened to him. "It wouldn't be pretty." He thought, "Hell, it aint very pretty now."

I walked in the door of the café and spotted Lancing right away. I think I had expected him to be sitting right where he was. I didn't really know this place. I knew where it was, but I had never stopped here before now. It looked clean and smelled good. I guess I was expecting some dive like you always see in those cop movies. This wasn't one of those places. This looked like a good spot to bring the family for breakfast. That is if I can get the family back together.

I walked up to Lancing and we smiled at each other. I could tell he was sizing me up and down, but I didn't take offense. That was his job. I knew he had to wonder some of the same things I wondered. Who were the good guys, and who were the bad guys? My bet is that the jury is still out on me with Lancing. I think he suspects everyone and everything until they can prove to him otherwise. I was okay with that. I suspected everyone, too.

Lancing looked tired as I walked up. Not tired from a bad night's sleep, but tired from too many bad nights. I think he takes his job very seriously, and I think that has taken a toll on him. I don't know how old he really is, but he looks about fifty five to me. Now that I know him better, I'll bet he is really only in his mid forties. I was happy about that and felt a little guilty for feeling that way. His lines and tired eyes told me that this guy was serious. I needed someone to take this case seriously, someone to help me find Sarah. I believe that Lancing is that man.

"Good morning, Jason. Please sit down."

"Thanks. Do you think this place is safe? I wonder if anyone was listening on the phone and knows we are here."

"Well, that's not a bad thing. I've been here quite a while, and I have a good feel for the clientele and the normal course of business for this place. If we get someone that gives us too much attention or is out of place, I think it will be easy to spot. Not only will we have the advantage because I will know who they are, but we will then know that the phone is tapped. That is an important piece of information.

"I guess you're right. I'm sorry about being late. I have so much to tell you, I don't even know where to start. I don't believe they have any intention of giving me Sarah back. I still don't know what they want, but this is an odd and dangerous group. You were right, I was contacted by them. They have made some requests, but nothing gives me the feeling that they intend to live up to their end of the bargain and return Sarah."

"Okay Jason, let's slow down. Why don't you fill me in on what you know? Tell me every detail you can think of whether you think it is important or not. I will listen, watch the room, and sort it out in my head. Don't hold back, Jason. The smallest detail may be just what we need."

I began to share everything with Officer Lancing. I told him about the chat room, the first contact, what I knew of the kidnapping, the chat this morning, and the book request made by the man called "Truth." I also shared with him my concerns about Ralph and Carol and the safety of my children. I was impressed by the way that he listened and took notes where appropriate. He seemed concerned about all the things I was concerned about, and I felt some comfort in that. I then gave him a copy of the printed conversation I had with "Truth." He scooped that up and immediately put it in his jacket pocket without glancing at it.

"Jason, I don't think you were followed here, and I don't think anyone here has paid much attention to us. I still wouldn't feel comfortable about that phone line though. They could tap into it at any time. I do think that you are safe right now to move your children as you planned. I also think that you need to go and get that book. It's already almost eleven, and you have some reading to get done. I will read this document you have given me and pull together my thoughts and notes on what you've told me so far. I will contact you and we should plan on getting together again later tonight. I have some information to share with you, but we have been here too long. I will find a different spot for our next meeting."

"I have so many questions, Officer Lancing. I mean, what do you think is going on? Why did they take her? Do you think we can save her?"

"Jason, I will give you more tonight. You have to trust me. If you are gone from home for too long, they will become suspicious. We want them to think you are lost in your grief. We can't let them know you are plotting their down fall. I will give you some answers to your questions tonight, but for now you have to go. By the way, Jason, my name is Ed. I would prefer you call me that."

We had clicked. I knew that Officer Lancing didn't give his first name out to too many people. He gave it to me. I felt that meant we had bonded somehow. I know how corny that sounds now days, but I don't know what else to call it. By Lancing letting me call him by his first name, it told me that he trusted me. He believed me. Now, we could work together. We shook hands and separated. I left immediately, and Ed Lancing stayed behind to pay the bill and watch me leave the lot. He wanted to watch the surrounding businesses to see if anyone pulled out behind me. He didn't believe I was followed, but he didn't just go with what he believed. He wanted proof.

I drove towards the library thinking about our meeting and all of the details that flashed before me. Did I leave anything out? Was there a detail I forgot? I also thought of my children. I had to get to the library, get the book, read it, and talk to Sarah. The next mission was to get my kids out of town. I needed to book their flights and get them out of state tonight. I was more convinced of their danger than ever before. Someone was attacking my family. I am not going to roll over and just allow it to happen. I am going to fight. I'm going to fight for Sarah and the children, for myself, and, yes, for God. This was a tangible battle of good and evil. I was convinced of it, and I believed God was on my side. We were fighting evil and there was too much to lose if we failed.

Chapter Thirteen

Sarah continued to lie silently on the bed even though she had been awake for what she thought was almost an hour. She just lay still and listened. Sarah hoped that they would think she was still sleeping and that they would talk amongst themselves. That didn't happen. These guys, assuming they were both still here, never said a word out loud to each other. The only time she ever heard them speak was last night when they untied her. She heard no T.V., no radio, no conversation. What were they doing? She tensed up as she thought about the fact that they might be in the same room with her, watching her. That thought made Sarah catch her breath. It clearly gave away that she was awake if they were watching. They didn't seem to be, as no one said anything or made any moves towards her. Her head was still covered by the "mask," as her captors called it. It was driving her nuts, and she wanted to just reach up and pull it off. She wasn't really excited or motivated about seeing her kidnappers, but she wanted to take a deep breath. Sarah felt that she now knew what it was like to fear closed in spaces like caves and elevators. She had never felt that fear before, but right now she wanted to scream. She had to keep talking to herself in a feeble attempt to calm her nerves. She couldn't allow her thoughts to go to dark places or become hysterical. Not now. They would just tie her back up and leave the covering on her head. It would only be worse.

The phone rang and the sound jolted her upward. She didn't want to sit up like that, but it was more of a reaction than a conscious effort. It was a reaction to a new sound; the outside world. Someone was calling. Someone from the outside was trying to reach them. "I hope it is the SWAT team and they have the house surrounded," she thought.

It took two rings and then she heard someone say, "Hello." She could tell it was the same voice as the man last night that seemed to be in charge. She listened intently. He didn't do much talking, mostly listening. Occasionally he would say, "Got it," "Yep," "Okay," but that was about it. Then he said something different. "Do you think that is wise?" Nothing came after that for a while. Sarah felt that the man was getting raked over the coals by the caller. It was as though he had questioned the decision of the man giving the instructions, and it didn't appear that that was acceptable. This was clearly not a democracy. There was a chain of command and you did not question it, you did not adlib, and you certainly did not circumvent it. Sarah could tell the man was still on the phone. She wasn't sure how she knew, but she knew. He was just being silent now. He was not even acknowledging the directions or instructions by the caller. It was clear that he had been put in his place and he was now just taking directions. After what felt like a lifetime to Sarah, he spoke again. "Okay, we are ready and will carry out your instructions exactly as you have given them to us. Anything further? Good bye."

Sarah realized that she was still sitting up, and she lay back down. She was sure this was a pretty transparent guise, and she wasn't really sure why she thought faking sleep was a good plan, but she just went with it anyway. She had nothing else to do; and she felt the longer they thought she was sleeping, the longer they would leave her alone.

"Come on, sweetheart, time to get up."

Sarah stirred slowly, continuing her game of artistic

sleeping. They apparently weren't impressed by it.

"I don't like to repeat myself, sweetheart. I know you are awake so let's just get up, have a stretch, a bathroom break if you need it, and prepare for our next move."

Sarah could tell that she was being spoken to by the dominant of the two men. She didn't want to make him regret the decision to free her hands. "I'm awake. Can you tell me what time it is?"

"Nine forty-five in the morning. You slept well. I'm glad of that. Now, I need you to push the sleep out of your head and get your wits about you. I let you sleep as long as I could, not that you need any extra beauty sleep, sweetheart."

"Can you call me by my name? I'm Sarah Shepard. That sweetheart line is going to get old fast."

"Whatever makes you happy, sweetheart. Sarah it is. Now, Sarah, do you have to use the bathroom?"

"Yes, I do. Listen, I know I've asked this before, but can I take this hood off? I'm going crazy in this thing."

"Not yet, but maybe soon, if you are a good girl. Stand up and I will show you where the bathroom is. I'll have to stay in there with you, but I won't watch, I promise."

He chuckled as he walked her around the bed and down a short hall. Sarah was humiliated that she would have to use the bathroom with a stranger watching, but she had no choice. She had to go, and she wasn't going to let him know that it bothered her. She didn't know what was in store for her; but if this was the worst of it, she felt pretty lucky. If this wasn't, then having a man watch her pee probably wasn't going to be something she worried about in the big scheme of things. Either way, she had to go and fighting with her kidnapper didn't seem too intelligent right at the moment.

While Sarah completed her personal tasks in the bathroom, she heard the outer door open and close and the sounds of someone else moving about in the outer room. The man in the bathroom with her moved towards the bathroom entrance, which had been left open. He spoke to the newcomer.

"Hey, hold up right there. She's using the bathroom. Everything okay outside? Are we ready to go?"

"Yep, we are ready. No problems. You want me to take over for you there?"

"Shut up, you idiot. Did you bring anything back with you to eat?"

"Oh, yeah, I left it in the car. I'll go get it."

"Sometimes I wonder what rock they found you under. You are as dumb as they come, pal. We got to be ready to rock and roll. We may not move at all. We may sit right here, but Simon wants us ready to go if the order is given to move."

"Okay, I'll go get the food. We're ready to go if we have to."

Sarah had finished and was floundering around the sink trying to wash her hands blindfolded. She heard the conversation and then heard the door close again as the man went out to get breakfast. She was hungry. She hated to admit it, but her hunger and the bathroom break made her realize how vulnerable she really was.

"That guy is an idiot. Sorry about him. I don't know what he bought for you to eat, but at least there will be something for you."

"Can you tell me your name or at least what you want me to call you?"

"You can call me Jack."

When he gave her his name, or pseudo name, it dawned on her that she had heard the name of the man in charge. Jack had called him Simon. She wondered if he did that by mistake and didn't realize it, or if that was a fake name too, and it didn't matter that she knew. Sarah realized that they were talking in front of her now. They were talking to her now. What did this change mean? They were so quiet before: didn't talk to each other, rarely spoke to her. Now they were talking to her, talking to each other, calling people by name.

Were they getting sloppy? Had the game changed and now it didn't matter? Was the fact that they were more open in front of her a danger sign? Sarah began to fear that they didn't have plans to send her home. If that was true, they may be more open, more willing to name names and talk in front of her. Sarah felt sick to her stomach. She felt Jack gently take her arm and guide her out of the bathroom. He took her to the kitchen, and sat her down at what felt like a small dining table. Jack rolled up her hood above her mouth so she could eat. It was her first chance to take a deep breath and fill her lungs. It brought tears to her eyes and caused her to weep silently, unable to speak.

Sarah began trying to size up her surroundings. The rooms were very small. The room she was currently in did not feel like a full kitchen. This had to be what Sarah called a kitchenette. There were definitely three rooms. A bedroom, where she spent the night, the bathroom she had just visited, and this room. She could smell coffee, but not much else. Sarah had the feeling that this was an efficiency apartment either at a motel or a small apartment complex somewhere in the mountains near her home. She could still smell the pine trees, and she could still hear the sound of gravel as the occasional car drove by. Sarah bet that it was a motel, a cheap motel with either cabins or rooms that lined the gravel road. The reason that she drew this conclusion was that she never heard anyone near their room. She could hear them drive by, but no one seemed to walk by their room as they would in a typical motel. In her mind she pictured a sleepy little motel with little cabins along the woods line. The place was probably frequented by skiers that would come in for the weekend. Sarah tried to think about what day it was. Friday was what she thought, but she couldn't be sure. This whole chain of events had confused her inner clock, and it disturbed her that she could not pinpoint the day, date and time. If it was Friday, that might explain why they may be moving. These guys probably don't like crowds and these places are pretty popular for the weekend warriors. Jason and Sarah had a favorite spot just like this, or what she perceived was just like this. They would run away on the weekends for a romantic getaway on occasion. It would never be the same for her now.

The door flew open again and she heard a man's steps in the room. He shut the door behind him. Sarah could feel his gaze as he walked in the room. He got to the table and put something down.

"Not a very exciting breakfast. I got some donuts and some fruit from the local market. Easy to eat, but not too exciting, I guess."

This was the same voice from last night: the younger guy. I guess these two were going to watch over her until the end. Sarah had this passing thought, and then wondered what she meant by "the end."

"I'm sure it will be fine, thank you," Sarah replied. "I'm very hungry, so I'm sure it will be great."

"I'll set you up with a plate and some coffee," Jack spoke up. "You can dig in whenever you like; we won't be saying grace before breakfast here." With that the two men broke into laughter.

Sarah didn't know what they were referring to, but she assumed that they were making fun of her religious beliefs. She didn't really know why they found prayer funny, and then how would they know whether she was religious or not? Sarah was confused, but ever since last night, confusion was nothing new.

"Sorry, Lady," the younger man uttered. "We just get a kick out of you people who believe in God. It's pretty funny stuff."

"You don't believe in God? What do you believe in? Do you think we are just accidents here? No divine intervention at all? I think that sounds like pretty funny stuff."

Sarah realized that she hadn't really prayed to God, and she hadn't even thought of talking to him through most of this mess. She felt some guilt over that, but quietly called to God under her breath at the table. She praised Him and promised that she would come back and talk to Him when she had time alone. She also told God that she loved and trusted Him. It was important to her that He know.

The young man started to speak again. "I don't believe in no God, that's for sure."

"Shut up, Pete!" This came from Jack and was forceful and mean. Pete did what he was told: he shut up. Now Sarah had three names, Simon, Jack and Pete. She didn't know if they were real names, but at least she could call them by name now.

"Sarah, eat up. You will need to keep your strength up. No good going hungry, and no good wasting time talking about things that we know we disagree on."

Sarah reached out, fumbled with the fruit and grabbed a piece. It turned out to be a plum, and it was a ripe one. It tasted wonderful as the juice ran down her chin and fingers. She felt around for a napkin, but she was surprised when someone began cleaning her face. She pulled away, but he grabbed her forcefully by the throat and kept wiping her face.

"Please, leave me alone. Please, don't hurt me."

"Just relax little, Sarah. I'm just cleaning you up. See how considerate I am? Am I hurting you? What are you whining about?" He then lowered his voice as though he was telling me a secret. "If you are good to me, missy, I could see that you get out of here alive."

This was Pete touching her and trying to engage her in some sick conversation. Where was Jack? She had to believe that Jack would never let him touch her or talk to her like this if he was around. "Oh, Lord, please help me."

Pete backed away and became silent. Sarah had to assume that Jack was coming back. Sarah heard his foot steps crossing the kitchen. Nothing was said. She wasn't hungry anymore.

After some time passed, Jack walked up and chastised her for not eating more.

"Sorry, Jack, I'm just not hungry anymore. I guess I'm just scared. Can we save it and I'll eat later? Is that okay?"

"Yeah, suit yourself." He reached over and began to adjust her mask.

"Oh please, Jack, can you leave it rolled up? I promise not to touch it, but I can breathe with it up. Please, Jack, I can't see. Please leave it up?

Sarah knew she was pleading, and she knew it was probably the wrong thing to do, but she needed to breathe. She needed that mask up. She didn't want to go backwards. Sarah felt she had earned the privilege of having the mask above her mouth, and she wasn't going back the other way without a fight. Well, a pleading anyway.

"Okay, Sarah. I'll leave it up for a while, but you understand if we have to move, I will be putting it back down. I won't have any argument or discussion about it when that happens. Let's make that clear now. I'll leave it up for you while we are here."

"Thank you, Jack. Oh, I appreciate it so much. God bless you."

"Well, I don't think God will be blessing me much, but you are welcome. I'm afraid there isn't much to do, but sit and wait. Just sit back and relax."

Sarah got bold after this little victory, and she began to push the envelope to see if she could develop a conversation and maybe a rapport with Jack. She didn't see much downside, and the upside might be that she finds out more about them and their plan. Even more important, she may develop a relationship with Jack, making it harder for him to hurt her. She had seen this in a few movies she had watched, and it always made sense to her.

"Jack, what did they say on the phone? Are you trying to get money from my husband? Are you planning a swap someplace: me for money?"

Sarah heard Pete start laughing, and this reminded her that she had him to tend with as well. He had stayed so silent that she had forgotten that he would hear everything she had to say. She didn't like Pete. He was more aggressive with her. It was clear that he wanted more than just the kidnapping, and she was sure that if Jack left them alone for any time at all, he would touch her, hurt her, or maybe more. She didn't trust him, and this caused her to draw even closer to Jack. At least he had treated her calmly and respectfully. Even during the bathroom incident, Jack was silent. He made no comments and did not try to touch her or humiliate her. She knew that it would have been a lot different if Pete had been with her. She also felt some comfort in the fact that Jack didn't like Pete either. Jack didn't trust him, and that may work in her favor later on.

"We don't need any of your stinking money, babe," Pete spouted. "We want much more than money; and what we want, your husband can supply. He is the key, and with you here, I'm sure he will see things our way."

"You want something that my husband can give you, but it's not money? I'm not following you. What could he possibly have that you would want?"

"Sorry, Sarah, Pete was way out of line and doesn't know half of what he is talking about. He just likes to talk, but I can promise you that if he keeps it up, if he keeps talking about things he doesn't know anything about, I will cut his tongue out. You hear me, Pete? Look at me, Pete. I'm telling you that if you open your mouth again without my okay, you will have opened it for the last time. Now look at me and acknowledge that you heard and understand what I just told you."

"I heard ya. I get it."

That was it. That was all he said. No argument, no machismo, just a quick "I get it," and silence. It was clear to Sarah that not only could Jack do what he threatened to do, but he also must have the authority to do it. That scared Sarah. She didn't like Pete, didn't like him at all, but she was with a man that obviously had the power of life and death over some people, and no doubt she was one of those people. Sarah realized that she and Pete were under Jack's control and authority, and that authority included the ability to execute a death sentence if need be. Sarah trembled visibly with that thought.

"What's the matter, Sarah," Jack asked. "You cold?"

"No, just scared. What's going to happen to me, Jack? What could my husband possibly have that is so important that you would kidnap me and force me to live like this to get it? Why won't you tell me? I mean, if you are telling my husband, why can't you tell me?"

"Maybe later, sweetheart. Right now I'm going to take a little walk. I need to get out of this hole in the wall for a few minutes."

Sarah panicked when she knew that she would be alone with Pete. "Please don't go, Jack! Please don't leave me in here!"

"What's the matter, Sarah? I'm just going for a little walk to look around. Pete will be here with you, and if he talks to you or touches you, or anything else, I will kill him. You do understand that don't you, Pete? No, Pete, shaking your head won't do. I want you to say it out loud so Sarah can hear you. That way if you do anything stupid when I'm gone, she can tell me and I can take appropriate action."

"I hear ya, Jack. I get it. I'm not going to touch her, and I won't tell her anything either. Why you got yourself all riled up? Just go out for a walk. We'll be fine. Sarah is as safe with me as she is with you."

"Okay, I hear you. I will hold you to that, Pete. I'll be

back in just a few minutes."

Sarah was in a panic, but she didn't feel she could protest any further without making Pete mad and guaranteeing trouble for herself at some point. She had to hope that Jack's threat would hold him back. The door opened and closed, and silence filled the room for several minutes.

"He thinks he's such a big shot. Thinks he can boss me around. Well, his time is coming. I know I'm going to get moved up, and when I do, I will be ahead of him. You can only imagine the hell on earth I am going to make his life." Pete chuckled.

"Sarah, remember what I told you? You be nice to me, and I can get you out of here. Jack's a fool, and he's on his way out. He's an old school type guy. Time he should retire and time guys like me should move up. I can get you back home, Sarah. I can make sure that you make it through this okay. Right now, chances are better than 60/40 that you are dead meat. Think about it, Sarah. You can't see me, but I'm good looking, and you and I could have some fun. Nobody would have to know. Then I could just make things good for you. Get you home and get you back to your husband, your kids, your friends, your God. Wouldn't that be nice?"

"Jack would probably kill you for even talking to me. Just leave me alone, Pete. I just want to be left alone."

"Okay, but don't you want to know what we are after? Don't you want to know what your husband has that we need? Aren't you interested in knowing what you're going to die for? I have that information, Sarah. I have lots of information. I could be your inside friend, your ace in the hole. You don't want that? Okay, baby, okay."

There was silence in the room. Sarah did want to know more. She wanted to understand why she was there. He told her that she only had a 40% chance of making it through. Why? Was that just a story of Pete's to scare her so he could get what he wanted, was it to make him feel important, or was it true? She didn't believe he could get her out of this place. He was the low man on the totem pole, so she wasn't falling for that. But he was talking. What did he know?

"Why am I here, Pete? What does my husband have that you want? Why did you take me?"

"Oh, baby wants to talk now? Good. I just want you to know that my information isn't free. I have a lot of information that I will share with you, but it isn't free. You will have to pay for it."

"I can give you money when I get out of here, Pete."

Pete cut her off. He was growing upset, and his voice sounded as though he was working himself up into an angry rage. "I told you I don't want your money. I don't need money. The family gives me plenty of money. They take care of me fine. No, baby, I'm looking at you and you are so pretty and sexy. I don't want your money. I want you."

This began to scare Sarah. She knew it was coming, but his tone, his state of mind made her even more nervous. She knew he wanted more than money. She knew he was attracted to her, but she also knew that Jack would be back in a few minutes. Sarah didn't believe that Pete could hurt her much now, and if she could get him to talk, get him to give her as much information as possible, maybe she could use it for her benefit down the road. Worst case she could use it against him with Jack if things started getting ugly.

"I'm just an old married woman, Pete. What do you want with a woman like me? I've got kids and a husband. Can't you tell me what you know? I'm not going to tell anyone. I mean, who would I tell? I just want to understand why I'm here?"

"Baby, you are fine. You may have kids and a husband, but you are a looker. You're not that much older than me, and I like older girls anyway. Besides, I'm not talking about running away with you or marrying you. I just want to spend a little time alone with you, if you get my drift. We could have some fun and no one would know."

"Tell me why I'm here, Pete. Tell me what they are going to do with me."

Pete grabbed her around the throat and held her while he leaned close to her. "I'll tell you, baby, but you know it aint free. You know I will want some fun later. We'll have plenty of time alone together, and I'm getting excited thinking about it."

Sarah squirmed and tried to pull away, and this seemed to infuriate Pete. He pulled her hood almost all the way off, and for the first time she could see his face. He was in his late twenties, and clean shaven. He had a crazed look in his eyes and she was lost in fear now. He held her by the throat and started to unbutton her blouse.

"You see baby. I'm going to be your savior. You don't have a chance without me. These people are going to kill you. They need to. They need a sacrifice. You were chosen. I'm the only guy that can get you out of here, and all I want is a little deposit for later."

He was still unbuttoning her blouse and he was getting rough. Pete leaned over and tried to kiss Sarah on the mouth. He became more forceful as she tried to resist.

"Don't you get it, baby? I'm your savior. I'm your Christ. The least you can do is give your savior a little lovin."

Sarah screamed and tried to resist. She tried to push back, but Pete only became more determined. It was clear that he had lost his ability to restrain his feelings. He was holding her as she fought, continuing to unbutton her blouse and trying to kiss her.

Sarah screamed again in total fear. This man was totally out of control.

Sarah didn't hear the door open, but she heard it as it slammed shut. She saw the surprise on Pete's face as a hand grabbed his hair and pulled his head back. Sarah saw a long knife blade cut into Pete's throat and tear deep into the skin.

Hot blood sprayed everywhere and Sarah could feel it hit her in the face. She could only watch in horror. Pete had a look of terror on his face, and the knife dug along the width of his neck. Someone had just slashed Pete's throat. The hand let go of Pete's hair, and Pete's hands came up to his throat as he dropped to his knees and fell to the ground. Sarah could hear him drowning in his own blood below the table as she stared at who she assumed was Jack standing above Pete with the knife in his hand.

"I told you that you would die if you touched her. Now embrace your fate. You were always a fool, Pete. Now you're a dead fool."

Jack looked over at Sarah and didn't seem too upset that she had her mask up above her eyes. "I'm sorry you had to see that, Sarah. He was a fool and a dangerous man. He didn't understand what we are doing. He was just a thug that they brought in. We don't have any room in our organization for thugs. You have to be committed; you have to believe. If you don't, you develop your own agenda's like this kid did. Did he hurt you? Are you okay?"

Sarah could only nod at Jack. She was in total shock. She had just watched a man get his throat cut, up close and personal. She assumed he was dead lying at her feet, and his murderer was standing there talking kindly to her with the knife in his hand.

"Sarah, button yourself up, sweetheart. You are showing. I'll get something to clean you up. I'm sorry I got blood on you like that. Let me get something."

Sarah looked down and saw that her blouse was unbuttoned and it was pulled back around her breasts. Her bra was showing, and that seemed to embarrass Jack. She covered herself back up and buttoned her blouse up. Jack came back with a warm rag and gave it too her to wipe the blood off her face. Her clothes had blood on them too, but neither she nor Jack seemed concerned about that now.

"Jack, thank you for coming back! He was in a rage! He was going to hurt me! Thank you for saving me!"

Jack had no comment this time. He only looked at her, smiled confidently, and nodded in response.

"He told me I was going to die. He told me I was going to be sacrificed, but that he could save me if I gave in to him. Am I going to die, Jack?"

"You're just in a little shock, Sarah. Don't listen to him. He was a fool. You're okay now. Just relax and let your heart slow down a bit."

To Sarah this sounded a lot like Jack was avoiding her questions. Sarah noticed that he looked about fifty. His eyes were tired, but he didn't look as though he felt any remorse about what he had just done. In fact, he looked as though he was comfortable with it and had done it many times before. He seemed relaxed with death and was just beginning to clean up the mess as though it was a food spill. He was working to mop up the blood and to pull Pete out from under the table.

"Jack, you didn't answer me. Am I going to die?"

Jack just looked back at Sarah and she read in his eyes that Pete had told her the truth. It was not their intention to let her go. She was going to be "sacrificed" according to Pete. What did he mean by sacrifice? Why? When? Where? Sarah began to cry, to sob, and Jack jumped up from what he was doing.

"Don't do that. I hate that. Look, I don't know what the plan is. I don't make the plans. I just carry them out. I'm sure if you are good and behave yourself, and your husband does what they want him to do, you will be sent home."

He wasn't convincing. Sarah felt she was doomed, and wasn't sure how to react to that. Right now all she could do was cry. She let it go. The tears that she had saved up and stored from the time she was first attacked and taken away poured down her face. She cried for herself, for her children, her husband, her parents. She was afraid of death only because of the unknown. How would they do it? Would it hurt? And she was afraid because she didn't think she would ever see her family again. That tore at her heart strings even more, and she sobbed unable to speak.

Jack watched for a while, tried to comfort her, and then felt it was best to let her have her cry. He turned away and began to deal with Pete again. He didn't know how to handle Sarah, but he was having trouble lying to her. Where was this thing going to end? What did the end game look like? He hoped Pete was wrong. He hoped they hadn't decided that Sarah would be the sacrifice. He had grown to enjoy her; to like her. It would be difficult for him to kill her. Of course, he would if he had to, but he would prefer picking someone else to die. Maybe Jason Shepard would be a good choice.

Chapter Fourteen

The book was right where it was supposed to be. The only copy the library had. I had thought that someone might try to contact me in the library, but it wasn't the case. I also looked the book over very carefully as I had an idea that a note might be waiting there for me. Wrong again. I guess these guys are serious. They really wanted me to read this book. Well, I won't let them down. I have to get it done by two o'clock so that I can talk to Sarah. I looked at the chapters, and they seemed relatively short. I had no doubt that I could accomplish their assignment in very short order. In addition to reading the book, I also needed to pick up my kids and make plans for their evening trip. It was now eleven o'clock. I had a lot to do, and only a few hours before Sarah would call. The car seemed to automatically turn for home and I drove as fast as I could back to what used to be 'home sweet home.'

When I got home, I pulled the car all the way into the garage. This was unusual and I hoped that nobody took note of it, but I wanted to be able to load the children's travel bags in the trunk without anyone seeing, including Ralph and Carol. That accomplished, I went inside to begin my reading assignment. The book was written as an introduction to Satan. Who was he, why did he exist, and why did he have the power he possessed? I took the book very seriously as I believe in his existence. The book began by confirming the story of the Bible, but with a substantially different spin on it. It told of Satan being an angelic leader and challenging God's authority. Very quickly I realized that this book was written by a follower of Satan. The writer had written the story as though God was jealous of Satan and it was this jealousy that lead to their argument and separation. The book presented the belief that Satan's exit from heaven was a mutual decision, and that God and Satan had agreed that Satan could rule the world while God ruled the heavens. I knew this version was in conflict with the Word of God, but I read anyway. What were these people after? What made them tick? Why would they kidnap my wife and then have me read this book? None of it made sense, but maybe I could discover a thing or two from the book anyway.

The first three chapters were filled with a distorted view of Satan. The facts were not 100% wrong, but they had a spin on them that made Satan appear as though he was in the driver's seat and in control of the world and the people in it. The Bible does reveal that the world is Satan's domain, but he doesn't own the people. People have choices, and we can choose between good and evil. This book seems to imply that it is already predestined, and to fight it is a waste of time and energy. The purpose of the first three chapters appeared to be to establish Satan as the being to worship. The book implied that Satan was made by God as his equal and separated from God because of God's jealousy. Nonsense, but it made me flip forward in the book to see where they were going with their line of thinking. Future chapters talked about the power of Satan, how to worship him, how to live in his world, and how to harness the power of Satan. These chapters seemed to encourage a life of debauchery and wonton abuse of most everything. The book told of Satan's desire to give his followers the world, and how he wanted them to enjoy all things to their maximum. This implied sex, drugs, alcohol, and anything else you could think of that people enjoyed, especially things that people enjoy to excess. The book was trash. It was just a book written to justify a life of use and abuse. I had to read it, as I didn't know if there would be any questions later, or some kind of test to ensure my compliance to their request. It was trash though. I quit looking ahead and decided I had spent enough time looking at this garbage. I felt some guilt for checking it out at all. Now my name would be listed in the library as a reader of this junk. I wanted to erase that and throw the book away. I knew I couldn't do that right now, but I might once this whole thing is over. It was time to put it away, as I had to redirect my thoughts to the children.

I had already acquired flights for both of the kids. They would be going to separate states. I needed to finish packing their bags and then get them into the trunk of the car. My plan was to go and pick them up and tell Ralph and Carol that I was going to take them to dinner. I would then head for the airport and get them out safe and sound. I would deal with the lie and the consequences after I got back. They never said not to send my kids away, so I wasn't doing anything they told me not to do. I also thought that my actions seemed quite reasonable since the press was going to go wild on this story as soon as it broke, and I would obviously want to protect my children from that. The truth is I just don't trust Ralph and Carol anymore, and if I am wrong, I will deal with that later too. If I am right, it reveals more problems than I can think about right now. They were friends, neighbors and local Church brethren. If they were a part of this craziness in anyway, then they were really none of those things. They were the enemy.

It was almost two o'clock now. I was supposed to hear from Sarah at two thirty. I didn't know if anyone would contact me before her call to verify the completion of my reading assignment, but I was ready. Ed Lancing wanted to be here for the call, but he was afraid that he would be seen and that could hurt us big time. If the kidnappers knew he was working closely with me, it could jeopardize everything, especially Sarah's safety. He did tell me to record it if I could, and if I couldn't, to write everything down that was said by anyone I talked to including Sarah. I was ready for that as well. I didn't really have a recording device, so I had a pad and pen sitting by the phone. I would be ready, whether it was just three words, or a book full of dialogue. Mostly, I was anxious to hear from Sarah. I was concerned about her emotional condition. Would she be crying, or angry because we hadn't rescued her yet, or would she be worried about the kids, or, or, or? I had no idea what her state of mind would be. I prayed that she would remain calm, and I hoped that she would tell me that she was being treated well and that she was in good physical and emotional shape. I didn't really expect all of that, but I hoped for it anyway.

I was surprised that I had not heard from Ralph or Carol since I got back. They seemed so driven to talk or help me earlier. My mind was filled with suspicious thoughts. Did they know I would have an important call coming in shortly? Is that why they didn't want to come by or call? Did they know I was at home reading the book that Sarah's captors had ordered me to read? Is that why they didn't want to disturb me? Of course, it was also possible that they didn't see me drive up the street, and since I parked my car in the garage, they may not even know I'm back home. It was hard for me to believe that I had slipped by old eagle eye Ralph though. Judging from the way he watched my house so closely from the darkness last night, I doubted that much slipped by without his notice. I knew my thoughts were sarcastic and harsh, but my thoughts were my thoughts. Until proven otherwise, everyone was under suspicion and considered my enemy. Ralph and Carol were no exception, and based on their recent behavior I was voting against them right now. Suddenly, my whole being was filled with dread and fear. What if they had left town with the children? What if my kids were gone? Fear began to turn to panic. I raced over to the window to have a peek across the street. I only had fifteen minutes before Sarah's call, so I couldn't go over and check on the children right now. Ralph's car was in the driveway. Carol's car was missing. This startled me and I didn't know how to read it. As I was watching and trying to determine the meaning of everything, Carol's car drove by my house and pulled in their driveway. I instinctively backed away from the window as I didn't really want her to know I was home if she didn't know already. She climbed out of the car with her groceries. She began to walk to the front door with a paper bag in each arm. She stopped and looked over at my house. My heart felt like it was beating through my chest. She stopped for a minute or so and just stared at the house. She then turned back to her front door and walked up the steps. I thought I saw her shaking her head, but I couldn't be sure. Her front door opened and Ralph had now joined her. He grabbed a sack and they stood on the porch talking for a minute. They were obviously talking about me as they kept turning and gesturing towards the house. I got the feeling that they didn't know I was home. They must think that I have been gone since this morning. I began to surmise that this could be a problem. If these two were part of the "Truth network," then "Truth" wouldn't know I was home either. If that were true, then maybe he wouldn't think I had done my homework and consequently there might be no phone call from Sarah. I wasn't sure what to do. I battled to stay calm, but I could feel the panic well up even more. Should I make myself known to Ralph and Carol so that they can deliver the message of my presence to "Truth?" Should I remain hidden and see what happens? What if "Truth" knew I was home, but Ralph and Carol didn't? I'm not sure exactly what that would tell me, but it gave me some new possibilities to ponder. I decided to remain hidden from my neighbors and await the call.

At exactly two-thirty the phone rang. I picked it up on the first ring, as I had been nervously anticipating the call.

"Hello?"

"Is this Jason Shepard?" the voice on the other end asked.

"Yes, it's me. Who is this?"

"Never mind that! Don't ask any more dumb questions! Are you alone?"

"Yes, I'm alone."

"Okay, here is your wife. You only get a few seconds so make them count."

There was a moment of silence that seemed to last forever. "Hello? Hello?" I kept asking.

"Hello, Jason," Sarah's tired and distraught voice sounded weak.

"Sarah, are you alright? Have they hurt you?"

"Jason, I'm okay. Tired and worn out, but I'm okay. How about you and the kids? Are you alright?"

"We are fine, don't worry about us. We are working to get you home, honey. Believe me; we are doing all we can."

"They say they want something from you first, Jason. Can you give it to them?"

"Honey, you know more than I do. They haven't told me anything yet. They just keep sending me on wild goose chases. No real requests yet, but don't you worry, Sarah; whatever they ask for, I'll get it for them. You will come home soon, honey. Don't worry about that.

"Jason, when I do get home, I want to go away together like we did a few months ago. I want to go to a place just like that place."

"Okay, honey. When you get home we can go anywhere you want to go."

"No, Jason, not anywhere! I want to go to a place just like that! Just the two of us, Jason. Do you remember?"

"Of course I remember, honey. It was a mountain cabin.

Just you and I. We'll make it a date. We will do it again, Sarah. We will do it just as soon as you get home. I promise."

I could hear her start to cry on the other side of the phone, and the frustration I was feeling became overwhelming. I wanted to help my wife, to protect her, but I was powerless. Anger began to well up inside me even though I knew that anger could only hurt me.

"Sarah. Sarah, are you alright?"

I could hear movement on the line, but no answer. "Sarah, are you there?"

"She is fine. I think we have proven that to you. Now, just do as you are told so that I can deliver her back to you."

The man's voice was matter of fact. Not mean, but not warm either. It contained virtually no emotion. The call was over. He made that clear. This man was apparently in charge of my wife's captivity and thus in charge of her care as well.

"Don't hurt her! Please, don't hurt her! I'll give you whatever you want.

"You just do as you are told." The phone went dead. That was it? That was all I was going to get? I didn't even get to say goodbye. I hope she knows I love her and that I'm doing all I can. At least I know she is alive. Praise God for that miracle!

I sat for several minutes taking stock of my emotions and trying to decide what to do next. I knew I needed to make the call to Ralph and Carol. I made the call filled with nervous anticipation.

"Hello," Ralph answered.

"Hi, Ralph, Jason here. How are the kids?"

"Jason, we have been worried sick about you. Where are you?"

"I'm home, Ralph. I've been home for hours."

"Oh, I didn't see your car."

I thought that Ralph sounded truly surprised. I didn't believe he was faking it. He didn't really know I was home.

I don't know what that means exactly, but I tucked it away in my memory so that I could share it with Lancing. He might know how to interpret it.

"Oh, I'm sorry Ralph. I parked my car in the garage. I didn't even think about the fact that you might not realize I was home. I'm sorry if I made you worry. I just called to get the kids. I would like them to come home for a few hours and then I want to take them to dinner."

"Well, Jason, Carol kind of thought you and the kids would join us for dinner. She went to the store and got stuff to make a big feast. Why don't you just come over here?"

"No, Ralph, I want some time alone with the kids. I need to talk to them now before this thing breaks in the press. I don't want them to hear it from anyone but me."

"Well, Jason, I kind of already told them. I told them that Sarah was missing and that everyone was looking for her."

I felt the anger rushing through my body. "Why would you do that, Ralph? I told Carol this morning that I wanted to pick them up this afternoon specifically to tell them about their mom. Why would you take it upon yourself to do that for me?"

"I don't know, Jason. I'm sorry. I'm kind of new at this too. I just thought that I could be of help. Why don't you just come over and spend some time here with all of us. We can have dinner together and then you can go back home and get some sleep."

"Ralph, I'm coming over, but I'm coming over to get my kids. I'm planning on spending time with them, and then I'm taking them to dinner as a special treat. I don't want any more discussions about it. I just want my kids. Understand?"

"Well, yeah, Jason. Don't get upset with me. I'm just trying to help. Trying to figure out what I can do to help you through this horrible mess. I don't mean to upset you. Come on over. Carol and I will get the kids ready. She can put the dinner on hold and we can do it tomorrow or the next night if you like."

"Thanks, Ralph, and I'm sorry. I'm just jumpy and nervous. I hope you can understand. Please ignore my rudeness."

"Don't mention another word about it. Just come on over. We'll be ready."

Ralph hung up the phone with no goodbye. I knew he was upset, but I didn't know any other way to stop his negotiations in their tracks. I had to get my kids. We had an appointment at the airport, and I wasn't about to share that fact with Ralph. He had no business telling my kids about Sarah. I didn't know what to expect when I saw them now. I hadn't decided whether I was going to tell them anything or not. Once I had made the decision I was sending them off to their Aunts, my thoughts of what I would say to them had become cloudy. Now, I would have to deal with their questions and emotional instability. That isn't what I needed right now with my own emotional state questionable at best. At least I can cling to the good news that the kids are still safe and sound.. In five minutes I would have them safely back in our house, and then shortly after that I will get them tucked away out-of-state, out of reach.

The phone rang and I immediately thought it was Ralph trying yet another approach to keep the children at home. I answered the phone with a curt hello.

"You okay, Jason? It's Ed here."

"Oh, yeah, I'm okay, Ed. What's up? You got anything new?"

"What time are you going to dinner tonight?"

I had to think for a minute to try and understand what Lancing was asking me. I wasn't that experienced at this cloak and dagger stuff, and I'm sure he didn't appreciate the slow response and the inherent breaks in the conversation.

"Oh, I'm leaving here at seven. Reservations are at eight."

"Good, I think I'll meet you at the restaurant."

"Okay, I will look for you."

"Good, see you then."

He was gone. Lancing had basically told me that he was going to meet me at the airport. At least that's what I hoped he was telling me. I would take my notes with me and be prepared to tell him everything that had happened. I was also anxious to find out if he had discovered anything new in his investigation.

I headed across the street to get the children back into my protective arms. I didn't really want to talk to Ralph or Carol, but I knew I had to. I would do my best to be gracious and thankful, but I would pull away as fast as I could so I could get some time alone with the children. I was also afraid that I might slip up and give something away while I was talking to them. I would keep the conversation short, sweet, and on topic. I needed to talk to my children, and then I needed to get them safely to the airport. It would be one less worry for me-actually two. I was anxious to chip away at the list of things that were weighing heavy on my mind and heart. This would start that process, and my heart was racing in anticipation of seeing their faces.

Chapter Fifteen

L ancing sat at his kitchen table, sorting through some documents and papers that were strewn in random order across the table. Seeing him like this might make one think that he was unorganized and that he couldn't possibly be an effective investigator. But Lancing had a system. True, nobody else could understand it and nobody else could follow it, but he had a system that he understood and used quite well. There had been some conflict back when he was a detective because his partner couldn't follow his investigative style, nor could he understand how to find anything in Lancing's desk or files. But Ed Lancing didn't have a partner now. He wasn't even an investigator anymore; just an ordinary street cop. Well, that suited him fine. He believed he could be just as effective on the streets, and it relieved him from having to wear that awful suit and tie everyday.

Mrs. Lancing was at work. She worked in a dental office nearby and she wouldn't be home until after six o'clock. Marion Lancing was the manager of a three doctor office, and she was doing very well for herself. Her pay wasn't all that great, but she enjoyed her work. There's a lot to be said for enjoying your work, pay or no pay. Ed Lancing had lost that joy many years back. He continued on, but mostly with his eyes on retirement. He realized that he would never be effective with the politics that some call police work today. So he kept his nose clean and just focused on crime and not promotions. Lancing was resigned to the fact that he would retire in patrol and that he would never make detective again-or sergeant for that matter, but who needed that anyway? He could do most of his detective work right from his patrol car, and when he discovered clues along the way he would pass on what he could to the guys upstairs. He would comfortably sit by while they made the arrest. It didn't bother him anymore. His thoughts wandered from his historic accomplishments to the case that currently lay before him. But Marion came to the forefront of his thoughts once again. She wouldn't be happy if she got home and found him using the kitchen as a "war room." She supported him 100%, but she didn't like to mix business with pleasure, and the home was supposed to be part of the pleasure. She also understood that he was no longer part of the upwardly mobile group in the police department, but she was okay with that. She was afraid for her husband's health, and the less stress he had to endure, the better. In her mind Ed didn't have the right personality make up for being a cop today. He was twenty or thirty years too late. He would have been one of the best back then in her mind. Now? Well, now it was all about being politically correct. It revolved around who you knew, how fast you could move up, and then how early you could retire. That's what it had become. Solving crimes had reduced itself to a part time job you endured while you worked the political system. Marion knew she was carrying her husband's emotional baggage, but that was okay too....They were in love. After thirty years of marriage, they were still in love. No job could duplicate that kind of satisfaction.

The phone rang and Lancing dropped the pile of papers he was looking at and picked it up.

"Lancing here."

"Well, Ed, that's one heck of a way to answer your home phone." Pastor Steve Krier was on the phone and he chuckled at his quip.

"Oh, hi, Steve. Sorry, forgot where I was. Thanks for getting back to me so fast."

"Hey, Ed, you are on my short list. Don't you know that? Whenever you call me, I'll do my best to be there for you. What can I do for you? You aren't calling because you want to come and hear one of my Sunday sermons are you?"

"Well, uh no, not right now, Steve. I mean I will, I'm sure, but right now I need your help."

"Okay, Ed, what is it?"

"Steve, I think we have another case associated with that group that killed Joe Deener."

"Are you talking about Jason's wife, Sarah? Please don't tell me you are. I knew she was missing, but I was hoping it was something else. Jason did call me and we are pulling together some help for him."

"Well, I don't know how much you know, but he is being contacted and they are saying some of the same satanic things that they said before they killed Joe. I need your help, Steve. I need you to help me decipher some of this stuff and help me with Jason. I don't want another death like Joe Deener's, and I especially don't want to see it be a woman, Steve."

There was a pause on the line as Steve tried to gather his thoughts and grasp the magnitude of the situation. His friend's wife had been taken. God forbid it be the same satanic group that killed Joe. Ed Lancing had called Steve in on Joe's case because it looked like a religious ceremony, and Steve was the only real religious scholar in town. There were obviously several very qualified ministers, pastors, and priests; but Steve Krier was the only one that had a Doctorate in Theology. Somehow Ed Lancing had found that out, and he used Steve to try and solve the Deener case. That was until Ed found himself removed from the case.

"Steve, are you there? Can you help?"

"I'm here, Ed. You know I will do everything in my

power. I wasn't much help with Joe's case, but I will give you all I have. You know that."

"Good. I need for you to meet with me and Jason at the airport at eight tonight. Can you do that?"

"Sure, Ed, but why the airport?"

"Steve, don't ask. You're on a need-to-know basis. I need you to keep this to yourself, Steve. We have a lot to lose, and we can't afford anyone slowing us down or getting in our way. You can't talk to anyone, Steve. I mean no one. Not your wife or your secretary or anyone in the Church. Okay?"

"I'll be there, Ed. Does Jason know I'm coming? Does he know about the Deener case and that it might be related?"

"No on both counts. He will find out about both tonight. He has shared a lot with me, and it's time I brought him up to speed on what I know. I need you there for two reasons. I think Jason may personally need your help when he finds out what we are up against, and I want to get you up to speed on the most recent contacts from these kooks. I am hoping you can help me decipher what the heck this group is going to do next."

"I'll be there, Ed, and I won't share anything with anyone. I was going to call Jason right after I talked to you, but I think I will postpone that until we meet tonight. Anything else, Ed?"

"Pray, Steve. You know I have never asked for that before, but we need some help here. If you have an inside track with the big guy upstairs, call on him now. Throw in all your markers, Steve. We need every advantage we can get to save this woman."

"I have been praying, Ed, but I will be more specific now that I know what I know. I don't know about the inside track part, Ed, but I will pray unceasingly to the Lord. Can I ask you to do the same? I'm not the only one He listens to you know."

"Well, I haven't prayed in a long time, but I will try for Mrs. Shepard. I want to bring her home, Steve. I have to believe that God wants to bring her home too."

"You're right, Ed. God loves Sarah, and he would want her home. Let's pray for her, and let's pray that God's will be done. I'll see you tonight, Ed, and I will come prepared to help in any way I can."

"Okay, Steve. See you then."

Lancing continued to go through the documents that were on the table before him. This was his personal file on the Joe Deener case along with the notes that he had taken thus far on the Shepard case. These two cases were connected. Lancing had no doubt about that. He reviewed the similarities. Both Deener and Shepard were Plant Managers of the same plant. They both attended the same church. They both seemed to be truly good men and strong believers in Jesus Christ. They not only believed in God quietly, they believed openly. They shared their faith with co-workers and with people they met. They weren't pastors by title, but they were men that openly talked about God, and they were men who seemed to practice what they preached. There was also evidence that the killers contacted Joe before they kidnapped and murdered him. It appeared that they had been having some type of on-going dialogue with him, but then the talking ended and the killing began. There was a twist in the Shepard case though. They had taken Jason's wife, not Jason. This was puzzling. With Joe it was very discreet and subtle until they killed him in the park. They had to know that Jason would report his wife's disappearance to the police. Why did they take her? Were they raising the stakes and implying that they didn't fear the police? Did they still intend to kill Jason but were using Sarah as a diversion?

This thought startled Lancing. This was actually the first time he had thought about that scenario. Jason Shepard could still be in grave danger. Lancing had put all of his thoughts on Sarah, but they could grab Jason at any time. If he wasn't careful, Lancing could be answering a call of a dead body in the park again. Lancing picked up the phone to call Jason but then thought better of it. If they were listening, they would note his change in concern for Jason. That change may cause a reaction and encourage them to step up the pace of their plan. Lancing didn't want that. He didn't want them moving any faster than they already were. He didn't know their current plan, and his hope was to continue to search these files to see if he could find a nugget in the Deener case that might match up to something in the Shepard case. A bit of a needle in a haystack no doubt, but it was all he had.

Lancing was disturbed because he didn't have any resources on this case. The detective bureau hadn't even contacted Jason as of yet. It was almost twenty four hours after she was kidnapped, and those idiots hadn't even gone out to the victim's house, set up phone taps, or interviewed anyone. It was a shame that his department's police work had eroded this far. It wasn't their fault entirely. Financial cut backs, poor leadership, too few detectives and too many cases. These were some of the things that got in the way of doing good police work. This was a big case for this town, though. Even in an inept police department this case should have gotten some attention and should have received some clear action from the investigators in charge. Something was wrong. Something smelled horribly wrong to Lancing. From what Jason had been telling him, it was pretty clear that this group, whoever they were, had someone on the inside. Lancing didn't have the luxury of trying to think about the identity of that inside person. He had no evidence of their identity, and he could only draw conclusions from his own personal likes and dislikes. There was no room for that. No time for that. Lancing would stick to what he did have. He had a lot of forensic evidence from the Deener case. He had a few witnesses who were able to help them put together what happened the days prior to the killing. He also had Steve. The question that Lancing was wrestling with was the motive. Why kill? Why kill the way they killed, where they killed, and who they killed? How can the answers to those questions in the Deener case help him find Sarah Shepard? Lancing had a strong intuition that he only had a day, or maybe two. These guys weren't kidnappers. They were killers. They were either planning on killing Mrs. Shepard or Mr. Shepard or maybe even both. He couldn't allow any of that to happen. Lancing's psyche could not even fathom it happening. It was his job to stop them. This thought overwhelmed Lancing and he wondered if he should take Steve's advice and try saying a prayer too. "Well, maybe later," he thought. "I've got plenty to do right now, and I'll bet God is busy listening to Steve anyway."

Lancing continued to go through the paperwork with one eye watching the clock. He had two deadlines. He had to get this mess cleaned up before his wife got home, and he had to ensure he was at the airport by eight o'clock. Actually, his plan was to be there around six thirty. He wanted to see who was there, and he wanted to watch Jason send his kids off to safety. Lancing wanted to make sure that they got on board safely and that no one was following or watching Jason during the process. Marion came first though. He would have to explain why he wasn't at work and why he was going out right after she got home. He would make up a story that she wouldn't believe, and then she would let him go anyway. She would know that he was following a lead on some case he shouldn't be working or interviewing a witness that he wasn't supposed to talk to. She knew it and accepted it. Lancing wouldn't tell her about this case though. Not until he had to. This was dangerous for everyone involved, and these people had already proven they were killers. No, he wouldn't tell her about this one right now. Let her think he was chasing a burglar or car thief. She would be happier, and he would be free to do what he had to do without being concerned about her fears or worrisome questions.

Time to start moving. The clock's ticking, and this mess needs to be filed away in such a way that he can find what he needs when he needs it again. It didn't matter if no one else understood his system. He was on this case alone. Lancing had the world heavily planted on his shoulders, and he felt that Sarah's life was his responsibility. Right or wrong he believed he was the key. It was his job. He would have to pull this together. He hoped Steve really had an inside track to the Almighty because right about now Lancing was feeling overwhelmed.

Chapter Sixteen

The little time I spent with Ralph and Carol was uncomfortable but not unbearable. They were gracious and had the kids ready as promised. The children were not as devastated as I anticipated, and I was obviously glad of that. I assumed that either Ralph had watered down the truth sizably, or it was just too much for them to fathom at their ages. I decided not to discuss it right away but to probe what they knew before I talked to them about it any further. I hoped their responses would help me understand how to proceed. I had to at least address the issue with them before they got on their respective planes. I couldn't let them go away without knowing whether they were really hurting and hiding it or just confused by the whole thing. The unplanned plane ride to visit family could add to their confusion and make matters worse. It's important that I understand exactly where their thoughts are before I let them go. I decided not to tell the children where they were going until we had left the house for the airport. I have planned to make it a big surprise for them. They both love visiting their Aunts and I'm sure they'll be excited about going. They might question why they are going alone, why they are being split up, and why they aren't traveling together. I will need to discuss all of that with them, but I need a little time to develop a story that is believable to my four and six year old children. Right now my mind is so muddled and confused that thinking like a child is probably as taxing a job as I can handle.

I told Ralph that I was taking them to dinner, and that I might send them back over later tonight. I felt it was important for them to think that the children would be coming back. I hope that will relieve any concerns they might have as they watch us drive away. By the time they find out that the children aren't coming back, the flights will be long gone. Look at me. I'm talking as though I know Ralph and Carol are the enemy. I don't know that at all. Yes, I find the things they are doing and the things they are saying very suspicious, but I also realize that I see everyone as suspicious right now. Ralph and Carol are no different. It is very disturbing to have nowhere to go; so few to confide in. I have one policeman that I believe I can talk to, albeit in code. Unfortunately, talking openly to him on the phone could jeopardize the safety of my wife, and being caught meeting with him would almost certainly guarantee her doom. It feels as if my world is imploding and falling in on me from every direction.

The children seem fine. They are playing in their rooms, and Jodie even asked when Mommy would be home. I was surprised by her question as it seems that the children have just blocked out whatever Ralph had told them. Right now that is a blessing. It is a blessing to both me and the kids. If I can just get them on those planes and off to the safety of family, I will feel that I have accomplished a lot. I asked my little munchkins if they wanted to go to McDonalds, and you would think that I had just promised them a trip to Disneyland! They jumped up and down running through the house yelling, "We're going to McDonalds, we're going to McDonalds!" I'm happy to see them excited and laughing, but their exuberance and behavior seem a little extreme for the occasion. I have to wonder if they are in denial and sending their emotions sky rocketing wildly on unrelated or unimportant events to overcompensate. The problem is I'm not a doctor. I'm a plant manager. I don't have time to take them for counseling or to give them the opportunity to talk it out. I will have to depend on their youthfulness to help them through this. My focus right now has to be on Sarah. I need to call both of my sisters to warn them of the children's possible fragility. My sisters don't know anything about what's going on, but I must ask them to watch the kid's behavior. I'll tell them that the children are going through some stressful times, and to let me know if they see anything that indicates they need professional help. I will call for the sake of both my sisters and for the sake of the children. No surprises. That's what I preach at work. I don't like surprises, and I don't like to give them to others. My sister's need a fighting chance to help my children, and that means I will have to give them a heads-up without giving them any details. Not an easy task. I need to go to the Lord for guidance, direction and comfort; but right now I need to focus on rounding these little ones up and getting them loaded into the car. Off to McDonalds, and then off to the airport. I needed to decide what I would tell the children about their surprise trip. That strategic planning would have to happen on the way to our little hamburger heaven.

Ed Lancing had already cleared his first hurdle. He had cleaned up his work mess and straightened the house to his wife's satisfaction. Not to her standards, of course, but he met the lower standard that she set for his efforts at cleaning. Hurdle two was cleared when, with little resistance, other than a raised eyebrow and a shake of the head, she accepted his plan to go out. It was about time he started for the airport. Ed planned to grab a little something to eat at the airport café and from there he had a bird's eye view of the airport activity. This was a small airport and it made his job easy. Only one concourse, one level for tickets and gates, and really only one way in or out for passengers and visitors. The only other way in would require police or airport identification. Lancing was not taking that lightly either. He knew this group had contacts inside the department. He knew he had enemies there as well. Since this case was too sensitive to call in help and since he couldn't trust anyone else at this point, he would have to just do the best he could with what he had. He would keep his eyes open for people he knew: off duty officers or known associates. At the same time he needed to look for people watchers, people out of place, or anyone appearing to follow Jason. He didn't have the capability to do much else, so he had to go with what he had. Ed kissed his wife goodbye and told her he would be late getting home. As she walked away from the door, she stopped and turned around. She looked at Ed and walked back to him, opened her arms, and enveloped him in one of her loving hugs.

"I love you, baby. You know that?"

"I know, hun, and you know it comes back at you, right?"

"Does that mean, "I love you too, sweetheart? Is that what you were trying to say?"

"Yep, I think you got it."

"Promise me you will be careful tonight. I don't know what you are working on, but it feels different. I know you won't tell me, but promise me you will be careful."

"I promise, hun, and don't worry about a thing. This is no big deal."

"You're a big deal to me, Ed Lancing. I could care less about your case. I just care about you. Be careful and come home to me tonight."

"I always do, hun. I always do. See you around ten o'clock. That's my best guess."

"Okay."

The door closed and Lancing almost flew to his car. He noted his wife's concerns and found her behavior to be new territory for him. He couldn't recall her ever acting like that before. He wondered what activated her internal warning system. He had a momentary concern about a woman's intuition or sixth sense and the reported accuracy of their hunches, but then he had no choice but to let it go and begin focusing on the task at hand. He poured into his front seat, started the car up, and headed west to the airport. That little event with Marion put him slightly behind schedule. He would make up the time as he drove. If he had one advantage from being a cop in a relatively small department, it was that he could push the envelope on the vehicular laws most of the time. He used that perk tonight and turned his thoughts to tonight's meeting.

Steve sat at home thinking about Jason and Sarah and then about Joe Deener and his wife Abigail. No one could have ever anticipated this type of chaos coming to a town like this, and no one could have foreseen the horror that was suffered by Joe and Abigail. Now, the thought that it may be happening again, and that it might involve another family from his flock was almost unbearable. He was due at the airport in an hour and a half, and he was dreading the meeting with Jason. What would he say? How could he possibly comfort him? Once Jason found out that this case might be related to Joe's, the anxiety level would triple and the concern for his wife would shoot off the charts. Steve's role was to help Jason deal with those facts and then to help Ed decipher the case's evidence if he could. Neither of the assignments was very appealing. There was so much at risk and one mistake with Jason or the case and things could boil over. People could die. Steve thought this through over and over. His heart grew heavy as the time drew closer. Steve picked up his Bible and began to study some more. He looked up every reference to Satan that he could find. His eyes glanced towards heaven as he whispered to himself, "What do you have to say, God?"

Steve had been praying almost unceasingly since he talked to Ed a few hours ago. He laid it all at God's feet and he gave God very specific requests.

"God, you say you want it all. You want us to give you all our burdens. Jason and Sarah are my burden tonight, Lord. Show me how to defeat your enemies. Show me how to be victorious in your name and bring your people home."

God hadn't revealed anything to Steve yet. He studied His word and waited patiently for God's voice. Steve believed in the power of prayer. Not just because he was a preacher and that was expected of a preacher, but because he had seen its power and he had witnessed miraculous results. He knew God heard him, and he knew that God would answer in good time. One thing about God, Steve thought, He is always on time. One Pastor he had listened to early in his walk with the Lord used to say, "God is never late, He is never early, He is always on time." Steve had never forgotten that, and he had seen the accuracy of those words over and over again in his life. He couldn't answer why Joe Deener had to die. Why he had to suffer so. He didn't understand why God did not intervene, but he did know that he would never understand the thoughts of God. God's thoughts and design were on a plain far above Steve's ability to comprehend, so he didn't argue. He just went on faith. God promises that he hears our prayers, and he promises that he will always work for good. Steve believed in those principles. He believed that God was listening; and if God was going to listen, Steve was going to give him something to listen to. He was a prayer warrior and he had dedicated the last several hours to the plight of Jason and Sarah. He also prayed for Ed Lancing, for his safety, for his investigative ability, and for his salvation. Steve believed that Ed was on the spiritual fence. Steve was concerned that Ed worked a dangerous job and that he was always in the line of fire. Now, Ed was in a fight with the Devil. Steve prayed that Ed would know that alone he couldn't defeat Satan. He prayed that Ed would turn to God. Steve believed that if Ed gave his life to God and accepted Jesus as his savior, together God and Ed could solve this case. "Heck, they could accomplish anything!" Steve spoke these words out loud, and then looked around sheepishly realizing that he had. There was no one else at home, so there was no one to make fun of his talking to himself.

Steve also had a sense of fear. He had seen what they did to Joe. He didn't believe that he had a true fear of death, but he had to admit that he did fear pain. Joe had suffered unbearable pain. Steve feared that Sarah or Jason might suffer the same fate. Privately, he feared that being on this case could bring his identity to the killer's attention as well. Steve knew he was not a brave man, but he had never run away from a responsibility before; and he wouldn't run now. He did confess his fear to God, though. He prayed for his safety, too.

Steve looked at the clock. He had enough time to shower and change and then head to the airport. No one said where they were meeting, but it wouldn't be hard to find them at this airport. It wouldn't be hard for anyone else to find them either. Steve put down the Bible, and headed into the bathroom. He would shower and change, but he wouldn't stop talking to God. That was the key thing that Steve thought that he brought to the table for these musketeers. He convened with God. When the others would be focused on strategy and planning, Steve would be meeting with God. Musketeers? Steve wasn't sure why that analogy had come to mind, but he only hoped that their performance would more closely mirror musketeers and not mouseketeers.

The dinner with the children was going wonderfully. They had their favorite foods, they were excited about their plane trips, and they were energized about seeing their cousins. I had forgotten all about their cousins being such an impact on them, but it was big. They were laughing and telling each other what they were going to do, how late they were going to stay up, and how many Cokes they would drink on the plane; all the fun stuff kids like to discuss. Nothing about Mommy, though. No questions, no concerns, no crying. I didn't know whether to be nervous or grateful. I just told them that Mommy and I would be at the airport to meet them when they got home. They seemed content with that. I left it alone.

The time had come to leave McDonalds and begin our short trek to the airport. With the security expanded at all airports since September 11th, I had to leave plenty of time for the airline check-in process. The kids were ready. They had their Happy Meal games, and they were buckling themselves in for the ride. All I had to do was double check their seat belts and focus on driving. Jodie and Tyler were growing up too fast. I needed to spend more time with them once this thing was all over. I need to spend more time with Sarah, too. We always think that time is on our side and that we have all the time in the world. In the last two days I have realized that time is fleeting. A "vapor" as it says in my Bible. I have read that passage many times, but it never sunk in until now. When this thing is over, we will be spending more time together as a family. This thing will be over soon and Sarah will be coming home. I refuse to think in any other terms. I will not let my 'glass half empty' mindset come into play here. "Everyone buckled in tight and ready to go?" We drive off towards the airport singing together. The two little ones start and I soon join in. "Jesus loves me this I know, "cuz" the Bible tells me so."

Chapter Seventeen

S arah remained in the chair at the kitchen table and just
sat dazed at all that was going on. She had talked to her
husband and tried to give him some clues as to where she
was, but she was pretty sure he hadn't gotten them. She
could hear it in his voice. He thought she was rambling on
about wanting to spend time with him, and she was sure he
hadn't picked up on the clues that she was trying to give
him. She felt frustrated and at times she felt anger well up
inside of her. "Why wouldn't he listen to me? Why does he
just dismiss everything I try to tell him? He could find me if
he would just try; if he would listen." Sarah found herself
talking out loud and immediately looked up to see if Jack
had heard her. She didn't want him to know that she was trying to give away hints as to where she was. If he thought
that, he would move her. She didn't want to move. She knew
the hood would be put back over her face and she would be
back in the trunk of the car. She didn't want any part of that.

Jack was still busy with Pete's body in the bedroom.
Sarah didn't know what he was doing with it, and she didn't
think she wanted to. This man was a professional, and this
wasn't the first person he had killed and clearly not the first
body he had to deal with. Jack came back into the room and
looked at her. Sarah had stopped crying, and she had come
to grips with the fact that a man was killed right in front of
her. Her emotions were all over the map, but for right now

crying was not one of them. Jack was happy about that.

"Feeling better, Sarah?"

Sarah just looked up at him and stared. What was there for her to feel better about? She didn't miss Pete staring at her and she was glad he was no longer a threat, but she wasn't happy that Jack had killed him right in front of her. She had determined that she was going to die; that they were going to kill her too. No, Sarah didn't feel better about anything.

"I'm sorry that had to happen, Sarah. The man was not in control of himself and he could have cost us all a lot. I had no choice but to get rid of him. I'm sorry that it had to be right in front of you. I'm also sorry that I left you alone and he tried to take advantage of that. That won't happen again as long as I'm around."

Sarah kept staring at Jack and then slowly responded, "I'm not happy about any of this, Jack. I told you not to leave me alone with him, but you went out anyway. I'm glad you came back when you did, but did you have to kill him like that? Couldn't you have just pulled him away and then sent him back to your home base, wherever that is?

"Sarah, Pete was a loser. I had to take him when I had the upper hand. He was so out of control that when I came back in he didn't even know I was in the room. He was so infatuated with you that he didn't know what was going on around him. That was the opportunity I needed to eliminate the threat. He was a threat, Sarah. A threat to you, to me, and to the cause. Pete was a fool, and I only did what had to be done. It would have been done eventually anyway. I'm just sorry that he had pulled your hood off and that you saw it. I didn't realize that at the time I cut him."

"He tried to rape me, Jack. Is that what this is all about? Was I kidnapped for sex? I mean, no one can seem to tell me why I am here. When I spoke to my husband, he told me no one had really made any requests of him yet. Why am I here, Jack?"

"Look, Sarah, I like you and I don't want to see you hurt, but you have to understand I don't call the shots around here. You're here because our leader wants you here. It's not about sex. I can promise you that. I won't let anybody touch you in that way. I'm sorry Pete got as close as he did. Your husband is the key, Sarah, not you. We need him. We need what he controls. If he joins us and helps us, you should be safe."

"Should be? You don't even know, do you, Jack? Look, I'm glad you came back when you did, and, God forgive me, but I am glad you saved me from Pete. I don't miss him and I don't think the world will miss him. I feel safe when I'm with you, Jack, but I don't think you are being honest. I'm just a middle class housewife! I don't have anything special. I'm not anyone special! My husband is a plant manager, not an executive. What do you want? Why would you have picked us to do this to?

"I didn't pick you, Sarah. You are here because your husband is the plant manager. You are here because we need his cooperation. We need him to join us. We don't want your money or anything you have. I'm glad you feel safe with me, Sarah. I will do my best to keep you safe, and I promise that as long as I am alive that no one will try to do that to you again. You are beautiful, Sarah, no doubt. Don't think I don't have urges when I am with you too, but I am in control. I am a man of my word. I will never let anyone hurt you in that way and you can feel safe with me."

"You won't let anyone hurt me in "that way," but you can't promise that I won't be hurt can you?"

"Sarah, I can't promise much. You're right. I told you, I'm not in control here. I can tell you that this is not about taking advantage of you or a sex thing. Pete was a loser with problems, and he wasn't really one of us. He was just a hired hand. It was a bad hire and a wrong fit. I eliminated the problem. I want to help you, Sarah. I want to make you feel better. All that said, I won't promise what I can't promise."

Sarah looked away and for the first time it registered that she could see where they were holding her. She didn't want to make it obvious that she was looking around for anything recognizable, so she talked to Jack while she studied her surroundings.

"Jack, I appreciate your honesty and your help. I do feel safe with you, and I want you to know that I am grateful for you saving me. I will never forget that for as long as I live. I only hope that I live long enough for it to be impactful."

There was silence in the room. No response. Sarah didn't want Jack to be silent. She didn't want him to be thinking. He might realize that she could see everything and that might prompt him to make her put her hood back on. She needed to keep him talking.

"Who are you and what is this group you belong to Jack? Are you hoods, gangsters, what?"

"Sarah, we are not hoods or gangsters. Everything we do, we do for a higher power. A greater one, if you will."

"A higher power? Jack, weren't you just laughing at me for believing in God? How can you believe in a higher power and then laugh at me for the same thing?"

"We believe in the one you call Satan. We believe that he is the ruler of this world and that God lost the battle with Satan so he had to forfeit much of his power. To worship God is to worship the loser."

"How do you come to that weird conclusion, Jack? What makes you believe such nonsense? Haven't you read the Bible? Don't you know that God threw Satan out of heaven and that Satan is doomed? Why would you worship an angel that was rejected by God?"

Jack smiled and walked over to the kitchen counter. He started to pour himself a cup of coffee when he turned around and looked at Sarah intently. "Sarah, you believe in the tooth fairy and Santa too, don't you? Why do you believe that the Bible is anything but a book written by fools? Just have a look at this world, Sarah. Are you going to tell me that your loving God is in charge? That everything that is going on in this hell hole is controlled by God? If so, why do you worship a God that could let so many people suffer? I worship Satan. He is a supreme being that says we should make the most of the mess that God has given us. He teaches us that we should enjoy life and that if we follow the requests of our leader, we will live forever. We will have everlasting life right here, not like you, in some mystical heaven or hell."

"How can you believe that? How can you kill a man like Pete and then say you will live forever? Don't you see that this life is temporal? Don't you see that you should resist the temptations of this world so that you may celebrate the joy of everlasting life outside of this world? I agree with you, Jack, this world is terrible. It is filled with hate and crime and evil. Why would you want everlasting life here? Why would you want to live forever in a world filled with people like Pete?"

Jack had his coffee and he walked to the window and pulled the curtains back just a little. Sarah tried to look outside, but she couldn't see much other than day light. She believed that she had gotten Jack to start thinking. She wasn't convinced that he really believed in the things he talked about, but this was a group that had accepted him and utilized his talents. He probably had difficulty fitting in anywhere else. Sarah could only imagine what kind of a childhood Jack must have had. She imagined that he had probably attended church sometime and was an outcast there. He probably grew up with so called friends that would not accept him and left him feeling unloved and cold. Clearly, the group he belonged to now liked him for who he was. He had reached some lower level of control in the group, and he seemed okay with the fact that he was not at the top spot. He followed orders and seemed okay with that too. They accepted him. They liked him. What she hoped

Jack understood was that they were using him. That was it in a nut shell. They found those who were lost and broken, and they brought them in and made them feel welcome and loved for who they were. They learned to serve through a chain of command, and they were obviously given access to whatever they enjoyed in this world. Sarah was glad that Jack was with her. Others could have desires like Pete. Sarah feared what was ahead. She couldn't stop thinking about the word "sacrifice." Now that she knew this was a satanic group, she feared the word even more.

"I'm going to let you leave your mask off, Sarah. I want you to stay away from the windows though. I told you that you can trust me. Can I trust you?"

"Jack, I will stay away from the windows. You can trust me, I promise. Thank you."

"I'm expecting a call soon. We may have to move to another spot then. I don't know. At some point we need to get you some new clothes so you don't have to wear Pete's blood around with you all day."

Sarah suspected this was said for its shock value. He wanted to give in to her about the hood, but he also wanted to let her know he was in control. He didn't want to threaten her, but by reminding her of what he had done to Pete and that she was wearing the evidence of his power, she felt he had effectively done the same thing.

"Just stay out of the bedroom, Sarah. No reason for you to wander in there. If you have to use the bathroom, go ahead. I won't need to watch you anymore. Just stay out of the bedroom and you will be okay."

Sarah had no desire to go in the bedroom. She knew Pete was in there. She believed she was making headway with Jack. He had changed the subject and reestablished himself as being in charge, but he had also let down his guard a little. Sarah felt that this was a good sign. She was hopeful that Jack would become her ally, and that she could help him see the error of his walk with Satan. She was convinced that he wasn't totally engulfed in the religion-if that's what it was, and she hoped to show him the truth.

Jack stood looking out the window. He thought maybe he could teach Sarah to be obedient and to follow his orders. Jack was hopeful that he could keep Sarah alive and that he could teach her the ways of Satan. He felt she was strong in her faith, but she was warming up to him. "Maybe I can teach her to conform, to follow? Maybe I can teach her true submission? Maybe she can become one of my wives?" Jack smiled as he had these thoughts. He liked her, and he felt that she liked him. Killing Pete was brilliant. Not only was he a loser, but Sarah knew that he had saved her. Those were her words. Jack was hopeful that Sarah would become his in time. But before anything like that could happen, they had to deal with this mess. They had to get Sarah's husband in line, or make him the next to go. Jack wasn't sure which he preferred.

Sarah prayed, "Oh Lord hear my prayer. A lot has happened already today, Lord. I need your help here, God. I'm fighting more than kidnappers. I'm fighting Satan. Lord, you know I have no power against the Evil One. Help me, Lord. Be with me. Show me what you want me to do." Sarah didn't have any words left. She felt the tears well up in her eyes again, but she didn't sob or cry out loud this time. Sarah couldn't tell why she was able to fight back the tears now, but she believed that there were some signs of hope and that God would help her. She had faith in that hope, and on that thought, tears of relief welled up in her eyes.

Chapter Eighteen

Ed Lancing sat in the coffee shop at the airport having a cup of coffee and a roast beef sandwich. He ate the sandwich and eyed the people coming and going. "So many people oblivious to the evil that lurks about, oblivious to the evil among us," he thought. Ed wished that he could be naïve again. He wished that he could trust his fellow man. and he also wished that he knew nothing about the wickedness in people and the horrible crimes that they could commit. He knew that he would never be naïve again. "You can't go backwards," he thought.

Ed watched and ate. He had seen nothing suspicious so far. He had been at the airport for about thirty minutes but had just made his way to the coffee shop. He had already walked around baggage claim, ticketing, the gift shop, and up to security. He didn't contact anyone. He didn't want to be noticed or recognized, but he had to check things out before he felt comfortable enough to sit down and eat. He kept his back to the wall and he had a good view of everyone coming and going from the airport as well as anyone entering the coffee shop. Lancing didn't feel that he had much time left. He had to get lucky soon. He needed to find a break in this case, or they needed to slip up some how, but he didn't believe that this current scenario would last much longer. He was surprised that they had not made any further requests of Jason. He was sure that they wanted something from the plant. That wasn't exactly rocket science. After all, you don't kill the Plant Manager and then kidnap his successor's wife without assuming that the common denominator is the plant. He thought that he could understand everything more clearly if they would just tell Jason what they wanted. So far they hadn't. He had gotten assigned to the Deener case too late, and he never did know whether there were any demands that Joe did not fulfill. The murder was made to appear like a religious event, but Ed Lancing was never convinced of that. He felt that the killers worked too hard to convince the police that this was something other than a cold blooded murder. He always believed that the killers wanted something from Joe that he refused to give them and so they killed him. What they wanted was the million dollar question.

Lancing saw Jason working his way through the baggage carrying group that had just come through the door. Lancing watched him check the children on to their flights and then walk each of them to their gates. Ed could see the concern and worry on Jason's face as he watched him continuously glancing over his shoulder and from side to side as he walked with the children. He was obviously nervous and frightened for the safety of his children. Jason hadn't made eye contact with Ed yet, but he knew right where to find him. There weren't many places to get lost in this airport, and there was only one coffee shop.

Jason dropped each child off at their assigned gates. He hugged them like he had never hugged them before. Tears filled his eyes as they said their goodbyes. The children seemed oblivious to all of it and were more focused on getting on board the plane. He handed each child over to a flight attendant as their time came, and watched as one by one they were escorted on to their planes. He gave each an "I love you" as they went off hand in hand with their assigned attendant, and he got a big smile and a small wave in return. Jason worried about their safety both on the flight and once they landed. He had no idea how big this group's web was, but he knew his wife was trapped in the middle of it and he had to move his children out of harms way in order to help her. Moving his children seemed right but he prayed that his good intentions weren't putting his children in worse danger. Jason watched, he waved and he cried. "Protect them, Lord God. Please, protect them."

When Jason had his children safely on their flights, he headed towards Lancing. Jason was walking at a pretty quick pace and hit the door of the coffee shop at almost a dead run. He worked his way through the shop to the atrium seating where he spotted Ed.

"Hi, Ed. I hope I'm not late." Jason was glad to see Ed, but he couldn't make his voice reflect that. He was apprehensive and scared, and he couldn't pretend anything else.

"You're not, Jason. You're right on time. Please sit down."

"I talked to Sarah, Ed." Jason wanted to tell Ed about his talk with Sarah. He found out that she was safe right now, but maybe even more importantly, there might have been something in that short phone conversation that could help Ed. He was both excited to share and fearful of what Ed might deduce from all of it.

"Hold that thought, Jason. We are waiting for one more. He just came in the door, and he will be here in just a minute or so. We can go over the details together."

Jason was surprised that someone else was joining them. He looked up towards the front door to see if he could spot anyone he knew, but he didn't see anyone. Just then he heard a voice behind him that he recognized.

"Hi, Jason. Hi, Ed. I hope I didn't keep you waiting."

"Nope. Jason just got here too. Now that the gang is all together, we need to cover what we need to cover and then break up. I will keep watching the airport while we talk, so don't think that I am being rude or not listening. I just want to know if anyone is watching us or otherwise acting suspicious.

I would prefer that you two do not do the same. If we are all watching the crowd and talking without looking at each other, we will be the ones that look suspicious. Now, Jason was about to tell us about his conversation with Sarah."

"Well, I have to admit, Ed, I'm a little surprised to find Steve here. Sorry, Pastor, no offense intended, but I thought we were going to keep the details of this case quiet until we had Sarah back? Why didn't you tell me Pastor Steve would be here?"

"I didn't think of it until after we talked, and I didn't want to call you back to tell you. Steve has been a big help to me on cases like this and frankly, Jason, I think this case may be related to one he and I worked some time ago. We hope to understand more after we go through what we know tonight. We will get you up to speed too, but right now we need to know about your call from Sarah. I want to know everything. Don't leave anything out, Jason!" Ed looked at Jason with a serious look. He had thrown an exclamation point on to the end of his last sentence. Jason understood that details were important to Ed.

"Well, we didn't have much time together. It only seemed like a few seconds. I didn't really get anything from her. I just tried to comfort her-to let her know we were going to find her."

"Details, Jason! I want the actual conversation, not your interpretation of it!"

"I know, Ed. I was just giving you a feel for it. I wrote everything down right here. Let me give you what I've got."

Jason took Ed and Steve through the conversation. He told them about Sarah's conversation and her desire to take a vacation as soon as she got home. He also told them about the comments from the man he talked to after Sarah started crying.

"I told you guys, there's not much here to sink your teeth into."

"Tell us about the last place that you and your wife went away together, Jason." Ed sounded excited.

"What? Look, Ed, I'll be glad to give you my vacation highlights, but I would rather focus on Sarah right now. What do we do now?"

"Look, Jason, your wife sounds like she was trying to give us a clue as to where she is. I don't think she was having a melancholy moment about your last vacation together. I think she is trying to tell you that she is being held in a place that is very similar to where you stayed together the last time you got away. Where was it, Jason? Tell us about it."

Steve reached over and gently touched Jason's shoulder. He was trying to reassure Jason as Ed was starting to get short with him. Steve was smart enough to know that no progress could be made if egos got bruised or a battle broke out between Jason and Ed.

"I'm sorry. I never even thought that she was trying to tell me something. I was just trying to comfort her. Let me see. We stayed at our little get away spot that we go to about once a year. It is a little cabin up in the mountains. You know, one of those motel type places that rents out cottages or cabins near the lake. Do you really think she is up there somewhere?"

Ed thought for a minute before answering. "Well, the time works out about right. She can't be too far away unless she is still moving, but I don't think so. I think they have her someplace fairly close and a cabin like that would be perfect: no maid service, no room right next door. Tell me the name of the place, Jason. We will check there first. I'm sure there are other spots up there like the one you stayed in. We need to check them all. That is obviously way out of my jurisdiction, but I have a friend up there that works for the local sheriff's department. I know I can trust him, and I'll call him and have him look for anything suspicious."

"Like what, Ed? I don't think they are going to be parading my wife around with her hands tied behind her back. What would he possibly look for?"

"Her car for one thing! We just have to start ruling places out. He can check to see who has checked in recently and what they are driving. This could rule out a lot of people. We can also rule out tourists that are playing by the pool or at the lake. We are looking for someone who checked in and has been virtually unseen since. We have to try, Jason. Yes, I could be wrong. Maybe your wife was just trying to tell you she missed you, but I think it's more than that. I think it's a clue. We would be idiots if we didn't get up there and have a look around."

"Who is this guy you trust in the Sheriff's office, Ed?" Steve was now jumping into the discussion. "You say you can trust him, but how do you know? You don't seem to believe like you can trust anyone around here. Why him?"

"He was a guy that left Los Angeles the same time I did. He once saved my life, and I trust him with everything I have, including my life. Jason, you will have to trust me here. I trust him with your wife's life too."

"If you say he is okay, Ed, then he is okay. I think the name of the place was "Cozy Cabins" right by the lake's edge. You're right though. We looked at several places before we picked that one. There are lots of places up there for the water lovers and skiers. You know, we may catch a little break if he can hurry. I can't imagine that there are that many people up there now, except over the weekends. If Sarah is there, I would think she would be a minority. During this part of the season those places are usually only used for weekend getaways."

"Okay, I will get him on it right away. Now, Jason, Steve and I think this case is related to another case we worked on together. We need to tell you about it. Maybe it will help trigger some thoughts of yours that could help us find out what they are looking for."

"I'm all ears, gentlemen. What is this case you keep talking about?"

"You knew Joe Deener didn't you?"

The blood ran from my face. I must have turned stark white. Joe Deener? He had died a horrible death. One that I assumed was a religious rite. Are their plans to treat Sarah the same way as Joe?

Steve saw the color change in Jason's face. He could do nothing but reach over and give him a reassuring grip on the arm. What a small gesture. He should be able to provide something better than that. As he battled with what he should say and do, Jason spoke up.

"Ed, what can you tell me about Joe's death? Why would it be related to Sarah? I thought that Joe was killed as some sacrifice for a religious sect?"

"Maybe so, Jason. I'll let Steve tell us more about that, but I think there was more than religion tied to his death. I think that they wanted something from Joe and he refused to give it to them. Then they sacrificed him, if you want to call it that. I think they still want the same thing, and I think they are trying another approach to get it. I think they took Sarah to convince you to give it to them."

"But what do they want me to give them?"

"We aren't sure, Jason, but Steve and I believe that it is related to the plant in some way. That seems to be the connection. Joe wouldn't give it to them, so now they want you to give it to them. They are trying a new approach by using Sarah, but ultimately I believe they still want the same thing. Finding out what that is specifically is critical. I had hoped that by now they would have contacted you and told you what they really wanted."

"Do you think if I give it to them, they will give Sarah back alive?"

"We don't know, Jason. I have asked Steve to pray about it and I know he is. Right now we have very little to go on.

Your wife's clue may be our biggest break. Jason, do you make anything special at your plant, anything that a group of crooks or a group of religious fanatics might want? Is there anything within your control that could bring others wealth or power?"

I sat there thinking for a time. It was frightening to think that there was something in my control that could set Sarah free or get her killed. It was hard for me to think of anything that someone might want bad enough to kill for it. They had already killed, too. If Ed was right, they had murdered Joe Deener because of it. Not just murdered him, but cut him open and staked him out for all to see and fear.

"I don't know, Ed. I don't know what they could want. I mean we do make some drugs that are worth some money, but nothing that is of real valuable and nothing that is a narcotic if that's what they are looking for. Geez, Ed, I just run a plant. I'm not an executive with Concord. I don't know what else is going on with the company. I only have control over this plant. I don't have the foggiest idea of anything here that is important enough to kill for."

"Steve helped me with the Deener case, Jason. Unfortunately, we both got tossed from the case because we weren't following the story line that the detectives and the bureau were trying to sell. Steve, do you want to take a minute and tell Jason what we do know and what your feelings about Joe's death are?"

Steve nodded, thought a minute and then progressed.

"Jason, Joe talked to me before he died about someone contacting him too. It was a little different. They didn't use the internet, but they were basing their beliefs on Satan as well. This is why I told you not to talk to the person in the chat room anymore. I didn't really feel it was connected at the time, but it just brought back bad memories for me. I didn't want you to get involved at all. Joe got phone calls at work from this group and they told him they believed in

Satan and that they wanted him to join them and to do something special for them. I, of course, told him to stay away, and then two nights later he was dead. I never did find out what they wanted. I do believe that they are followers of Satan, but I don't believe that Joe's death was the result of some ritual sacrifice. I believe that they wanted something from him, and he refused to give it to them or do it for them. I think they killed him for that and used his death as a statement of sorts. If you remember, it did put fear in the community for some time afterwards. His wife, Abigail, left town because she could not live with the memory or put up with the way people looked at her. It was fear in their eyes and somehow she felt she was tainted by the death of her husband. She wasn't much help. Joe apparently didn't confide in her about their demands either. He went to his grave without leaving us any clues as to what they wanted. Jason, we think the same people are after the same thing only they want it from you this time. They knew the first way didn't work, so they decided to kidnap your wife and use her as leverage. They are dangerous people, Jason. They have killed and they do not fear hurting others. Sarah is in grave danger, and, frankly, I believe you are too." Steve turned to Ed and finished by saying, "I think you are a known factor too, Ed. I have to be honest. I have some fear that our whole little group is in some level of danger. I'm not trying to be an alarmist, but I think we need to be realists, and we need to be careful about what we do and who we talk to for now."

There was silence at the table for a minute or two. I tried to grasp all that Steve had told me and all that it implied. It was a bit overwhelming. Joe had lived through it all alone. He had gone to his death with all these secrets that he had not felt safe or capable of sharing with his wife, his Pastor, or his friend. I'm glad I trusted Ed, and I'm glad I had this small group that would know the truth no matter what happened.

"Look, we need to get out of here. I need each of you to

get to work on different aspects of this case. I'm going to call my friend at the Sheriff's office. He will get started right away. Jason, I need you to start acting like a frantic husband. I want you to reach out to this guy calling himself "Truth." We need him to tell you what they want as quickly as possible. The sooner we know, the sooner we can develop a plan to find out who they are. Steve, I need you to continue your efforts studying the different satanic groups that may be running around. We need to know as much about them as possible. The more we can find out about what they believe the better. Boys, we can't trust anyone. I know that seems a little paranoid, but it is a fact. I think they have someone on the inside of the police department, and they may have people in your church as well, Steve. We just don't know. Here, I brought both of you a cell phone and here are all of our numbers. We will only talk with each other on these phones. Jason, I agree with Steve that we are all in some level of danger, but I particularly fear for your safety. Don't go anywhere with anybody without letting me know about it. This is not a game. It is about life and death. Time is of the essence. Sarah's life and your life, Jason may lie in the balance. Any questions?"

There was silence for a minute after Ed's sobering comments, but the realism of its intent was not lost by anyone. Steve was the first to speak.

"I hope you are wrong, Ed. I hope the group is small and that they have very few people on the inside of your department or my congregation. I am hopeful that their impact on the community and the people in it is small. I do understand your concern, however, and I promise to you and Jason that I will not talk to anyone about this case. Jason, I know that you are concerned about your neighbors Ralph and Carol. I have prayed about it and can't believe that they are involved in any way, but again, I understand the concern and think we should play the most conservative cards. I will only talk to you on these cell phones, and I will also use it for my inquiries into the satanic sects. I don't want anything traced back to the church just in case they have my phones tapped or they are tracking inquiries. I will continue praying for both you as well as Sarah. These people are evil. I have no doubt about that. We will need God's help if we are going to have a chance of defeating them."

"I'm good to go, too." I volunteered. "I'll only use the phone to reach both of you. Please keep me posted, Ed, and you too, Steve. Don't wait until you have everything buttoned down before you call me. I need to know how this is progressing as we go. I promise to do the same. I'm going home to see if I can reach "Truth" and see what he really wants from me. I will call when I know anything. Ed, please find my wife. I know she is out there, and now that you've told me what you think Sarah was saying, I trust your instincts. God give us the strength to bring her home."

"Ed, Jason, do we have time for a prayer together?"

"Steve," Ed answered, "I have to ask that we postpone the prayer. Maybe we can have a short one in the parking lot. I just don't want to attract attention to us here. I haven't seen any indication of anyone watching us, but if they show up later, someone might remember three guys praying in the coffee shop. I don't think they will remember three guys having a conversation near as easy."

"I understand. Well, I will be praying for all of us. Just know that."

"Thanks, Steve," I was moved by his obvious love for us. "I have been praying, and I know Sarah is too. Thank you for everything you are doing. Especially your prayers."

The three got up and drifted off to the door. No further words were spoken, and they fanned out as they left the building and headed to their own cars. No one appeared to be watching, but often the unseen is more dangerous than what we see.

Ed climbed in his car and looked for evidence that someone might have been there before him. He saw nothing, but it didn't really make him feel any better. He was leaving with some hope, though, thanks to Sarah's comments to Jason. Maybe they could find her. Maybe Ed could make this case turn out different than Joe's. Ed paused a minute and then bowed his head. "God, you know I don't pray very often, and I know I am not very good at getting to church like you want, but I'm not praying for me, I'm praying for Sarah Shepard. Help us find her. Lead us to where they are holding her. She does love you and lives her life like you want her to. Don't let these Satan worshippers take one of yours away from you."

Jason got into his car. His head was filled with thoughts of Joe, Sarah, the mountain retreat, his work, and how they were all related. I've got to get them to talk to me. I have to get them to tell me what they want. Ed is afraid that the more time that goes by, the worse things will get. I have to get them to tell me what they want now! "Lord, give me the strength and the faith to follow your will. I know with you we can defeat these followers of Satan, and without you we have no hope. Please, God, let me listen for your intervention. Show me the way you want me to go. Let my words be your words, Lord. Amen." I have to get home and see if I can find "Truth." If I can, I know God will help me find out what they want.

Steve stood at his car door but didn't open it. He had his head bowed in prayer. He was the Pastor. He needed to be the strongest, but he felt the weakest. His faith was at an all time low. His people were being defeated by Satan, and he didn't know who he could trust and who he couldn't. Prayer was the only place he knew he could go and be with someone he trusted. "If you are willing, God, we can overcome this. If it is your will, God, we can beat Satan. Let your people have a victory over this evil, oh Lord. Give us the knowledge, the faith, the insight, and the desire to fight the fight; to fight the good fight, to fight the battle that needs to be fought. We are your people, oh Lord. We praise you, Lord and we bow before you. We know you have a plan, and we ask that you share that plan with us so that we might have a victory over our foes. Your will be done, Lord, YOUR will be done."

The three cars pulled out of the parking lot in random order, but their presence was noted by the lone man in the car near the toll booth. He was writing down license plates of who came and went. All three passed before him, and all three were duly recorded.

Chapter Nineteen

A thousand thoughts ran through my mind as I drove from the airport. I was excited that I had the children off on their adventures, and I felt that they were safe now. I knew I needed to deal with Ralph and Carol when I got back because they would be waiting for the kids to come back over. No doubt they will be waiting for me and be over as soon as I pull up. I think I should pull into the garage again just in hopes they don't see me come in. That will hide the car and hopefully give me a little time before I have to deal with them. I doubt that they will let me slip by twice unnoticed, but if God wills it, it can happen. The balance of my thoughts all revolve around my meeting this evening. I was shocked to find out that Steve and Ed believed this case was related to the death of Joe Deener. A chill ran down my spine as I thought about Joe again. I missed him and was sorry that he died such a horrible death, but I realize now that my life just went on. I wasn't much help to his family. I tried to calm the fears at the plant, but really my objective was to get people back to work and back to working efficiently. It all sounded so cold now. It sounded as though Joe and Abigail didn't mean anything to me, but they really did. But what could I have done? The church and the community were working with Abigail, or so I thought, but then she left town never to be heard of again. Now, I hear from Steve that she felt driven out; that she felt people were looking at her differently because of Joe's death. Now the shoe was on the other foot. It was on my foot. My wife was kidnapped, and if God chooses not to intervene, she could be murdered too. Will people forget her so quickly too? Will someone else jump in to keep the plant operating at full efficiency? Guilt filled my heart as I thought of Joe and how quickly the memory of his life had come to an end.

There was no traffic this late, so I was making pretty good time getting across town. I really hoped that I could get on the computer quickly tonight to see what the next move was going to be. I believed that Sarah was in more danger than ever now, and I also felt that my life was at risk too. If there was something at the plant these people wanted and I didn't give it to them, not only would they kill my wife, but they would then have no choice but to come after me. I couldn't believe how vulnerable I felt right now. They took my wife without much effort at all. They could be at the house waiting for me right now. I wouldn't be very hard to find or to kill. I was puzzled by one thing, though. Why did they take my wife so quickly? They had just engaged me in conversation. I hadn't refused any requests they had and I hadn't stopped talking to them, but they took my wife anyway. Why? Did they think that I would refuse their request? Why did they decide to save some time and move on Sarah? Was I too strong with "Truth" about my beliefs and my distain for Satan? Could Sarah be where she is now because of something I said? My whole body ached with remorse, guilt, and anxiety. I will give them whatever they want, whatever they ask for. Nothing means more to me than Sarah, Tyler, and Jodie. Two out of three were safe now, and I had to work hard to make Sarah safe too.

I pulled up to the house and hit the garage door opener, but I hadn't even turned into the driveway before I saw Ralph heading across the street with Carol an arms distance behind. I pulled the car into the drive and right into the garage anyway. They were standing beside the car by the time I shut off the engine and opened the door.

"Where are the kids, Jason? I thought you were bringing them back over tonight?" Ralph barked.

"Sorry, I didn't call you guys. I've just had a ton on my mind as I'm sure you can understand. I sent the kids out of town to be with family while this mess is going on."

Carol interrupted me, "Why? Why wouldn't you let us help you, Jason? We were right here for you. Where did you send them?"

"Carol, you two have been great, and I thank you for everything. I just felt that the children would be better off away from here. They would have heard things if they had stayed. They would have seen things on the news. My mind is on Sarah, and I had no time to worry about giving them attention or making sure it was okay with you if I brought them over. I sent them out of state where they can keep their minds on kid stuff and away from all the garbage that they might hear around here. I'm sorry if that offends you. It wasn't about you. It was about what was best for me, and what I thought was best for the kids."

"Are they with family, Jason? Carol and I are just worried about them, and we are worried about you too. We don't know how to help you, and watching Tyler and Jodie was our little way of being there for you."

"Thanks, Ralph. I know you are here for me. I know you want to help. Right now, though, I don't know how to ask for help. I don't know what I need. I'm just thankful to know you are there. If I need something, I'll call. I promise. But unless you know where my wife is, there isn't much you can do for me right now."

I stared at them both after that last remark to see if I could read any type of reaction. I couldn't see anything but sorrow in their eyes. I saw frustration in their body language, but their eyes were filled with sorrow. I was happy to see that. Maybe I had read them wrong. Maybe I had just been paranoid about them. Maybe, just maybe, they were the friends I thought I had.

"Where did you send them Jason?" Carol pursued.

I looked her directly in the eye and responded. "Away Carol. Out of state. Someplace where I believe they will be safe and free from the stress that currently surrounds all of us."

She persisted, "But, Jason, if you tell us where they are, we can check up on them for you. You won't have to worry about them at all."

"Listen, I appreciate what you are trying to do, but I think it is best for me not to share where the children are with anyone. I believe they are safe, and I want them to stay that way. I am not saying or implying that you would do anything to harm them. On the contrary, you were there for me when I needed you, but the fewer people that know where the children are the better. If one person knows, then it could slip out to others. Since I don't know who the bad guys are right now, I think it is best to keep their whereabouts a secret. I hope you understand."

I could see anger well up in Ralph's face, but I saw Carol nodding as though she understood.

"Look, I want you to know that I am thankful-very thankful to both of you for everything. I may need to call on you again before this thing is through, and I hope you will be there for me. I also may do some things or say some things that might offend you over the next few days. If I do, I want to apologize in advance. You are my friends and neighbors, and I need you by me, but I'm under a great deal of stress right now. I strongly believe that there is a very short timeline for this thing to play itself out. I have been praying and am hopeful that God will show himself. Right now I am making decisions very quickly and moving swiftly. I am very hopeful that you understand and will be there for me when the time comes."

I could see the anger subsiding in Ralph's face, and Carol broke into tears. "We're sorry, Jason. Ralph and I were just trying to help. We got selfish and were worried about what role we would play instead of worrying about you. We will be there for you, Jason. We are your friends. Call us anytime. Whatever you need, we will do our best to provide it."

"Yeah, Jason, we're here for you. If we got out of line, we apologize. We haven't been through this before either. Not sure exactly what we should be doing. Whatever you need, don't be afraid to ask."

They both started walking towards the driveway. They had their heads down and seemed dejected. They were acting like my old friends again. I had judged them too harshly. Steve had been right. They are good people. Before they got too far away, I walked after them and called to Ralph.

"Hey, Ralph. Can you help me with something now?"

"Sure, Jason. What do you need?"

"The other night when Officer Lancing came back to my house to interview me again about Sarah's kidnapping, I looked out the window and thought I saw someone standing in your bushes. I got the phone and started to call 911, and then I saw you step into the light. Can you tell me what you were doing? Why were you out there so late?"

Ralph seemed stunned by the question. His eyes were moving as his mind was working. I glanced at Carol and she was looking at Ralph with nervous anticipation.

"Ah, so you caught me spying on you. I thought I was pretty clever and that no one would be able to spot me watching you. The cop that left didn't see me, so I guess I just got a little full of myself when he left. I must have slipped up."

"What are you talking about, Ralph? Why would you be spying on me?"

Carol was nervous now and her eyes filled with tears

again. I could tell I wasn't going to like what I was going to hear from Ralph. I braced myself for what he would tell me.

"Jason, I have to be honest with you. When this thing first happened, I suspected you. I have seen all the shows on Court TV, and in most cases it is the husband or wife that kills their spouse. I racked my brain trying to figure out who would want to kidnap Sarah and why, but I didn't come up with anything. I decided that I would watch you closely and try to see if I could spot anything suspicious, you know, like a girl friend, or some seedy visitor that you might have hired to take her away. When I saw the car parked at your house so late, I assumed it was a girl, and so I hid to watch and see if I could get some evidence. I had my video camera hidden behind the bushes too. I'm sorry, Jason, I'm so sorry. I know you are a good man, and I know now that you didn't have anything to do with her disappearance, but I didn't know at first and I was worried."

Carol spoke up, "I told him he was wrong, Jason. I told him you were a good Christian brother and that you would never do anything like that, but he watches so much of that stupid television that he begins to suspect everybody for every crime. He thinks he is Sherlock Holmes. Please don't hate us, Jason. We are your friends and we are here for you. Please, forgive us."

Tears filled my eyes and I could think of nothing else to do but to walk up and hug Ralph and Carol. We stood together in the driveway in a group hug. Carol was crying, Ralph kept saying he was sorry, and I just lost myself in the hug.

"Thank you. Both of you. Thank you for caring that much about Sarah. I don't hate you. I love both of you. This is a crazy time for all of us. None of us has had to deal with anything like this before, but I just want you to know that I am thankful. Ralph, this thing isn't over yet. People may still be coming to the house, and quite frankly, some of them may be bad guys. I would appreciate it if you would keep being that spy and keep track of who comes and goes whether I am here or not. It would be a big relief for me to know you are there watching. I don't know how this thing is going to end yet, but I know it isn't over. Can you do that for me?"

Ralph's chest swelled with pride in knowing he was needed and his snoopy and suspicious ways would be an asset here. He looked at Carol with a little "I told you so" look and then looked back at me.

"You can count on me, Jason. I'm your man. No one will get on or off of this street without me knowing it. No way will anyone get within 100 yards of your house without me having them on film, including their license plate numbers."

"Great, Ralph. Thanks. Thanks again to both of you. I need to get inside and see if I have any messages. I will keep you posted as best I can."

Carol spoke up, "Jason, there is some food on your front porch. We saw one of the ladies from church stop by and drop it off. It will be cold, but I can come in and warm it for you if you want."

"Thanks, Carol, but I'll be fine. Thanks for telling me. I wouldn't have looked at the front door since I parked in the garage."

"Hey, Jason, I noticed that," Ralph blurted out as though he wanted to show me just how good a sleuth he was. "Why have you all of a sudden started parking in the garage? I haven't seen you do that since you started living here."

I chuckled inside, but decided I wouldn't tell him that he was the actual cause. "I just thought it best if people didn't always know if I was home or not. Now that I know you will be watching, I am less concerned about it. I'll probably go back to my lazy old ways."

"Okay, we're going to get out of your hair now, Jason. Come on, Carol. Call us if you need us, and I will let you know if I see anything that looks off color."

"Good night, you two, and thanks."

I got a wave from both and they turned and headed down the driveway. I hadn't wanted to spend that much time talking to them, but the results were worth the delay. They were loyal friends. The fact that they didn't trust me made me laugh as I walked into the laundry room from the garage. Someday I would share with them about my lack of trust for them too. We could all have a laugh together. Laughs would have to wait for now. First we had to bring Sarah home.

The phone in the kitchen showed three new messages. I walked by the phone and directly to my computer and turned it on so that it could start booting up. I went outside the front door, gathered up the dish that someone had left and took it back to the kitchen. I wasn't very hungry, so I looked at it, rewrapped it, and put it in the fridge. There was no note, so I had no idea who had prepared it, but Steve had told me they were going to bring meals for me. I need to be sensitive to that and not leave them sitting out on the front porch. Once I got the food taken care of, I checked the phone messages. The first was from a friend at church just telling me that he and the men's group were praying for me, and that he was there if I needed anything. The second was my sister just wanting to know if the kids got on the plane. The third was a distorted voice. It sounded like it had been run through a machine to mix and disguise the voice. It had worked very effectively. I almost couldn't understand the message much less recognize the voice.

"You went on an unauthorized trip today, Jason. Unauthorized trips could have dire consequences. It is time we talked. Check for me as soon as you get home. I'm waiting, and I don't like to be kept waiting!"

The phone went dead. I deleted the first two messages and listened to this one about three times. I saved it and then headed to my computer. I grabbed the cell phone that Ed gave me and dialed his number. He picked it up first ring. I told him about the message and that I was headed to the chat room as we spoke.

"Jason, I know it is hard but don't be confrontational with him. He wants to dominate you. He is trying to make you submissive to him and he wants you impressed by his ability to know everything about you. Let him think you are exactly that. Let him think you are broken. Don't give in 100% at first, but let him know you don't care about anything except getting Sarah back. Don't lie about the airport either. They may already know where you went and may use that to test your honesty. I need you to play along with them, Jason. Trust me."

"I trust you, Ed and I will play along. I will call you back as soon as I know something."

"Why not keep me on the phone. He can't hear you."

"I know, Ed, but I can't hold the phone and type at the same time. It will just be something else to stress out about. If I run into a jam, I'll call you back before answering. Trust me on this one."

"You got it, Jason. Good luck. I'll stand by the phone."

After hanging up, I got on my computer to find "Truth." I found the chat site "Looking for Christians" and logged on. I found that there were two people in the room besides the host this time so I didn't say anything at first.

"We have been waiting for you, Jason. Where have you been?"

"Are the others in this room with you? I hate talking with people I don't know."

"I don't care what you hate or love, Jason. I asked you a question, and I'm still waiting for an answer."

I remembered that Ed told me to be submissive, and I blew my first attempt. I had to try and regroup.

"I'm sorry. I just wanted to make sure it was safe. I was

at the airport. I sent my children away for awhile."

"I know you were at the airport. Why did you send your children away?"

"I didn't want them to hear the news or see me in such a frazzle. I felt if they were away on a little vacation, you and I could have this resolved by the time they got back."

"Very good, Jason. I think that was a very sound move. The next time you decide to do something like that, however; you will contact me first, won't you?"

"Yes, I will, Truth. I just haven't been thinking clearly since you took Sarah."

"You may call me Simon. Truth is what I am, but Simon will be easier for you to say. It will also help you remember that anytime you want to do something, anything, remember to wait until "Simon says" it is okay. Kind of cleaver, don't you think?

"Thank you. Yes, very cleaver. Tell me, Simon, how do I get my wife back?"

"Sorry, Jason, you are out of line again. I have more questions for you first. Why was your pastor, Steve Krier, at the airport too?"

I was a bit startled that they knew Steve was there, and I tried to grab the phone to call Ed for some coaching. Simon wasn't being patient though.

"Jason, your answers need to come faster, otherwise I may think you are making them up. That could be very costly, Jason."

I began to type. I didn't really know what I was going to say and didn't know what I did say until I read what I typed. I went with it and sent it.

"Steve went with me to send the children off. He is my Pastor. He is my counselor. I needed him to help me emotionally as I saw my children leave, and then we prayed together."

"You spend so much time in that worthless effort you call

prayer, Jason. Your God isn't listening. I'm listening. I know what you are doing and with whom. I am just testing you to see if you know how to be honest with me. If you can't be honest with me, Jason, we might as well call the game off now and send Sarah to her death. I would suggest that you spend more time focusing on the things I tell you than praying to the being you call God. He forgot about you a long time ago. Jason, your God is not dead. He just doesn't care."

I didn't know how to respond to that. I wanted to reach through the computer screen and rip his tongue out. I began to type in a lashing response and then realized what I was doing and deleted it. I couldn't agree with him as I felt that would have been blasphemy, but I had to do something. Silence, that was my only answer. I would remain submissively silent. One day I hoped to get Simon alone somewhere. "Forgive me, God, but my urge for violence is overwhelming."

"Very good, Jason. Your answer about Steve was honest. That is a good start. Now, I have another. Why was Officer Lancing at the airport?"

Here we go again I thought. No time to call for tutoring and no time to stall. I would have to go with whatever I could come up with on my own.

"I don't know why he was there. He did approach me though and wanted to know if I had heard from my wife's kidnappers. I don't know how he knew I would be at the airport, unless maybe he was there for other reasons and saw me. He was surprised I had not heard from you. He also wanted to know if any detectives had contacted me yet. When I told him no, he seemed to get angry."

"His anger will be his downfall someday. He makes a good point though, Jason. I think it is time that the detectives come out to investigate. Expect them tomorrow. I think Officer Lancing is a frustrated old cop that needs to retire. One day his irritating ways will cost him his life. I have tried to tell him that through various methods, but he is not very good at understanding my messages. I will have to take note of that. Okay, Jason, you have done everything we have asked and you have been honest with me. I am happy to see that you are coming along. It is time that we got down to business don't you think?"

"Yes, I just want Sarah. I will do whatever you ask."

"Be careful, Jason. I can ask for some things which may be difficult to deliver, but your intent and willingness are good to see. I want you to get Sarah back too. She is still safe just as I promised. That can't last much longer, though. We have to decide which way we are going to go-you and I, and then fish or cut bait. Isn't that the saying, fish or cut bait? I like that."

"I'm ready to fulfill your requests, if I can. Nothing is more important to me than Sarah. I would do anything in my power to get her home safely."

"Very good, Jason. Soon we will meet. I think you are going to enjoy being one of us. I know you love Sarah, but there are many other joys in the world that you can have along with your Sarah. Life can be very good for you, but first you must become one of us and you must deliver something to us."

"I am ready to do as you ask. Just ask! I will join you. I will do whatever you like, but I don't understand what you are asking. When will you tell me exactly what you want so my wife can come home?"

"Soon, Jason, soon. I think tomorrow is the day. It is too late tonight. The moon is not in proper alignment, and I think you will be better prepared and ready to serve tomorrow. Come to this site again tomorrow at 9am, Jason. We will be ready to discuss the details then."

I noted that none of the others in the room had spoken during our chat. They just sat silently. None of them had profiles, but they did have chat names. One called himself "The

Enforcer," and the other was "Death Angel." Both names made my blood run cold. I obviously didn't know who they were, but their names indicated that they might be there to carry out any sentence that Simon would order. Would he have given the death sentence to Sarah if he caught me lying? I was in fact lying to him, but I realized that he didn't know it. That made him human, and if he was human, he possessed no higher power than I. He was beatable.

"I will be here as you wish. Simon, I'm ready now if you want to save a day."

"I appreciate your anxiety, Jason, but we have to do things when the time is right. Rushing anything has never brought good to anyone. This will begin to move quickly, Jason. I promise you that this will not last much longer. You are coming along just fine-better than I expected really. I think that we will all be happy again soon; and though this has been painful, it will lead to a higher peace that you can not fathom quite yet. I will speak to you at 9am."

"Goodnight, then." I didn't know what else to say.

"One more thing, Jason. I want you to lose that "Jesse James" chat name that you are using. It just makes me feel like you are going to try to ride in and save your little Sarah. That would be a deadly mistake. Change it before tomorrow, Jason. I like the name "Seeker." Use that, Jason. It shows me that you are seeking the truth; and that you have a mind that is open to knowing the real truth, not just what you have heard or learned so far. You may have to add some numbers to it, as I'm sure it is a popular name; but "Seeker" would make me happy."

"I will change it tonight."

With that all three of them exited the chat room. I went to my profile and played with it for a few minutes until I could find a chat name that was not taken. I changed it to "Seeker 77," for no reason other than it was available. I printed all of the chat, and then closed off my computer. I phoned Ed back and gave him all the details.

"We're getting close, Jason. We have to be ready. I'll call Steve and tell him everything you have told me. Maybe he can find something in their names. I've got my friend doing a search up in the mountains right now. He promised me he would cover all of the sites that fit the "Cozy Cabin" profile. He knows the area well and told me he would have some news first thing in the morning, if not sooner. Keep your cell phone on. Just plug it in the charger but leave it on in case I need you. Be careful, Jason. This is going to get dicey pretty soon."

"I'll be honest, Ed, I'm scared; but I'll do anything to get Sarah back and to put these freaks behind bars. Any special instructions when I talk to the detectives tomorrow?"

"No, just tell them what happened. Tell them just like you told me. Try to leave me out except where you have to. Remember, I don't know if these detectives are in this game or whether Simon is their boss or anything else for that matter. Right now we have to assume that we are always talking to the enemy. You did fine with Simon tonight, so I believe you must be good at thinking on your feet. Just go with your intuition. It has worked well so far. Keep in touch, though, just like tonight. The three of us need to keep each other informed. Now try to get some rest, if you can. Tomorrow could be a very interesting day."

"Okay, Ed. I'll talk with you tomorrow. Hey, Ed. Be careful. These guys know who you are and I think you are getting on their nerves. You need to watch your back as much as I do."

"I will, Jason, and thanks. Get me off your mind, though. I know how to take care of myself. You just do what you have to do to stay safe while we are trying to get Sarah home. The last thing we need is for you to get into trouble at the same time. We only have a small team and you're one third of it. We can't afford to lose any of us."

"Okay, Ed. Thanks for everything. Talk to you tomorrow."

"You got it, Jason. Call me before 9, if I haven't called you yet. Goodnight."

Chapter Twenty

S imon paced back and forth in front of the computer that sat on a folding table near the middle of the room. The room held little else. There was a chair, a phone, and a coffee pot that sat on the kitchen sink next to a dirty mug. It was a dark, damp, tiny apartment that felt gloomy and cold, but it served as a temporary headquarters for the group that Simon liked to call "Satan's Den." Simon wasn't sure about Jason Shepard. He was saying all of the right things, and Simon was hopeful that he was coming along as quickly as he appeared, but the big question was how he would act if he got his precious Sarah back. That was very doubtful. Jason had to become dependent on the group. He would have to see that there was no other way, and that the only people that cared about him were Simon and the Den. It was already apparent that Jason wanted to do anything to get Sarah back. He was frustrated with the police, which was by design, and Simon thought that Jason was beginning to believe in the power and control that Simon possessed.

Simon knew that Jason had met with Officer Lancing and Steve Krier at the airport. He was surprised to find that Jason didn't deny it. His story was plausible, and since none of Simon's people saw anything to refute it, they would have to accept his story as fact. It is understandable that someone like Jason, under a great deal of stress and emotionally distraught, would call for his Pastor to add comfort and support. It was also clear that Officer Lancing was becoming increasingly difficult, and it appeared that there was nothing left to do but eliminate him. Simon didn't like killing police officers, but Lancing was going to have to be an exception. He just wouldn't let the Deener case die, and it's clear that he isn't going to let this one die either.

Joe Deener. What a waste. He had it easy. All he had to do was agree to the terms that were presented to him and join the team. He could have had everything. Life would have been his to control. He wouldn't do it, though. He stayed loyal to his God and his Christ, and it cost him his life. Even at the end, when he knew there was no turning back, when he knew the truth and the shock wore off, he stuck to his faith. He died calling out Christ's name. Silly man. Of course, no Christ came to save him. Of course, this God of his remained quiet and still. He died a painful death, and it wasn't what Simon wanted. Simon had hoped that the pain would break Joe and that he would come to his senses before he died. He didn't. He was a foolish man.

Then Jason Shepard took his place. That wasn't in the plan either. Gene Rikes was supposed to get the job. The Den could have controlled Gene easily enough. He was a weak man and would have done anything the Den wanted to keep from having to suffer like Joe suffered. That was ultimately the reason the final decision was made to leave Joe's body in the park and display him in a way that Gene and the community would fear. It worked great. The community was locked down in fear for several weeks. The plan was to watch as Gene got the promotion, and then to strike while the iron was hot.

Joe Deener could have taken the lead position in the Den. He could have been Simon. All he had to do was accept the truth and deliver on the demands of the Den. He would have had to get over some of the surprises and shocks that are associated with learning the truth, but he could have been a leader. He could have had anything he wanted, anyone he wanted, anytime he wanted it. He chose death instead and that made Simon angry.

Gene Rikes could never have been the leader. He would have just been one of the pack, but he could never have been Simon. He was not strong enough or convicted enough. He would have been the perfect man at the helm of the plant though. The Den could have had free access to worship on the sacred ground that happened to fall inside the plant property. They would have received on-going supplies of the drug that the Concord Company was about to release. This was a very exciting drug. Simon had sampled it personally. The drug would enhance the lifestyle of the Den, freed up the sexual inhibitions of some in the pack, and would have allowed them to worship openly as Satan had intended. This was a very exciting drug that was being developed by Concord for the purpose of helping paraplegics regain feeling through spinal cord rejuvenation. Simon tried the drug and the effects to a healthy person were miraculous. The drug stimulated every nerve in the body, and it freed the spirit so that one could worship Satan just as he would want his people to worship him. Worship free of inhibitions, free of restrictions, and free of the binds of those that worship the one called God. Gene Rikes would have delivered all of this willingly, and on top of that, he would have been required to funnel cash to the Den from Concord through some creative accounting practices. This cash would be used to support the work and the efforts of the Den. Simon had already created the accounting method that would siphon the money to the proper accounts, and the money trail would not be traceable.

It was a wonderful plan. It would have worked beautifully if Joe Deener would have accepted his role as leader, or if Gene Rikes was promoted after Joe's death, but neither of these came to fruition. Jason Shepard was promoted.

Simon knew as soon as Jason was promoted that there

was going to be a problem. The decision was then made to draw back and regroup. Jason was known in the community as a believer in Christ, and he would take much more work to convert than Gene Rikes. The outcome was clearly not as predictable as with Gene. The decision was made to wait, watch, and develop a plan that would either convert Jason or remove him permanently. The plan was good. They would hit him where he was most vulnerable: his family. Sarah was the first strike. The children were next. Simon had the strike force ready to go if Jason needed more convincing. The children would have disappeared right from their school. Jason was smart. He took the child card away. Now that option didn't exist, but they still held the strongest card of all, Sarah. Of course, if that didn't get the job done, they would take Jason himself. If worse came to worse, Jason would have to suffer the same fate as poor Joe. If that happened, then the Den would take their chances with Jason's replacement. There was no way that Concord could find another God fearing, Christ preaching, Bible believing plant manager. Simon believed the odds of that happening again were low.

Jason was saying all the right things now. He sounded as though his psyche was exactly where it should be for a proper conversion. He was wounded, broken, hurt, and becoming more and more dependent on Simon. That was good, but Jason was no dummy. Simon needed to proceed with caution. Jason could take over leadership of the Den once he grew in his knowledge of the truth. That didn't upset Simon. In fact, it would be just fine. Simon knew that following Jason would be exhilarating, and there was no inner battle or ego that caused Simon to want to hoard power. Simon just wanted to worship Satan and to do it in a way that would be most effective. That was why this plan was developed a few years ago. Simon had created the plan with the expectation that Joe would join the team. There had been some obvious set backs thus far, but they would be overcome and the end result would be the same.

Simon kept pacing around the room looking at all the options over and over again, continually thinking through the next steps. Simon would welcome someone like Jason to the leadership team. In Simon's mind, it was a relatively weak leadership team thus far. No one in the Den was even close to having the knowledge, skill or drive, to take the leadership role away from Simon. That didn't make Simon happy. The Den would grow with the right leadership. The pack's power would intertwine all through the community and could then begin to impact the politics and ultimately the creation of laws. Simon was very proud of the evolution of the group thus far. They had people in the local police department, the Christian school, and even City Hall. They weren't high level people yet, but they were the eyes and ears for the Den. One day they would grow in their power and influence, and Satan's Den could come out of the shadows and be known for who they were. Satan would then be given the credit he deserved. People would fear Satan and support his people. Everyone would begin to see the power of Satan and the imperfections of their God. The Den was small now, but it had proven that it could strike hard and fast and that it could create fear in the community. Fear was power. Simon kept the pack inline with fear, and Satan's Den would keep the community in line with fear someday as well. It was exciting for Simon to think about all the future possibilities.

Simon's thoughts kept bouncing from Joe to Gene to Jason. Simon forced thoughts of the future and past back to the present. Simon had made some decisions. Jason was ready. Simon believed that he was going to break and would give in to their demands. Jason would be the future of the Den. Sarah would have to die. Simon had less faith in her ability to accept Jason's conversion. She would be a distraction, and neither the Den nor Jason needed any distractions right now. Simon would give the order for her death tomorrow. She was of no value any more, and she was tying up valuable resources in Jack. Pete was not such a valuable resource and seemed clumsy and foolish. Simon would have him eliminated along with Sarah. The other person that had to go was Officer Lancing. Simon didn't like making this decision, but it had to be done. Lancing was in the way and could stumble on something that would bring the rest of the boys in blue down on their necks. His death sentence would be issued tonight. Simon would have Pastor Steve Krier watched carefully as well. It wouldn't be a good idea to kill a clergyman, but he had been involved in Joe's investigation, and he seems too close to this one as well. Of course, both Joe and Jason came from the Pastor's flock, so Simon understood why this Pastor would be involved, but he needed to be watched. If he got too involved or too close, he would be visited. If that visit didn't resolve the issue, then his passing would. Simon was pleased that Satan had revealed the truth and made it visible and clear to him. This allowed Simon to make these important and appropriate decisions. Action needed to be taken to start things in motion. Simon picked up the phone.

"Hello, Enforcer here."

"This is Simon. It is time for Officer Lancing to go."

"Understood. Are there any special orders?"

"No. Make it happen quickly and with as little fanfare as possible."

"I'm on it."

The phone went dead. Simon walked over and shut down the computer. There was nothing more to do tonight. Tomorrow would be a big day and it could be a major milestone for the future of Satan's Den. Death would play a role, but Simon had gotten used to death and the power it wielded. Death didn't come easy to Simon in the beginning. Death was always a difficult decision, especially early on.

Especially Joe Deener's death. It was all for the glory of Satan, and Simon had determined that death was a small price to pay for the expansion of Satan's kingdom.

Simon smiled at the thought of playing a role in bringing Satan's kingdom out of the shadows and into the light. Simon almost laughed when he thought about God shirking back from the power of Satan. "We are coming God. You have time to gather your people and run. We will grant you that, but we are coming to assume our rightful place. You will serve Satan just as it was always intended." Simon spoke this out loud and then laughed eerily as visions of God cowering in the corner became visible. The lights went out and the door was locked. Simon drifted back into the darkness.

Chapter Twenty One

At 3am Ed Lancing's phone rang. He jolted up from his sleep and grabbed the phone all in one move.

"Hello, Lancing here."

"Officer Lancing, this is the Sheriff's department. Sgt. Ted Dalton wanted us to patch through a call to you. I know it's late, but will you take it?"

"Yes. Yes, patch him in."

A few seconds went by while the dispatcher patched Ted into the phone line from the field. Lancing knew that Ted wouldn't be calling this late and using official channels without a reason. Lancing began to feel his adrenalin rising. He believed Ted must have something.

"Hello, Ed. You there?"

"I'm here, Ted. Go ahead."

"Ed, we found the car. Your victim's car."

"Great, Ted. What can you tell me?"

"At some point we will impound it for evidence, Ed, even though there is no official kidnapping report on the wire yet. The car was found parked in the woods. Ed, it was just a short walk up the hill to a motel that rents cabins. We may have something here."

"Ted, you are making me feel warm and fuzzy all over. Have you checked out the motel yet?"

"Yeah, I personally slipped up there and talked to the manager. Two men checked in to one of the cabins for one night, but they keep extending there stay one day at a time. The manager has never seen them go down to the lake or even to the café. She did spot both of them on different occasions, but always one at a time. She described one of them as older and polite. Probably mid-forties-a large, strong man. The second guy was younger and she just said he looked like trouble. He drove a green van, and it's in front of the cabin now. I have a couple of guys watching the grounds. What do you want us to do?"

"That's got to be them, Ted. This is awesome! How long would it take me to get up to where you are?"

"You're about two hours away Ed. Are you coming up? Ed, I got to tell you that I have a few men deployed on this thing. I'm not sure how far to push this. We don't even have a missing person report yet. What's holding up that detective bureau down there? Why don't they have this thing on the wire?"

"I know. I know, Ted. You have to hang in there with me. You have to trust me. I filed the report myself, so I know it is a real kidnapping. The fact that you have found her car up there ought to tell you something. The fact that we have our suspects holed up right where Mrs. Shepard said they would be should make you feel some level of confidence as well."

"Ed, I'm not walking away from this. You know me better than that! It's one thing, however, to find the car and watch the grounds. It is another to kick in the door and start shooting if it comes to that. We need an official case filed, Ed. I need to cover my butt. In the mean time, I promise you no one will leave this place. I'm not going to tow the car in either until we have made our move. I don't want them to find the car missing or hear the tow trucks. Right now, we have just backed off and I have my boys watching the place. If anyone moves, we will be all over them."

"Great Ted. The report should get filed tomorrow. Something tells me that the detective bureau is going to work this weekend, and this case will be the reason. I think the best thing to do right now is to wait and watch anyway. It might sound a little calloused, but I want the ring leader of this group. I think they are behind other murders, and I want to bring them all down. I think the guys up there holding Mrs. Shepard are just pawns. If she is safe, I want to buy us some time."

"Okay, Ed. We will stay on it and wait to hear from you. Get that case filed as fast as you can. I have to answer to a Lieutenant up here who likes everything buttoned down and in order. I have no problem right now because it is the weekend and it buys me some time. There will be hell to pay, though, if I have to explain that I have all these men deployed up here with no official crime. Are you coming up?"

"I don't know, Ted. Let me see how things develop down here. I think it's all coming to a head tomorrow, and I believe that the big play is down here. If it looks otherwise, I'll be up. I know you can handle the situation up there, Ted, but I'll call you and let you know what I'm doing as soon as I can. I can't tell you how much I appreciate your help. Bailing me out of tight spots is becoming pretty common place, isn't it?"

"No thanks required. It's what we do. You'd do the same for me. Keep me posted, Ed and I will call you if anything moves here. I won't take them down unless I have no choice. I'll try to give you the time you need to make your play down there. Be careful, Ed, and let's bring all these boys down."

"You got it, Ted. I'll call you right after daybreak."

Lancing gave Sgt Dalton his cell phone number and told him he could reach him on it twenty four hours a day but not to give it to anyone else. The two agreed on their plan and then hung up.

Lancing sat at the edge of the bed thinking through what he had just heard. He turned and saw Marion wide awake and staring at him.

"I'm sorry that woke you up, honey. You know how I hate to get those calls here at home."

"Sounded to me like you were excited about that call, Ed. Are you going to tell me what's going on, or are you going to tell me to just roll over and go back to sleep?"

"Honey, I'm working a kidnapping case, and the Sheriff's Department just found the victim's car. It's a break through, so I guess I am a little excited."

"Well, I'm glad to hear something is going right for you, but I'm sure you aren't supposed to be involved in this case, at least not at this level. Since when does a patrolman get phone calls in the middle of the night from outside agencies on a case? That was Ted Dalton wasn't it. You two are working together again, aren't you?"

Lancing smiled at his wife. She wasn't going to dig anymore, but she had to make her point.

"Okay, honey, roll over and go back to sleep."

Marion smiled and started to roll over. She stopped and asked, "You're not going anywhere now are you?"

"I'm just going to get up for a little while. I need to think through a few things and maybe make a call or two, but I'm not leaving the house."

"Okay then, Sherlock. I'm going to try to get some sleep. I know I'm off tomorrow, but I want to get enough sleep so I can enjoy the day. You know I need all the beauty sleep I can get."

"You don't need any at all. You're beautiful just as you are. Any more beauty sleep and you may disrupt the whole natural course of mankind. What will the world come to if every man is attracted to the same woman?" I already have more competition than I can handle.

Marion Lancing laughed and waved Ed away. "Get out of here, Ed Lancing, or I'll disrupt your natural course." She rolled over and Ed could hear a little chuckle as he slipped out of the room and quietly closed the door.

Ed felt exhilarated and alive. This was a big break through and he had to think it through carefully. He needed to play this just right or it could turn into a disaster. There was no question in Ed's mind that he needed to try and find out who the leader of this group was. It appeared that they had located Mrs. Shepard, and that was a good thing. Locating her and saving her were not the same. He had to break this down and decide which way to go and what strings to pull. If they moved on the cabin too fast, then this Simon character might break off contact with Jason and they would drift away just like they did after Joe's death. Ed hoped he could just get lucky and capture one or two of the kidnappers. If they could do that, maybe they might turn this Simon in to help their cause. He also had another concern. They could move on the cabin and Mrs. Shepard-Sarah could be killed in the exercise. Waiting was a better idea. He was sure of it.

He wasn't sure whether to call Jason or to keep this lit-tle tidbit to himself. Lancing was afraid that this information could make Jason act differently when he talked to Simon. Any changes in his tone or actions now could result in a death sentence for both Jason and his wife. Ed felt that it was better to hold back this information right now. Tomorrow was looking like the big day. Simon had indi-cated that the Detective Bureau would be out tomorrow. It made Ed mad to think this Simon character could hold power over his department. He didn't know if the detectives were involved, or if it was just someone controlling the information flow within the department. Either way, they had lost valuable time on this case. Ed was glad he was there to fill the gap. Simon had also indicated that the time was coming for Jason to receive his final instructions. Of course, no one knew what those would be, but Ed was hopeful that those instructions would lead to the identity of next level in the organization.

Lancing wasn't sure if he could take Simon down because he didn't know how many layers existed in this organization. All he could do was try and take out as many layers as possible. The more layers he could reach the better chance he had of finding a weak link. He hoped he could cripple the organization and maybe someone would give Simon up. He knew that his first concern had to be Mrs. Shepard, but he also knew that if he didn't drive a stake into the heart of this organization, there could be another Mrs. Shepard or Joe Deener down the road.

Ed went into the kitchen, put on a pot of coffee, and broke out the file again. He knew his sleep was done so he might as well use the time to study his files again. The more he knew about the Deener case, the more he felt he could connect the dots to Simon. That was the first time this group had revealed themselves, and then they went into hibernation. Now they have come out one more time. There must be a reason. Ed Lancing settled down at the kitchen table and broke out the file one more time. He felt energized now. They weren't invincible. For the first time he began to feel that this adversary was beatable. They weren't particularly good kidnappers. They got to Sarah alright, but to leave the car so close to where they were staying seemed amateurish. To allow Mrs. Shepard to ramble on about a vacation she wanted to take while she was on the phone with her husband also showed signs that they weren't as professional as he once thought. He always believed that they weren't kidnappers by design and that this was always about something else. He didn't understand it all, but he knew that they had made some big mistakes, and he could only hope and pray that he could capitalize on them.

Ed sat at the table and realized that he had asked God for help while he was in the airport parking lot. That was the first time he had talked to God in a decade. Was it possible that God heard him-listened to him? Was it possible that God had led Ted to the car and motel?

Ed bowed his head. "Thank you God. If you are helping us, God thank you. Don't leave us now. There is a lot more to do. Lead me, God. Tell me what to do. Help me make the right decisions. Amen."

Ed lifted his head and looked around to see if anyone noticed. He then realized that he was in his kitchen at 3:30 in the morning and the only other person in the house was his wife who he hoped was sound asleep. He felt relieved, silly, and then guilty for worrying about what others might think of his talking to God. If God had helped them on this case, then God was real. If He was real, then He had heard Ed's prayers. If He could hear prayers, then what fool wouldn't want to talk to Him?

Ed turned back to the open file. He would look for a clue; look for something to help him understand this man called Simon.

Outside, there was movement in the shadows. Ed could not see it, but it was there. Eyes watched him closely with alarm as the kitchen light went on and Ed seated himself at the table. The plan was to slip in and kill Lancing and his wife in their sleep. Why was he up at this hour? The inevitable would have to wait. Moving in when he was awake didn't make any sense. A fight could ensue, shots could be fired, the police called. None of that made sense at all. After all, Simon's directions were clear: make it quick and quiet. Officer Lancing has forced a change in the plan because he can't sleep, but the outcome will be the same. "Have your coffee, read your paper, and enjoy your last moments. None of it will change your destiny," the shadow whispered aloud. "Today you will die Officer Lancing."

Chapter Twenty Two

I woke up early from what little sleep I was able to steal during the night. I was sure that today would be the turning point. Today, I pray I get Sarah back. I am nervous because I still question Simon's true intention. Will he send her home to me alive? But I also have faith in Ed Lancing. I believe he is working hard to find Sarah. Though he wasn't able to do much for Joe Deener, I have a fairly high level of confidence that he will somehow help me.

I wasn't really sure how I was functioning at all really. At times I have surges of strength and endurance, and at other times I just want to go hide under my pillow until this all goes away. My emotions have run wild too: from rage to sorrow, guilt and self pity. Through all this I manage to keep going because I know that Sarah needs me. I know that after this is all over there will be plenty of time to look back and search for answers; but now I just need to stay focused on getting Sarah back. Nothing else matters. I can't allow anything else to sneak into my mind or heart right now. I don't need the distraction. Everything else is just noise. The only thing that matters is doing everything in my power to help my wife.

I got up early for three reasons really. I couldn't sleep anyway so what's the point, I had to begin to think about how I would handle my next interaction with Simon-I had the feeling that every word and even choosing the appropriate time to be silent was important, and I needed some quiet time with God. I had only spoken to God in short panic prayers and always while I was on the run. I needed some quality time with my Lord; not only to ask Him for help, but to listen for His direction. I knew that today would be fast paced, edgy, and undoubtedly dangerous. I need to talk to God, to read His word, to see what He wants me to know before I even start the day.

After about an hour I rose from my chair in the living room and felt empowered by God. I knew today wasn't going to be easy, and I knew there were no guarantees how it would turn out; but I believe that God's Spirit now empowers me to get through it no matter what. I don't know why I feel so confident; but by reading how God supported so many people in the Bible and how he delivered so many from their enemies, I just knew God would be there for me too. This was Sunday, the Lord's day, and I just couldn't believe that God would allow Satan a victory on His day. I got up with a new sense of purpose and peace. I knew that I couldn't afford to let my attitude evolve into arrogance because that would offend God. I also knew that God did not guarantee things would turn out just the way I wanted them to. The death of a believer was not a bad thing to God. It was really just bringing one of his children home to Him, so I didn't pray for the life of Sarah for her sake. I prayed for her life for my sake and the sake of the children. I prayed that God would spare her life for us. I would be lost without her, and I believed that together we could be more effective for God's kingdom. Although I knew it was a selfish prayer, God tells us to ask Him for what we want, and I want Sarah. I believe no matter what happens God is with me. Because of this, I would do my very best today. I would give everything within me and would listen and watch for God's lead. If Sarah was going to come home safely, it was because God wanted it to be so.

I walked into the kitchen and began rummaging around for something to do as much as looking for something to eat. My cell phone began ringing and I realized that I had left it in the living room. I sprinted around the corner. Maybe Ed had found Sarah. Maybe she was already safe? God could do awesome things if he wanted to.

"Hello, Jason here."

"Jason, it's Steve. You sound out of breath. Are you alright?"

"I'm okay, Steve. I just left the phone in another room and had to run to catch it. What's up?"

"I just wanted to see how you are holding up, Jason. It has been an unbelievably stressful time for you, and I wanted to make sure you were okay."

"Thanks, Steve. I'm holding up pretty well right now. I had a great quiet time with God this morning. I feel He is alive and well and on this case with us. I don't know how this will turn out yet, but I believe God will be a part of it no matter what."

"Your strength and faithfulness are an inspiration to me, Jason. I'm so glad that you haven't forgotten God during all of this. For many people it would be easy to leave him out all together. Is there anything you need from me? Anything I can do for you personally?"

"No, not that I can think of, Steve. Your being here with me during all of this is special in itself. I don't feel that I'm alone. At one time I thought I had no one I could trust. Not only do I have Ed, who I think cares about Sarah almost as much as I do, but I have you. Just hang in there with me, Steve. We will beat this thing."

"I'll be there with you at the finish line, Jason. You can count on that. Well, I know you have a lot going today. Call me anytime you need me. I'll be preaching today, as you know, but I will have the phone on all the rest of the time. I will break away from whatever I'm doing to help. I only wish I could do more."

"I wish I could explain to you how much help you are, Steve. Don't minimize your importance to me, Sarah, and this case. Hey, Steve. There is one thing you can do for me. I would appreciate it if you had the ladies group stop making the meals for me right now. It is a wonderful gesture, but I have no time to think of food right now, and I don't want their efforts to sit spoiling on the front porch. Could you pass on my thanks and love, but let them know I just can't think about food right now?"

"You got it, Jason. They'll understand. Don't worry about that little thing. Anything else?"

"Oh, yeah, I wanted you to know that I think I have resolved everything with Ralph and Carol. Things are fine there, and I thought you should know."

"Praise God, Jason. Praise God. I just didn't want to believe that any of our flock could possibly be involved in this awful thing. I'm so happy you have reconciled with them."

"Yeah me too, Steve. Well I have to go and you have to prepare for your sermon. Wish I could be there to hear it but save me a tape. Sarah and I will want to hear it together when this thing is over."

"Ok, Jason. Call me if you need me. Good bye and may God bless you today."

I hung up the phone feeling warm and loved by not only a man, but by a congregation of God's people who cared about one of their lost sheep. It was a wonderfully euphoric feeling, but I couldn't allow myself to enjoy that feeling for too long. I had to get my thoughts focused on the up-coming chat with Simon and the visit I expected from the Detectives.

It was now 7:30am, and I was struggling with how I would handle Simon when we talked again. How could I plan for something that I wasn't controlling? He would ask the questions, and he would make the demands. I would just have to react. How can I plan for that? I came to the conclusion that the important thing for me to do was to remain calm and composed. I couldn't allow my anger and frustration to impact my reaction to Simon. If I did, it could set us back, it could even hurt Sarah. I had to appear to be cooperative; to be falling in line. I had to make him think that I was mentally and emotionally right where he wanted me.

My cell phone rang again and I picked it up on the first ring. I assumed it was Steve calling back with one more thought.

"Hello, Jason here."

"Good morning, Jason, this is Ed. How you feeling this morning?"

"I'm good, Ed. I'm ready to bring this thing to a close. I just spoke to Steve and he thinks today is going to be a big day too."

"Well, that makes three of us. I think that today is the day. My friend at the sheriff's department is making some headway up near the lake, and I am hopeful that he will have something to report to us real soon."

"You mean he has found Sarah? Ed, tell me what's going on!"

"Jason, stay calm. Take a deep breath. We don't have anything yet, but he thinks that he is getting close. I need you to keep your mind focused on your job. This is very important for us, and you are the key to finding out who Simon is."

"I will do my best. You know that, but my main concern is obviously Sarah. If you get her back, I'm going to be focusing on that and only that!"

"Listen to me, Jason. Getting Sarah back and getting her back safe is the goal for all of us. But there is another very important side of the coin. If we get her back and we don't find Simon and take him out, who's to say that they won't just come and take her again? Who's to say that the next time they won't go after the kids or you? They want something from you, Jason. I think they wanted the same thing from Joe. They didn't get it, and I believe they will keep trying until they do. Getting Sarah back is what we plan to do, but we also have to plan to take Simon down. You and your family will not be happy or safe until we are able to do both."

I sat quietly for a minute reflecting on what Ed had said. He was right of course. This wasn't just about getting Sarah. This was about destroying this group and their leader. We would never be able to relax until that happened. It was a sobering thought and the first time I had thought about it from that perspective.

"You still with me, Jason?"

"I'm here, Ed. You're right. Of course, you're right. I just never thought of it in those terms before. I'll stay focused, Ed. I will do the best I can."

"I know you will, Jason. Look, I plan to be with you when you contact Simon this morning. I will be able to better support you and I will get a first hand view of where he might be trying to lead us. I think I can park a block or so away and sneak into your house without attracting too much attention."

"That would be great, Ed. I would love to have you here. I'm afraid I might make a mistake that could set us all back and possibly hurt Sarah in the long run. It would be great if you were here."

"Okay, Jason. Well I had better get going if I'm going to get there in time. I'll try to be there by 8:30 or so. See you then."

I felt like a million bucks for that one short minute. Now I didn't have to face Simon alone. Since our communication was going to be on the computer, Ed would be able to help me and coach me before I answered Simon's questions. It was like a weight was lifted off my shoulders. I wanted to bring Sarah home, but I now understood that it was also very important to find Simon and put him out of business. This was now part of my responsibility, and I would do everything in my power to make it happen. I will do everything in my power to stay out of God's way so that He can make it happen.

The front door bell rang and I practically jumped out of my skin. I'll be happy when this thing is all over so that I can regain control of my emotions and stop the jitters every time the phone rings or the door bell chimes. I have no idea who might be at my door at this hour, so I cautiously move towards the front door to the find out.

Two men stood at the door looking somber and serious. I immediately assumed that these were the detectives that Simon said would come today. I had no way of knowing whether they were good guys or bad guys, but I knew I had to be careful with whatever I told them.

"Mr. Shepard?"

"Yes, I am Jason Shepard. Who are you?"

"Sir, I'm Detective Kyle and this is Detective Fisher. We are here to follow up on the disappearance of your wife, Sarah Shepard."

"Well, it's about time. I don't understand how so many days could have gone by before you would come and see me. I still don't know where she is. Nobody has told me anything. What is going on?"

"Can we come in, Mr. Shepard? We are as much in the dark as you about why we weren't given this case earlier. We should have been out here that very first day, sir, but for some reason no one ever gave it to us. We're here now. Can we come in?"

"Yes, of course. Let's go into the living room. I have given everything I know to Officers Lancing and Devoy. I don't know that I have much to add, and I haven't heard a thing since she was first reported missing."

"Lancing was here?" The two detectives looked at each

other and I saw them shake their heads ever so slightly. "Maybe he is why we didn't get the case until now. He seems to enjoy doing some of the detective work himself before he hands his reports over to us. Maybe he just turned the report in. Who knows."

I could feel my temper rising while I listened to these two men. They were automatically dropping the blame on Ed Lancing. Their reaction did convince me that these two were not stone walling this case on purpose. I believed that they had just received the case and were now following up on it as soon as they found out about it. But I didn't like their willingness to just dismiss the delay in the filing of the case and assume the cause was Ed Lancing. I had to let my personal feelings go. Ed was big enough to take care of himself. What I realized was that I had to make sure these two didn't stay around too long. Ed was on his way, and I had to contact Simon at 9am. I didn't think that Simon would like being kept waiting. Right now, it was all about keeping Simon happy.

The meeting with the detectives lasted about forty five minutes, and their questions lead in a predictable way. They tried to determine if I was involved in any way. They wanted to know if Sarah had any enemies. They seemed surprised that the kidnappers had not contacted me by now, and that her car had not turned up some where. They assumed that the kidnappers had abandoned it right after taking it. Of course, they then realized that the kidnapping and the car theft had not even been reported to other jurisdictions yet. That meant that even if someone found the car, it wouldn't come back as stolen or wanted. Sarah wasn't even listed as a missing person. Detectives Kyle and Fisher seemed upset over this and left leaving verbal assurances that they would get it posted within the hour. They apologized for the delay and promised that they would get on the case immediately. They also promised that they would report the delay in receiving the case to their supervisors, and the reason for the delay would be thoroughly investigated. They shook my hand and promised to stay on top of it until Sarah was found. They gave me their card and asked me to call them if I thought of anything else or if I was contacted through any means. They would come back with phone tapping equipment and tracers once they knew that the kidnappers intended to contact me. They tried to reassure me that most of the time the kidnap victims came home unharmed, but it was obvious that they were stumped by this case. I felt a little guilty that I was not giving them all of the facts. I knew we were close to finishing this thing, and although I didn't believe either of these officers was involved, I couldn't trust anyone outside of our small circle this late in the game.

The detectives left and I went inside to grab the cell phone to let Ed know they had come and gone. It was now 8:40 and I had expected him to be here by now. I was grateful that he was late. I didn't want him wandering up while the detectives were here. The doorbell rang again. I knew the detectives were gone because I watched through the window as they drove away, so I assumed this was Ed.

When I opened the door, I was surprised to find Ralph standing there. He had his hunting rifle in his hand.

"You okay, Jason? I saw those two guys here and I just wanted to make sure you were okay."

I smiled. I couldn't do anything but smile. Ralph had been given an assignment, and he was taking it seriously.

"I'm good, Ralph. Thanks for checking up on me. They were detectives following up on the case."

"Oh, okay. I saw them pull up. I came across the street when you let them in and I saw all of you in the living room. I got the license number just in case they were threatening you or anything. Glad to hear it was nothing like that."

I wasn't so sure that Ralph was glad it wasn't something more. He looked ready and armed for battle. Although he acted as though he was relieved, I read a little disappointment in his manner. He liked being involved and he wanted to be called into the fight.

"Thanks, Ralph. Thanks for being there for me. I feel a lot safer knowing you are watching over things for me. By the way, I'm expecting another man to visit me as well. He may walk up to the house, but he's a good guy, Ralph. He's with us." I gave Ralph a description of Ed which he immediately internalize and just nodded back in response.

"Okay, Jason, I'll keep at it. Any news yet? Anything good or bad?"

"Not much yet, Ralph, but today could be a big day. Keep a sharp eye out for me, Ralph. I think this thing is going to come to a head today. I don't know if that means they will come to the house or not, but we all need to be ready."

"You got it. I'll head back over to my place now. I want to get back into position. If they are going to come today, I'll be ready for them. You'll be fine, Jason. Don't you worry about that."

Ralph marched off gun in hand. I smiled and had to admit that I did feel just a little safer with Ralph on the job. It was a bit comical, but his heart was bigger than I had realized, and he was ready to stand up and fight by my side. That said a lot about the man, and it said a lot about the woman that stood by his side as well.

I walked back into the house and was jolted by the sight of Ed Lancing sitting at my kitchen table drinking some orange juice. He looked up and smiled when I walked in.

"Who the heck was that guy?" he questioned.

"My neighbor, Ralph. You met him the first night you were here. He means well. He's keeping an eye on me until this mess comes to an end."

"He's doing a great job if the bad guy comes in the front door." Ed chuckled a little and then looked up as though he needed to apologize for making light of the situation.

I had to chuckle back and he seemed relieved. "His heart is in the right place, and he's doing what he thinks he can do to help me right now. It's a tough time for everyone."

"I thought you didn't trust him?"

"I was wrong, Ed. He and Carol are good people."

"Okay, good. I saw Kyle and Fisher were here. Anything there?"

"Just what I expected. I think they are good guys, Ed. They were very upset that no one had notified them of this case until now. They told me it would be sent out to all police departments nationwide within the hour.

"Good, that's very good. After this is all over, I need to find out why this got held up too. Someone inside the department is involved. I need to find out who that is and weed them out."

"Well, they seemed to imply that it must have been because of your ineptness. Once they heard you were on the case, they assumed you were doing some of your off the cuff detective work before you turned it over to them. They plan to report it when they get back."

Ed started to get angry and his anger turned to a quick laugh. "What can you say when you're in the dog house. Everyone likes to have a kick at you. I just have to learn to enjoy the pain. Now, let's get ready for Simon, Jason. I don't know how this computer stuff works, but show me so I understand before you make the contact. Jason, I believe I know who Simon is now. I was studying the files of the Deener case just like I have done for the past few years. All of a sudden it just jumped out at me. It came to me like a revelation or vision, and then as I followed up on it and studied it more. It seemed so obvious to me. I should have seen it before, Jason, but it was like a fog was lifted from my eyes and I saw it for the first time. Now I think I know. I can't be positive, but I'm about 85% sure anyway. Get this computer up and running and I will tell you what I know. You won't believe me at first, Jason, but I think I'm right and I'm convinced we will take this Simon character down before this thing is done. I should also tell you that I had a very exciting ride over here today. I'll give you the low down on that as well. I told you today would be the day, and I am more convinced than ever that I'm right. They want to make their move today. I feel it in my bones. You will need to convince them that you are ready; that you are theirs to control. We can do this, Jason, and we can get Sarah back. Today is our day. I don't know how I know it, but I know it.

I started up the computer as I turned to listen to Ed tell me all he had discovered. I was excited, nervous with anticipation, and a bit scared. I was a little afraid that Simon might be someone that I knew; someone that I cared about.

"Well, come on, Ed. Don't leave me hanging!"

Chapter Twenty Three

Just a few hours before his meeting with Jason, Ed sat in his kitchen pouring over the Deener and Shepard files looking for that one clue, that one piece of information that had escaped him until now. He needed something; something to help him discover the identity of Simon. He thought he would find out what they were really up to once he and Jason contacted Simon later this morning. But he needed something more. He needed something that might give him the upper hand. He had just hung up with Jason, and Ed thought that he sounded as though he were in pretty good shape emotionally. That would be very important. Ed believed that today was the day that this group would reveal themselves, and everyone was going to have to be sharp as a tack if good was going to overcome evil.

Ed was just wrapping things up and he began to think about cleaning up his mess so that he could prepare for his drive to Jason's. That's when it happened. That's when it just jumped off the page at him. He yelled out in excitement and disbelief when he saw it and that caused Marion Lancing to call out from the bedroom.

"What are you doing now, Ed? I had a perfectly good nightmare going on when you interrupted it by your scream. Are you okay?"

"Sorry, honey. I'm not just okay, I'm great! I think I found something I have been looking for in a case I've been working. I don't know how I overlooked it up until now, but I think I'm on to something. I have to study it a little more, but I'll try to be quiet. Besides, I have to get dressed and get over to a friend's house this morning. He needs me to give him a hand, and that will leave the house nice and quiet for you."

"That's nice, dear. Go back to your work, but no more screaming. I have a dream to finish."

Ed looked down at his report. He moved from one page to the next, flipping back and forth between different reports. "Of course," he whispered. He had to be right. It was never even considered when the Deener case was open, and it would have never hit the radar screen in the Shepard case, but there were connectors. They were small-almost microscopic, but something made them jump off the page at him this morning. How had he discovered this now after all of these years? Why this morning, right when it was needed most? Ed didn't know why, but didn't have time to understand it all now. He believed he had just discovered the identity of Simon. Ed thought he knew who was behind Joe Deener's murder and the kidnapping of Sarah Shepard. This was big, but he wasn't sure who would believe him. It would take someone with an open mind; someone enlightened. This wasn't easy to swallow, not even for Ed.

Ed cleaned up his mess in the kitchen, as he knew Marion would not appreciate getting up to case files lying all over her kitchen. He couldn't dilly dally, though. He wanted to get over to Jason's with plenty of time to spare. He would want to toss his theory about Simon's identity around with Jason. Jason was bright and he would be a man that could effectively challenge Ed's thought process. That would be good. Ed wanted to be 100% sure he was headed down the right path. He wanted to be sure he wasn't seeing things that didn't really exist. Ed was pretty sure that it wasn't the case, but he would talk it through with Jason, and that would either help shore up his hypothesis or it would help him see the flaws in his thinking. He was excited about his find and excited to share it with someone.

Ed kissed Marion goodbye and went to the garage to get his car. He backed out of the garage and headed south to catch one of the main streets that would lead him across town. As Ed hit the first stop sign, he looked at his rear view mirror and spotted a car pulling away from the curb just down the block from his house. He waited at the stop sign longer than he had to so that he could get a closer look at the car. It did not pull up directly behind him but slowed down as though the driver was waiting for Ed to proceed. The car looked liked a dark green newer model Mercury Sable or Ford Taurus. It was a four door and appeared that the driver was the only one in the car. Ed pulled away from the stop sign and watched as the car then accelerated and practically ran the stop sign following in the same direction. The car looked like a typical rental car and did not look familiar in the neighborhood. Ed was sure that he was being followed but by whom? There was only one way to find out. He continued to drive south until he came to State St, and he then turned east. While Ed drove he watched the car follow at a safe distance. Ed developed his plan of attack.

Ed continued eastbound until he was outside of the city limits and into county territory. He knew he could get help here. He wasn't sure who to trust in his own city and that was a shame, but he knew Ted would get him some help. Ed drove to a nearby grocery store and parked in a row that was relatively close to the front door. He watched as the man following him and parked at a safe distance a few aisles away. Ed got out of his car and walked towards the front door of the store. He was careful to watch his reflection in the store's glass windows to see if the man exited the car and followed him. Ed didn't want to be caught in the open parking lot. He not only took great caution in watching this man's actions, but he kept attentive for any other suspicious activity that might be going on around him. There was nothing to say this man was working alone, but he was the only one Ed could see right now. Ed stood inside the door of the store and looked out through the smoked glass. He watched as the man got out of his car and walked over to Ed's. He watched as the man checked to see if the car was unlocked. Finding it locked, he walked back to his car and then moved it closer to where Ed was parked. Ed's experience and intuition told him that this man had come to kill him. From the man's actions, Ed thought that his pursuer had chosen this parking lot as the place for it to happen. Ed didn't believe he had ever seen this man before. He was in his mid thirties, partially balding, and not very distinct in any particular way.

Ed used his cell phone and called Ted Dalton. He explained the circumstances to Ted and told him where he was. Ted would get some deputies to him right away. Ed hung up and headed for the back door of the store.

As Ed Lancing circled around the store parking lot, he was very careful to watch everything to his sides as well as in front of him. He didn't want to stumble into anything because he was only focused on this one man. He might have reinforcements as well. If he was going to lose his life, it wasn't going to happen because he was caught unawares. If he lost in a gun battle, then so be it; but he wasn't going to lose because somebody out thought him. He kept his head down and ducked from car to car until he circled to the end of the aisle where both his car and the mystery man were parked. He could see the man sitting in his car smoking a cigarette. Ed eased his way down the aisle closer to the man in the car. Ed drew his gun and moved quickly now. The man in the green Taurus had his window down and was taking a deep drag on his cigarette. Ed quickly moved up to the driver's door and jammed his 9mm into the side of the man's head. The man froze immediately.

"If you so much as move a muscle, I'll blow your head off!"

There was no response. The man just sat in the car holding the cigarette in the air. Ed looked down at his other hand and it was gripping a small caliber revolver which lay in his lap.

"You can raise your other hand nice and slow and leave the gun on your lap, or you can try to make a move and make this your last day on earth."

The man said nothing but raised his hand slowly to the level of the one with the cigarette. Ed slowly opened the man's car door. The man just continued to sit quietly with his hands in the air. This man was no professional. He was probably pretty good at killing people when they didn't expect it, but he had no stomach for a fight. He didn't want to die, and he wasn't going to protest the fact that Ed was in control. Just then the cavalry poured into the parking lot with lights flashing and deputies bailing out of their cars with guns ready. Of course, they didn't know who Ed was either, so they not-so-gently told him to drop his weapon. Before Ed responded he announced that he was a police officer and that the man in the car had a gun lying in his lap. The deputies had both men covered effectively, so Ed felt safe to lower his weapon and lay it on the ground.

After the arrest was made and identities verified, the deputies were very helpful and told Ed that Sgt Dalton had given them the call. It turned out that the man in the car was wanted on several warrants including two for murder. He was wanted in Tennessee for murdering a man and his wife in their sleep. He was apparently a gun for hire. Lancing gave the officers a statement, told them he would follow up with them if they needed anything else, but they could always reach him through Sgt Dalton. Ed told them that he was currently working on another big case and that he believed that this man was hired to eliminate him because he was getting too close. Ed made one request.

"I need one big favor from you. Don't let this man make his phone calls right away. If he notifies his boss that I'm alive and that he got caught, it could blow this whole thing." Ed told them he was on a kidnapping case and that the life of the victim was at risk.

"Don't worry," one of the deputies volunteered. "We are very good at losing paperwork and getting behind on things. We will have to give him his calls sooner or later, but later is okay with us. How about if I promise no earlier than 5 pm tonight? I'll try to make it later if I can."

"That would be a big help. I really appreciate it. I don't have time to call Ted, but would you let him know I appreciate his help? He has bailed me out more times than I care to count."

"You got it. Well, we're just about done here. We'll take this guy in and see what else we can find out about him. His car looks like a rental, but we will tow it in for a more thorough search. You can get out of here if you want."

"Thanks. I'm sure we'll run into each other again."

Ed climbed into his car and turned it back in the direction of Jason's house. This was more evidence that today was a big day in this case. Ed parked a block away from Jason's just as he said and worked his way up the street along the car line. He saw a detective's car in front of the house and decided it would be better to go through the back. As he got to the nearby intersection he planned to move down the fence line towards the back of the house. Before he started to move he spotted a man with a rifle behind a bush near Jason's front window. Ed drew his gun and prepared to move. He was grateful that it was a Sunday morning. There was very little traffic and no other people out that he could see. He hated standing in the middle of a quiet neighborhood with his 9mm drawn; but if this guy raised that rifle, he was going to start pumping shells at him. He was a little farther away than Ed preferred, but he was pretty sure he could hit him. Ed hoped the noise of his gun fire would warn those inside and scare the hell out of the suspect if he didn't hit him. The man with the rifle suddenly ducked down and Ed saw Detectives Kyle and Fisher come out the front door. He used that opportunity to go over the fence and into the back yard. Kyle and Fisher could handle the guy with the rifle if he showed himself, but Ed wanted inside the house in case the guy waited for the detectives to leave before he made a move on Jason. Getting into Jason's house was not complicated. A sliding glass door with no slide lock made easy access. He applied a little pressure and a pull at the same time. The door slid open easily, and just as important, quietly. Ed slipped into the house. Jason was closing the door as Ed slipped through the kitchen to a laundry room that gave him a view of the man in the bushes. The man with the rifle watched the detectives drive away and then got up. Seeing the man walk towards the front door, Ed readied himself. The doorbell rang and Ed moved behind Jason as he opened the door. He watched the man and saw that the rifle was not being held in a threatening manner. He kept his 9mm ready until he heard Jason talking to him as though he was an old friend. When Ed figured out that this was a neighborhood watch militiaman, he holstered his gun, walked back into the kitchen, found some orange juice, and sat down at the kitchen table.

This was going to be a busy day. Ed knew he was going to have to stay sharp so that he could identify the good guys from the bad guys. As soon as Jason finishes up with Daniel Boone out there, we'll get down to business and get ready for Simon. Ed Lancing wasn't sure why the name Simon was used, but he believed he knew the real name. He not only knew the name, but he knew the person behind the name. He only hoped that he could get Jason to see it and believe it. Jason shut the door and came towards the kitchen. Ed couldn't wait to see his face. He loved surprising people.

Chapter Twenty Four

S teve sat in his church office. He had just hung up the phone with Jason, and he felt inspired by Jason's strength and drive. Steve was feeling as though he wasn't of much help to Jason or Ed. He knew there wasn't going to be enough time for him to study the details of this case to help Ed Lancing solve it. He agreed with Ed, this thing was coming to a head quickly. Steve felt frustrated that he couldn't help them in a more hard and tangible way. Then he realized that he could help them in a way that he didn't even think of before. He could help them, not only through his prayers, but he could call on a congregation of believers to pray for them too. They could pray for Sarah and her safety. They could pray for Jason and his strength. They could pray for the skill and knowledge of Ed Lancing. They could pray for the will of God.

Steve realized that he could not give a lot of information to the congregation because very little was actually public knowledge yet, but he could give them enough to send them to their knees. God would know what they were praying for. God would know what needed to be done. Steve picked up the phone and began to call each of his Elders and Deacons. To those he could catch, he explained what details he could and told them to pray. He asked them to stop what they were doing immediately, and go to God in prayer. Steve then called the leader of the Woman's ministry and explained the same thing. He asked her to call as many women as possible. "We need prayer and we need it now." He also asked that the support meals for the Shepard's stop for now. "I may call on you to start them again soon, but let's wait to see what the family's needs are going to be." Everything was agreed upon and prayer was set in motion.

Steve then got up and walked the halls of the church. He found some of the men he was looking for earlier already setting up for classes and preparing for another Lord's Day. Steve talked to each of them. They all stopped what they were doing and went to God in prayer.

Steve knew he couldn't solve the case for Jason and Ed, but he knew who could. God knew what we all needed. We didn't really have to ask for it. But the Bible says he wants us to ask. God wants us to be persistent and to ask for what we want. God tells us that we do not receive because we do not ask.

"Well, God, we are asking. We are all going to ask together as a family. Your people need you now, God. Sarah needs you, Jason needs you, and Ed needs you. God, we pray that your will be done, and we pray that your will is to bring Sarah home and to find and punish those responsible for this terrible crime."

Steve then went back to his office, scrapped the sermon he had prepared for today, and began to jot some notes on a new sermon. Jason and Sarah were going to be the focus of the day. This couple was going to be our constant petition for the day. We were here to worship God, and he would receive all of our worship and glory, but Jason and Sarah needed the help and focus of their church family. They needed us even though they weren't here with us. They needed our prayers. Through the power of prayer, we could provide them love, caring, and nourishment that many outside of the Lord's Church couldn't even fathom. His Church would come together this day. God's people would come to the defense of one of his lost sheep. Our weapon would be our knees, our hearts, our faithfulness, and our prayers. The power would come from God.

Steve reminisced about why he had become a Pastor. He remembered why he had gotten into ministry in the beginning. It was to fight Satan, to save souls, to serve people, and to honor God. This fight would be the biggest of his life. Satan was alive and active, souls were at risk, God's people needed to be served, and Steve knew that all of this was to the glory of the Father. Steve felt alive. He knew that God had stirred his spirit and given him direction. Today would prove a victory for God and his people! Steve's role? Steve's role would be as it should be; that of a servant.

Steve's eyes filled with tears as he felt God working inside of him. He knew his purpose and he knew the purpose of the Church that Christ first created. None of the programs, budgets, or building projects seemed important now. Of course they were important, but Steve had realized that he had momentarily lost sight of the purpose of his calling. He had gotten so caught up in running the business of the church that he had forgotten what it felt like to serve the people of Christ's Church. God had awakened his spirit and allowed him to feel the need to serve again. It was overwhelming to Steve and he could not hold back the tears. In fact, he didn't want to hold them back. He fell to his knees and thanked God. He would pastor this congregation through this crisis, and he would continue efforts to effectively run the business of the Church. Steve knew he would strive to develop good programs and he would continue to work hard to expand the church body, but he knew that he had turned a corner. He knew this was a special day. God's Spirit had filled him to overflowing. He knew his calling, and he knew what God wanted him to do. He was to serve, to lead through prayer, to meet the needs of God's people, and to find lost souls to bring into the Lord's family. It isn't that Steve didn't know all of this. He knew it and lived it everyday, but to feel it, to feel it from the Spirit, to have your heart overflowing and your mind and heart in step. This new energy and expanded understanding were reborn in Steve. He was excited. "God is at work on this day. I know it. If Satan isn't already aware, he will know it soon enough."

Chapter Twenty Five

I just sat there at the computer staring at Ed, listening to him explain his morning ordeal, and his theory on the identity of Simon. The computer was flashing signs requesting my log in password, but I ignored it and focused on Ed.

"Ed, this is getting serious! You could have been killed! They mean business, and you are on their list of trouble makers. You have to be careful, Ed, but then I guess you know that don't you. I just can't believe I have gotten myself into such a mess. I knew Simon and his group were dangerous, but now we know their intention is to kill. How the heck did you come up with your conclusion, or guess, on Simon's identity, Ed? It just seems so far fetched. I'm not sure I can get my mind around it."

"I kind of thought your reaction would go something like that, Jason. Mine was pretty much the same when I first stumbled on it. Think about it for a minute, though. I'll be glad to take you through the details, but we have to get on-line with Simon. I'm pretty sure about this, Jason, so be thinking about it as you talk to Simon. See if anything that is said either affirms my hypothesis or discounts it. I do agree with you that we all have to be careful: you, me and Steve. They are looking to clean house, and death is not a card they are afraid to play."

"I will see if I find a connection, Ed, but it seems like a stretch to me. I just don't get the motive for killing Joe. Have you come to grips with that yet? If it is who you think it is, why come after me and my family?"

"I didn't say I had all of the answers, Jason. I just said I was pretty sure who was behind the whole mess. I'm not sure what the motivating factors are for the crimes just yet. I hope we find that out today. I expect that Simon, whoever Simon ends up being, will spell out what these people want. I'm hopeful that we can try to force this thing to a head today. Jason, you have to keep pushing Simon to bring this to a close. It's very important if we expect to get Sarah back and catch them all at the same time."

I turned back to the computer and logged in. My mind was running wildly over all of the things that Ed had shared with me. I couldn't quite get my mind around his prognosis on Simon's identity, and I'm not sure I believed it. But right now, I have to let it go. I can only hope that Simon is at his chat site. I maneuver through the log in process and head to the chat sites. Ed leans over my shoulder and watches as though this whole thing is new to him. I find Simon's site and sign in. He is there, alone, and waiting.

"I'm here, Simon, as promised."

"Glad to see you are so punctual. That is a good sign. In the past, though, you were always at the site several minutes early. What have you been up to this morning, Jason?"

"The detectives were here this morning. They only left a short time ago. I was actually afraid they were going to make me late. I'm here now. Let's do what we have to do. I want Sarah to come home."

"Any surprises with the detectives?"

"No, they were just mad that they weren't called in earlier. How did you do that by the way?"

"Jason, I have many powers and many ways that you don't understand. You will though, Jason. You will. In fact, I have to tell you I am very hopeful that once you join us, you will join us in a leadership role. I think you could be dynamic, Jason."

"Leader of what? You haven't really told me anything, Simon. What do you want of me? What do you want me to join? Who is it that you want me to lead?"

"All good and fair questions, Jason. I will share a little with you now, but I think it is important that we meet. This computer chat is pretty good, but it is nothing like a face to face meeting, especially if we think this can evolve to a lasting relationship."

I felt the tingles of fear run up my spine at the thought of meeting Simon. He seemed to have so much control over so many people. I found it difficult to believe that this person called Simon would believe that I could be changed so quickly, that I would join their group and forsake my God without a fight. Of course they are holding the ace in the hole. They have Sarah. They must know that I would do anything, say anything to get her back. But what do they think I will do once I get her? Do they really think that I would stay with them and be loyal to them? How could they be so naïve? Is it possible that the face to face meeting is to complete the process using hypnosis or brainwashing, or is it just a ruse and what they really want is to sacrifice me the way they did Joe Deener?

I felt a nudging on my arm and turned to look at Ed. He just nodded at the screen as if to get my attention back to Simon.

"You know, Ed, you and I can talk out loud while this is going on. They can't hear us."

Ed thought for a second and then smiled. "I guess I wasn't thinking very well. This computer stuff is all pretty new to me. Don't keep Simon waiting like that, Jason. You have to keep the conversation going. Don't leave any time for them to get second thoughts or nervous."

"I'm the one who is scared and nervous, Ed." I began typing again.

"Simon, I will meet you wherever you want, whenever you want. There is nothing more important than resolving this and bringing Sarah home."

"I know, Jason. I know. Let me try to explain. Let me try to tell you what we are about, who we are, and what we want. I want you to understand what you could be a part of; what you must be a part of. I know you want Sarah back, and we are working on that as we speak, but there is so much more. You can have the world, Jason. You can have anything in it whenever you want it. That means money, women, men, toys, whatever your heart desires."

I knew that Simon was looking for a reaction. I knew what my natural reaction would be, but I knew that Ed wanted me to keep Simon happy, to convince Simon I was one that he could convert. I also knew that if I was too agreeable, too fast, Simon could become suspicious and back away.

"I'm listening, Simon."

"Good. Good Jason. You see, we worship the one that you have been taught to hate throughout your life. We worship the true ruler of this world. That ruler is Satan, Jason. I know you will have an immediate reaction to that name and what you think it stands for, but give me a little time. Try not to get tied up in the fairy tales that you have learned through your upbringing and your churches. Try to keep an open mind. If you do, you can receive the true gifts of life, Jason. You can have the kind of power you never dreamed of. Whatever you wish for can be yours, whenever you wish it."

"You are right, Simon. My first reaction to the name Satan is just what you describe. I will wait to cast final judgment, however. I will wait for you to help me understand why you worship him and what your purpose in this life is."

"Very good, Jason. You want to know our purpose? Our purpose is to enjoy what Satan has freely given us. This world is a gift to his followers. We are here to enjoy it and worship him. There is no other purpose. The reason we are approaching you is that you control some very important facets of our worship Jason. When you join our group, we will have freedom to worship on what we believe to be holy ground. We will have enhancement to our worship and our play, and finally we will have financial support that will help us grow and acquire whatever we need in the future."

"I don't understand what I control? I don't understand why you kidnapped my wife? Why didn't you just talk to me about these things?"

"Jason, do you think that you would be here talking with me about joining our group and taking a leadership role if we didn't do something to get your attention? Sarah was just an attention getter. She is safe and sound. We just needed you to seriously listen and think openly about the issues we want you to consider. I agree that we had just started talking when some of my team jumped the gun. They weren't supposed to take her when they did, but they got their signals mixed up. As you know, I was trying to talk to you right here on this site before she was taken. I apologize for that, but I do believe the outcome would have been the same. You weren't listening with an open mind when we first started talking. Not like you are now. It is very exciting to think about you joining us."

"You talk like you know me, Simon. Do we know each other?"

"I know all people, Jason. I know them by what they want and what they desire. I know you, yes. We will meet in person, Jason, and then you will know me. You believe what you believe today because it is what you were taught from childhood. You live your life filled with guilt and pain. What if I were to tell you that you could live guilt free? You could do and have whatever you wanted? You can have money overflowing from your pockets and bank accounts. Jason, you can have women. All types of women, for any purpose you want them for. You can have power Jason, power over men and women. Power over companies. Power over governments. You will be in a position to make and carry out decisions that will impact the course of our world. Your decisions will impact the lives and deaths of the people in it. You can have whatever makes you happy. You can have power, sex, drugs, or money. What is it, Jason? What sounds good to you?"

I hated this conversation and I hated what Simon was trying to imply. He was trying to stir up worldly desires and lusts inside of me. He wanted to see what turned me on: greed, sex, or power. I wanted to turn off the computer and tell Simon that he was a loser, a liar, and lost forever in the eyes of God. I knew I couldn't do that. I knew it wasn't even an option right now. Even if I wanted to, Ed was sitting right next to me with his eyes glued on me and everything I wrote. He was a constant reminder of what my job really was. Of course breaking it off with Simon wasn't a choice anyway. After all, he had Sarah. I will continue to play the game. I will keep this charade going. I had to give Ed and his friends a chance to find Sarah and find her alive. I began to type again.

"If you know me as well as you say you do, Simon, you should know what motivates me."

"Touché, Jason. I think I know several things that will motivate you. What I'm telling you though, is that whatever it is, you can have it."

"Okay, you have me intrigued. I have to confess, I'm interested. So tell me, what is it that you want from me, and when do I get to see Sarah?"

"Sarah, precious Sarah! I want you to forget about Sarah for a minute! This is much bigger than Sarah! If you still want her when this is all over, you can have her. But my guess is you will see that the horizon is much bigger, and you will want to indulge in all that the world has to offer."

I realized that Sarah was a sore spot with Simon. I decided to change tactics and to start focusing on our meeting and the future he kept going on about. Simon had said that once all was finished, if I wanted Sarah, I could have her. I will want her, and he doesn't know yet, but I am coming to get her.

"Okay, Simon, fair enough. Let's talk about how we move on from here. What do you want from me, and when do we meet so we can have that face to face meeting you said was so important. I'm tired of this computer and all the secrecy. You are offering me a lot, and I want to find out more about it.

Simon grew excited upon reading Jason's last note. Jason was ready. He could be converted and his leadership would guarantee that the Den's sanctity and growth were assured. Simon would set up a meeting with Jason today. This was going to be exciting. After this chat was over, Simon would have to call Jack and have Sarah eliminated. This was an unavoidable payment for the security of the pack. Jack would have to make it look like an accident, or better yet, like the police did it by mistake. That would assure that Jason remained loyal.

"Jason, I will tell you three things that we want from you. In return, you will have all that I have told you about thus far and more. First, we need regular access to your plant. I will explain more when we are together, but we believe that there is a certain place on that plant's site that is sacred soil. We believe that an awe inspiring event occurred there years ago before the plant was built. Satan revealed himself to several followers on that specific site, and we have been trying to get back to that site to worship him for years. We believe that he will appear to us if we can worship him there in mass. We would not be disruptive. We would only come after hours, but we would need access twice a week to fulfill our worship and love rituals. I won't go into the details now but you will understand once you become one of us. Okay so far?"

"That doesn't seem like a major stumbling block. I control who comes and goes, I think we can overcome that obstacle. What are the other two?"

"Second, we would need access to the new drug that your company is developing to assist in spinal chord restoration. I know it isn't released yet, but it should be soon. When you start production of the product in your plant, we will want a regular supply. I will move to item number three when you are clear about this request."

"I know the drug you are referring to, but the company has been working on that for at least 6 years. It is up for approval with the FDA, but who knows how long that will take and whether they will approve it at all. Why would you want that stuff anyway?"

"We understand you don't control the release of the drug. What I said was that we wanted your intervention when it is released. I believe it will be released this year, and when your plant starts to produce it, we will want an ongoing supply. I will explain the benefits of the drug to you at a later time, but I will say that it stimulates all of your senses and nerves. It is a wonderful stimulant for love rituals and expanded forms of recreation, if you get my drift."

"Okay, I can get you the supply once we start making it. That won't be a problem unless the amount you want is so large that it would be noticed by others. I have to ask though, how do you know what the pills do? How do you know how you feel when you take them?"

"You still don't seem to understand, Jason, I know many things. How I know and what I know will be saved until you are officially one of us. Then I will share many things with you, and you will be overwhelmed at the knowledge and power you can possess. Third, we will agree on a modest financial sum that you will forward to us from your business. This money will be used to support our efforts and activities. I have the plan and a sum in mind, and I believe that it will appropriately support the efforts of our group while being small enough to fall below the radar screen of your controller and auditors. Now, those are the three things we want from you in return for all that I have promised."

"I have to admit, the first two were a surprise, but the third was expected. I can manage all three assuming that you can deliver on your promises. You have promised a lot by the way."

"Very good, Jason. Don't you worry about my promises. You will get all that I have told you. I'm sure your fantasies and inner thoughts have desires I have not even touched upon. If you think it, it can be yours. The details of that and how we begin our walk together are too important to discuss in a chat room like this. I would like to meet with you, today."

I got excited and looked over at Ed. He was grinning from ear to ear. They were going right where Ed wanted them to go. "Jason, make it happen early this afternoon if you can. We need to do some planning, so not too soon. But make it happen as early as possible-sometime after noon or 1pm if possible. I don't know where they will want to meet, but I would like it to be before dark, if you can make it happen." I nodded and went back to my chat.

"I have nothing on my agenda today except you, Simon. Tell me when and where, and I'll be there."

"I can't tell you how happy I am that you have come so far so fast, Jason. It pleases me and I know it pleases him."

"Him?"

"Haha...Satan, of course!"

"Oh, sorry.....well, Simon, you got my attention pretty quick by taking my wife. Now, your offer sounds too good to be true. I tend to believe that most things that are too good to be true usually are, so I have to admit I am skeptical; but if you can deliver on what you have promised, I am very interested in pursuing our discussions."

"Good, Jason. I am going to sign off now. I will call you on your home phone in two minutes. I will give you instructions on when and where we will meet. You will not be sorry. This is a very exciting time."

"Okay, I will be waiting for your call."

"I know I don't have to say this, Jason, but you can't tell anyone and you must come alone. If you don't, you will miss out on the opportunity of a life time, and, of course, Sarah will die. You may not care about her much longer, not once you see what else you can have. You may find you are better off without a wife, or maybe with two or three, but either way you have to come alone. Any questions?"

"No, I understand. I will wait for your call."

Simon signed off. I printed the conversation and then logged off the computer. I turned to Ed and he seemed puzzled. "Why did they want to call you instead of type the directions Jason? Why talk to you about everything and then at the last minute move to the phone?"

"I think they probably wanted to make sure I'm at home, Ed. I could have accessed this site from any computer on earth, including one sitting right in the middle of the police department. I think Simon wants to make sure I'm home where I belong. I assume it's another one of his tests."

"Good point, Jason. I'm sure you're right. I just don't understand how this computer stuff works. You really mean that you could access this site or any site from all computers?"

"Well, yes, if they are logged on the internet or have internet access. That's all it takes. Once you have that, you can surf all over the net for good and evil. I certainly stumbled on evil when I met this Simon."

"Don't feel bad, Jason. I think they were lying in wait for you. If they didn't get you on the computer, they would have moved to another medium. But they were after you from the beginning. Look what they asked you for. All three things required help from the plant manager of the site. That would be you, Jason. Everything else is hocus pocus. They want access to the plant for some reason. Who knows what Simon was really talking about, but they want frequent and regular visits to the plant. They want your drugs, and they want your company's money. Nothing too surprising with any of the requests except the plant visits. I will need to know more about this drug they are talking about, but I assume there aren't too many people that are even aware of the drug yet. Am I right, Jason? Don't you think it supports my theory on Simon's identity?"

"I don't know, Ed. It could be anybody that works with the company. I just don't know. I'm not ruling it out, but I'm not sold either. Now, how do you want to handle this? Do you want to pick up on an extension phone?"

"No, too much risk. They may hear it, or they may have a device that tells them how many lines are open. It is a tool that is easy to acquire. I think you're right, this may be a test. We want to make sure you pass it."

The phone rang and I automatically looked at Ed. I must have had panic in my eyes because he told me to calm down and pick up the phone on the third ring. I did what I was told. "Hello?"

A deep and distorted voice answered, "You waited for the third ring. I would have bet that you would have answered on the first. You are constantly surprising me, Jason. I am not 100% sure whether that is good or bad at this point."

"Nothing near as exciting as you think, Simon. A Girl Scout was at the door selling cookies. I had to chase her away before I could get to the phone. I'm here though, what now?"

"There is an old abandoned warehouse at the East end of town. It is located on Holly St. There is no name on it anymore, but it used to be a paper stock warehouse for the newspaper. Do you know it?"

"Yes, I know where it is."

"Good, I want you to be there at 6pm tonight. I want you to drive up with your lights on. You will be watched to make sure you're alone. Come inside the south entrance. It will be a little dark, but not completely. Don't bring any friends. Enter through the south entrance and walk to the main warehouse floor. Wait for me there. I will greet you personally. Any questions?"

"Do we have to wait so late? Why can't we get together earlier? I'm anxious to meet you."

"We wait because I say we wait. I want the evening to settle in. You should know in your Bible studies that Satan rules the world, but he especially rules the night. I want the advantage of his power and the benefit of darkness. I want that advantage just in the off chance you might try something stupid. Be there on time. We can put this all behind us very quickly."

"I won't try anything, Simon. I just want to find out more about all those promises you made me. Like I said, they seem too good to be true. I want to know if you can really deliver."

"Enough talk for now, Jason, I am anxious to meet you as well. I think we can do some great things together. A lot is at risk here, Jason. I am putting a lot of trust in you. If you disappoint me; Sarah will be killed, you will be killed, and we will visit your sisters and kill your children. Understood?"

The phone went dead. Simon had made his point and there was nothing left to be said.

"Jason, you all right?" Ed was staring at me with a worried look on his face.

"I'm okay, Ed, but they threatened to kill me, Sarah, and the children if I try to trick them during this visit. Simon even knew the children were with my sisters. What do we do?"

"Jason, I know this is tough. We are all in extreme danger here. But we have to fight this. If we don't, this evil will continue to grow and others will no doubt suffer because of it. They are only surmising that you sent your children to your sisters. That would be the obvious guess. I'm sure they know a lot about you. They have done their research. They have had plenty of time to plan and think through this since you were promoted to plant manager two years ago. I was able to hear most of what was said. Simon used a voice scrambler to disguise the voice. Do you know why? Because you would know the voice if you heard it, that's why. I'm telling you I know who this is. We have got to stop them. We have to stop them all."

I knew Ed Lancing was right. I knew we had to do everything in our power to kill this beast before it continued to grow. He was also right when he said we were all at risk. They had already tried to kill Ed, and Simon promised to kill me and all my family if he had to. I believe him. I believe this group could kill all of us, including the children, with little or no remorse. It is for that reason that I have to go through with this.

"With any luck at all, Ed, your friends will find Sarah before we have to meet Simon."

Ed looked at me and I thought I saw a small smile pass his lips. "We are close, Jason. We are very close."

Chapter Twenty Six

S arah sat in her chair at the kitchen table mesmerized by
the television program Jack had allowed her to watch. It
was 9:30 on Sunday morning, and she was watching some
silly, mindless children's show. Sarah had slept on the fold
out couch in the large room that shared the kitchen. It had
been a fitful night, and she awoke tired and depressed. Jack
had slept, if you want to call it that, at the kitchen table. He
looked worse than she felt. Jack had allowed Sarah to turn
on the television, but he would not allow her to watch any
religious programming. Jack and Sarah were eating whatever they could find. They had shared the last of the food
that Pete had purchased at the store, and the balance of their
food had come from remnants from Pete's car. Jack
promised if they didn't get a call soon, they would go to the
store and get something substantial to eat. Sarah felt weak
and tired, and she wondered if anyone was even looking for
her. Jack continued to watch over her and to take care of her.
Nobody else seemed to care.

Jack wondered what was going on. He had hoped that
this mess would have been over by now. He was anxious to
move on to something more his speed. Kidnapping was not
his cup of tea. He wasn't afraid of it, but it wasn't his field
of expertise. Murder was what he did best, but he had no
taste for Sarah's blood. Pete's death had been exciting, however. Pete had it coming. He was a loser and would only

bring grief to people in this world. Let the afterworld take responsibility for him. Killing pond scum like Pete didn't bother Jack at all; in fact, he really got a charge out of it sometimes. Killing innocent people was not what he wanted, and killing Sarah would be the hardest of all. Jack had grown to like Sarah. Jack believed Sarah liked him too. Jack thought that when this thing was all over, maybe, just maybe, Sarah would go away with him. He knew she wasn't ready now, but he also knew that she liked him. Jack believed that this like could grow into love, couldn't it?

Sarah had no hood on anymore, and she was given free reign to move around the small cabin. No one followed her to the bathroom. No one tried to force her to do anything. All she had to promise was to stay inside and away from the door and windows. It was worth it to get the freedom that Jack gave her now. Where was Jason? Had he just forgotten about her? How were her children? She wondered where they were and who was watching them. She was tired, hungry, and mad at everyone right now. Jack was the only one who seemed to care about her.

"Jack, can we go to the store and get something to eat? I'm feeling weak and light headed."

"I know, Sarah. Just wait a little while. If we don't hear anything by noon, we will go to the store together. You can pick out your favorite food, and I will cook it up for you. Is that okay?"

"Okay, Jack." Sarah's mind wandered off to what she would buy. What was her favorite food? Jack was going to cook whatever she wanted. He was a sweet man.

Jack's cell phone rang and he looked down at it almost startled by the noise it made. It had been almost two days since they had received any contact from the outside and Jack knew this would be Simon.

"Hello?"

"Jack, Simon here. How is our little prize?"

"She is holding up. She's no trouble; just waiting to go home."

Sarah was listening to the conversation, but it frustrated her that she could only hear one side of it. What was Simon saying? What did he want? Jack would have to tell Simon that he killed Pete. What would Simon's reaction be? Sarah worried about all of it. She pretended to watch television, but she listened intently to Jack. She didn't want Simon to get mad at Jack. He was doing the best he could. She knew Jack was smart. She convinced herself that he would be fine. She drifted back to the puppet show on television, but she kept one ear on the conversation. Were they going to move now? Was she going home?

"Well, Jack, things are moving very well at this end. I think it is time that we rid ourselves of the baggage. I don't think Pete is bringing us any value, Jack. I think it would be best if he didn't come back to the next meeting."

"That has been taken care of already, Simon. He got out of line here and almost jeopardized the plan. I had to take him out."

"You killed him? What would make you think that you could do that without authority from me, Jack? You have really overstepped your bounds this time."

Jack found himself getting a little red in the face, and Sarah noticed the change in his demeanor.

"Simon, maybe you don't understand. It was a split second decision. He was trying to rape Sarah. She was screaming and it could have ruined the whole thing. I did what I felt I had to do under the circumstances. Besides, Simon, it's all a moot point anyway. You wanted him dead."

"Sarah? You called her Sarah. Are you two on a first name basis now, Jack? I am beginning to grow concerned about you, Jack. I am beginning to wonder whether you can handle this assignment. Yes, I wanted Pete dead, but I decide who dies and when, not you! Do you understand that?"

"Yeah, sure I understand."

"Good, Jack. Understanding that will be important going forward. Why did you stop Pete from raping Sarah; or as the rest of us like to refer to her, Mrs. Shepard? Why would you care? I could have cared less if he wanted her or if both of you took turns with her. She is ours to do with as we please. I didn't ask you to pamper her, Jack, just to hold her. What you wanted to do with her while you were holding her was your business. What I don't understand is why she had the ability to scream? Why wasn't she wearing her mask?"

"That's what I'm trying to tell you, Simon. He ripped it off her. He was out of control. I could hear her screaming from outside the cabin. I ran in and I couldn't get him to stop. I couldn't get him to settle down. I killed him. It was my decision and I stand by it. So I have actually taken care of your order before you asked for it. It wasn't how you wanted it to happen, but the results are the same either way. Pete is dead."

"True, Jack, the results are the same. I would like to mention that there have been two major mistakes that have occurred under your command. This is very concerning to me. One was that you took Mrs. Shepard at least a day too early. I never gave you the green light, but you and Pete made that decision on your own. Then you killed Pete. Two major mistakes in my book. I agree that the results are the same, but discipline and carrying out orders as they are given are important to the sanctity of our organization. In addition to those two mistakes, you don't appear remorseful about what you have done. You seem argumentative. That is unacceptable, Jack. You must know that I can not tolerate this type of behavior or attitude."

Jack was pacing the floor and Sarah saw a side of Jack she had not seen before. He was mad and red faced. He was controlled, but he was arguing with this man Simon. On earlier calls he was placid and controlled. She watched and listened in between watching the puppet in the tree house and looking at the food they kept showing on commercials. Sarah still hadn't figured out what she wanted Jack to cook for her after they went shopping. She had never been so excited about going to the store before, but she was bubbling over with excitement in anticipation of the event. Sarah knew she was so frightened, tired, and hungry that she wasn't making much sense; but she didn't care. Right now she went with what felt good. Thinking about food and a trip to the grocery store was the highlight of her last three days. She was going to stay focused on that. Sarah kept an ear towards Jack. She was afraid he was going to overstep his bounds with Simon and get himself in real trouble. She didn't want that. They might send someone to replace Jack. She liked Jack; she wanted to stay with him.

"I understand, Simon. The first was a mistake. We thought we got the green light, and obviously we didn't. The second was a decision I felt I had to make. I understand that you are now telling me it was a bad decision, but I can't reverse it. I am not trying to be argumentative with you, Simon. I am only trying to explain why things happened the way they did. I'm sorry about the mistakes. What do you want me to do now?"

"Okay, Jack, I will accept that as your apology and we can move on. We can discuss this in more detail when we get together later today. It is now time to eliminate Mrs. Shepard. I want you to do that today, and then I want you to come back to town. I have a meeting with Jason Shepard, and I would like you to be there."

Jack sat dumbfounded listening to Simon. Kill Mrs. Shepard? Kill Sarah? There must be some mistake, a bad connection on the phone. Simon said there was a follow-up meeting with Jason Shepard. So it was proceeding. Why kill Sarah?

"I think I heard you wrong, Simon. Could you say that again?"

"Yes, with all the mistakes we have had, I think that is wise, Jack. I want you to kill Mrs. Shepard. I would like for you to make it look like she had an accident. Or better yet, make it look like the police did it. It will really help if Jason thinks the police are against him."

"I don't understand, Simon? It sounds like things are progressing well. Why are you calling for this action if we are moving along with our plan?"

"How dare you question me, Jack? When you get back here, we are going to have to have a major performance review. You aren't thinking clearly, Jack, and your behavior is not what I have grown accustomed to expecting from you. I don't know what is going on, but you had better get in line right now! I want you to kill her, Jack. Do it like I tell you to do it. Get it done by early afternoon because I want you back here for our meeting with Jason. Is that clear this time?"

Jack paced back and forth. He couldn't believe what he was being ordered to do by Simon. He hadn't really expected it to come to this. Jack had no problem with killing, but killing a woman? Killing a woman that hadn't hurt anyone? Kill Sarah? Jack could feel anger building, and he wanted to lash out at Simon. He didn't like being talked to like a child, and he didn't like being scolded like one either. He had no problem killing for Simon. He had already killed for Simon, but this was going to be hard. He would make it painless. He promised himself that, and then he glanced over to Sarah. Sarah was looking at him and their eyes met. At that moment Sarah knew. She knew that Simon had just given Jack her death sentence. She had no strength to scream or run, and she had no interest in the food or the television anymore. Jack had just been ordered to kill her. She knew she had very little time left.

"I understand, Simon. Your instructions are clear."

"Good, I'm glad to see we are communicating. Once you have finished there, head back to town and meet me at the old paper warehouse on Holly St. I want you there by 5pm. I'm scheduled to meet Jason at 6pm and I want you in place before hand in case anything goes wrong."

"Okay, I know the place. I will be there by 5. Anything else?"

"No, Jack, nothing else. Try to make this happen smoothly this time. No mistakes. You and I will need to spend some time together when this is over, Jack. I think you have forgotten who you are serving. It's not about you, and it's not about me. It is about serving our all powerful overseer. You must not forget who you are doing this for. You must remember that your actions will please him and you will be honored for your work. Do it right this time, Jack. Get it done and get back here."

"I understand." It was all Jack could say. His head was spinning and he wasn't sure what he would do next. He had to kill Sarah. He had to make it look like the police did it. Worse yet, she knew it. He could tell when he looked her in the eyes. She knew.

"Good bye, Jack. See you this afternoon."

Jack hung up with no response. He had a lot on his mind. He turned and looked at Sarah. She looked beautiful but sad. He didn't like to see her sad. He hoped she didn't cry. He hated that most of all. She knew she was about to die and he didn't know what to say to her. He walked into the back room and started gathering up some of his belongings.

Sarah sat frozen in the chair. She should jump up and run. Head for the door and run out into the road yelling for help. She knew he would catch her. If he did, he would kill her just like he did Pete. Sarah didn't want to die that way. She wasn't sure how she preferred to die, but she knew it wasn't the way Pete died. Sarah was at a point of giving up. Her strength was gone, she felt deserted by the ones she loved, and now the one man that stood by her and cared for her was going to hurt her-kill her. She had nothing left to do but prepare herself for the inevitable. She needed to talk to her Father in Heaven. Jesus Christ had walked this walk. He went to his death willingly. He went for the sake of all the people of the world. She was going to her death now, but she didn't really know why. She didn't understand why she was going to be killed, but she went to her knees to talk to Jesus. He had felt the hands of death, and she knew he would comfort her.

"Lord God, I don't know why this is happening to me, but you know. I just pray that you stay with me until the end, God. I fear death God; I don't mind admitting it to you. I fear the pain of it. I fear leaving my children and my husband. God, I trust you, but I fear the unknown. Give me peace, Lord. Stand close to me now. If there is anyway you can let this pass, I pray for your intervention. May I honor you in death as I have tried in life. Forgive me of my sins and stay close to Jason and the children, Father. I don't know where Jason is, but I'm sure he is doing his best." Sarah had to stop because she was crying now. She felt guilty for crying in the middle of her prayer. They weren't tears of love for God. They were tears of fear. She didn't want to die, but she didn't know what to do about it now.

Jack came flying out of the back room and saw her down on her knees. "Get up from there, Sarah. You don't have to pray to your God, we are going to get out of here. This is stupid, crazy. There is no reason for you to die. They are just doing it because they can. I won't be a part of it. Get up and get ready. I have a plan, but you will have to make me some promises."

"I will promise you anything, Jack. You saved my life; you have cared for me and protected me. Just tell me what to do and I'll do it, Jack! Please, help me get out of here!"

Jack looked at her and he knew he loved her. Maybe he would come back and maybe they could be together someday. Jack didn't really believe it, but stranger things had happened in his life. It was about time something good happened to him. Having Sarah would be a good thing.

"We will jump in Pete's van and get out of here. Your car is at the bottom of the hill, Sarah. I will drop you there, and you should head right to the police department. Don't go anywhere else. I don't want you to go home until the police say it's safe. Once they find out I have let you go, these people may come after you again. I wouldn't want that to happen. Do you understand?"

"Yes, Jack, but where will you go? What will you do? Simon will be angry."

"Simon can go to hell. I have had enough of this whole thing, Sarah. I don't know what I believe anymore, but I don't believe in Simon. That I know for sure. Now, you have to promise me that you won't describe me or my car to the police for a few hours. I'm just asking for a head start, Sarah, that's all."

"Oh, Jack, I promise I won't tell them about you. I'll tell them I never saw you, that I always had a hood over my eyes. You have been so good to me, Jack, so kind. Words can never express how thankful I am."

Sarah went to Jack and put her arms around him hugging him tightly. She had strong feelings for this man in some distant way. While she was embraced in her hug with Jack, she raised her eyes towards heaven, and mouthed the words, "Thank You Lord."

Jack felt her embrace and he wanted to melt. It was a hug like he had never had before. No one had ever hugged him like that, and he didn't know how to react to it. He slowly just relaxed and enjoyed the moment. He had fallen for her, as he had never fallen before in his life. It was a new, strange, and exciting feeling. He knew now that he would come back for her. He was sure that she loved him too.

"Sarah, we had better get moving. I have to put some miles between me, you, and Simon before this afternoon.

Have you got everything you need?"

"I have my life thanks to you, Jack. I don't need anything else."

"Okay, let's go. Here are your keys, Sarah. I won't spend any time down at the bottom of the hill saying goodbye. I will just drop you off and move on. I love you Sarah, and I'm sorry for what I have done to you."

Sarah was surprised by his expression of love. It struck her because it was said with such conviction and passion. Jack cared for her. She hadn't realized how much until now. She took the keys, smiled at him, and followed him outside to the car. Her mind and heart were being pulled in a thousand directions.

The sun was bright for both of them. The temperature was cool but not cold. Sarah breathed in the fresh air and took a look around at her surroundings. She didn't recognize the place, but it looked just like she had imagined. Why didn't Jason listen to her? He should have come and saved her. He should have taken her away from all this, but he didn't listen. Jack yelled for her to get in the car and she did as she was told.

Sarah was suddenly struck by the concern that maybe this was all a trick to get her to go quietly. Maybe he was luring her to her death. Maybe this was all just a game. She discounted those thoughts quickly by remembering his words just a few minutes ago. "I love you, Sarah." She knew he wasn't acting when he said those words. She felt it as much as heard it. She was going to be set free. She knew God was making it happen, but she couldn't help but feel close to the man that she had spent so much time with over the past several days. This man had protected her and finally saved her from Pete, and he was saving her once again. She hoped he got away. Sarah hoped that she would see him again. She prayed that she would someday have the chance to really share her faith with him. "God could help this man," she thought. "Only God can help him."

They reached the bottom of the hill and Jack turned right. He pulled over to the side of the road and she looked up a gravel path and saw the back of her car sitting in the woods. Sarah leaned over and kissed Jack on the cheek, climbed out of the van, and walked towards her car without looking back. Jack watched her and knew he would be back. She was worth fighting for. He would come back for her. Once Sarah reached her car, Jack pulled out onto the road. He had to get out of here but he wasn't completely sure where he was going to go. Jack knew he needed to get across the state line as quickly as possible so he didn't wait to watch her back her car out of the woods and down to the road. Jack just drove off knowing she would be alright. The sooner he got out of the state; the sooner things would cool off. The sooner they cooled off; the sooner he could come back-back for Sarah.

Chapter Twenty Seven

Ted Dalton heard the crack of his radio, and he listened as one of his men spoke. "I've got movement, Ted. The door is opening. I have a male and a female exiting the room. They appear to be walking towards the van."

"Is she tied up or handcuffed? Is it Mrs. Shepard?"

"I can't tell, Ted. She definitely is not being confined. She seems to be moving slow though, kind of in a daze if you ask me. She's just staring at the rest of the motel as though she has never seen it before. The sunlight is hurting her eyes. I don't have a picture of Mrs. Shepard, but my bet is that this is her. She matches the description you gave me. I just don't see that he is openly controlling her in anyway. She is getting into the van that was parked in front of the cabin. Stand by."

"Okay, troops. We will watch for a little while. We can't let them get far though. I just want to know what is going on. I hate trying to stop the car with her in it, but we will if they are going any farther than the local grocery store. I will give the order to make the stop. Everybody move as planned. Get ready."

"Okay, Ted. They are coming down the hill right at you. Have you picked up visual yet?"

"Yep, I got them. Thanks, Tony. Get down here as soon as you can. Okay, folks. Here we go. The car is turning right out of the motel driveway. It is coming at you, Greg."

"I hear ya, Ted. I can see it making the turn now."

"Wait a minute, everybody. They're stopping. Ted was getting excited. He had yet to receive any official report of Mrs. Shepard's kidnapping. He was taking a big chance here. He was really going out on a limb, but in his estimation, Ed Lancing was worth it. Ted trusted him with his life, and if Lancing said this woman had been kidnapped, then that was good enough for him. The van pulled over to the side of the road right where Mrs. Shepard's car had been abandoned. Everyone was watching the car now. The airwaves were silent. Ted was in control. His team waited for his instructions.

Ted was watching with binoculars from behind the trees at the bottom of the driveway. He thought he saw Mrs. Shepard lean over and either whisper something to the male driver or kiss him. This was getting confusing. Ted wasn't sure about anything right now, but he was sure he wasn't going to let these two out of his sight. He saw who he believed to be Mrs. Shepard get out of the car and walk towards the car parked in the woods. She had a set of keys in her hand. The driver in the van began to pull away.

"They're separating! Take him down, Greg. Take him down now! Tony, you and I will go for the woman. Remember, I think she is Mrs. Shepard, but don't let your guard down. I don't know for sure." The entire team was moving now. No time to call Ed Lancing. It was now or never.

The car pulled away from the side of the road and accelerated. Two sheriff units blasted out of the woods, and one pulled across the road ahead of the van blocking its path. The driver slammed on his brakes and turned his car sharply to avoid hitting the sheriff's car. The van's driver was obviously surprised by the move. He looked in his rear view mirror and saw the two units that had pulled out of the woods and were now behind him. He was trapped. Jack grabbed his gun and opened his door. He would not give up without a fight. While exiting the van, he raised his gun at the officer in front of him and there was a barrage of gun fire that came at him from behind. Jack never got a round off. He was struck several times from behind and once from the officer in front of him. They were ready for him. He never had a chance. He dropped his gun and crumpled to the ground. He rolled over on his back and watched as police approached from every direction with their guns drawn. "How did they find me? How did they know?" Jack couldn't grasp the answers to his own questions. They were standing around him with their guns out. He knew he wasn't going anywhere, and the police knew it too. Jack was bleeding to death. One officer searched him and he removed Jack's final weapon of defense; his knife. Jack heard the cop yell, "He's clean!" Jack thought he could hear Sarah in the distance. He thought he heard her screaming and crying. "What were they doing to her?"

As soon as the van pulled away, Ted had moved towards Sarah. He pulled his car behind the one she was getting into. She looked up at him with a shocked look on her face and then he recognized relief as it replaced the shock. She smiled and started walking to him waving at him with her keys in her hand. A second officer pulled in behind Ted, and Sarah knew she was safe. As she walked towards the officers, she heard the screech of cars stopping. She turned and looked up the street and saw that they had surrounded Jack. She watched in what seemed to be slow motion, as Jack came out of the van with his gun drawn. She saw the hail of gunfire from the officers, and finally witnessed Jack falling to the ground.

Sarah felt herself being pulled and restrained by officers, and then she realized that she had run screaming and crying towards Jack's car. "Don't kill him. He let me go! Please, he saved my life. Don't hurt him!" She was crying and fighting the officers, trying to get closer to Jack. They were having no part of it. She could hear Jack yelling.

"Sarah! I'm dying Sarah. I love you!"

Sarah turned to the officer that was holding her. She begged him to let her go to Jack so she could comfort him while they waited for the ambulance. Ted couldn't let that happen. He wouldn't let it happen. He was sure this was Sarah Shepard, but he was also sure that these two had developed some kind of bond. He wasn't taking any chances. She wasn't going anywhere. Sarah began to sob. She quit fighting and held on to Sgt. Dalton with all of her strength. It was all too real for her. They had kidnapped her, put her in her car's trunk, held her hostage for several days, murdered a man in front of her, and now she was involved in a police shoot out. Sarah didn't think she could take anymore. She broke down. She had had enough. She felt safe in this officer's arms. Ted Dalton felt her transformation. She was helpless now, sobbing and gripping him so tightly it almost hurt. "No one will hurt you anymore, Mrs. Shepard. We came here to get you. We came to take you home."

Sarah knew now that Jason had not given up. He had been searching for her, and he had found her. God was at work. He had touched Jack's heart and had led these officers to her. Sarah couldn't speak at all. She continued to cry uncontrollably. She simply raised her eyes to heaven. God would know what was on her heart.

Jack lay in a pool of his own blood. He began drifting in and out of consciousness. He knew he was losing blood fast. The officers were trying to keep him alive, but they had no chance. He was riddled with bullets, and his life was slipping away. It didn't hurt very much. Jack had always wondered about that. He could feel his strength slipping and he still heard no ambulance siren. He knew they were a good distance from that kind of service, and he believed he would be dead on arrival at the nearest hospital. That would be the term they used for him: dead on arrival. He could hear Sarah crying a short distance away. He didn't have the strength to yell at her anymore. Her crying had changed though. She was no longer screaming. She was just sobbing. Jack figured that she saw him and knew he was going to die too. "She is in grief," he thought. No one had ever grieved over Jack before. He was comforted by it. Jack was sure the tears were for him, and that proved that Sarah loved him. He wouldn't ever get to experience her love, but he would die knowing he was loved. That was a new experience for him, and he felt warmed by it.

Jack lay in the street in an ever increasing pool of blood, and drifted off to unconsciousness.

"Sergeant, this guy is gone. Nothing we can do for him. He's dead."

There was no reaction from Sarah on the news. She just continued to cry softly. She was helpless now. One of Ted's men had confirmed her identify while Ted was comforting her, and he was glad that he at least had the right girl. They were running checks on Jack, but he possessed four different driver's licenses and several other pieces of identification, so it would take a while before they knew who he really was. He was a bad guy, Ted was sure of that. Ted knew he had a lot of explaining to do to his superiors, but he was confident that Ed Lancing was on top of things, and he and his team had saved Sarah Shepard. It looked like this guy was letting her go, but Ted would have to get more details about all of that when Mrs. Shepard was able to talk. Right now he was just happy she was safe.

Ted needed to call Ed and give him a heads-up about everything. Although several officers tried to help, Sarah Shepard was not letting go of Ted Dalton. That was okay with Ted; he had as much time as she needed. She was distraught, tired, hungry, and emotionally shot. Ted thought she would need some help once she got back to her family. This wouldn't be easy to forget.

"Hey, Sarge, it just came out on an APB. Sarah Shepard is listed as kidnapped and her car is listed as stolen. You did it, Sarge. Congratulations!"

Ted sighed with relief. He still had some spin he would have to put on this for his boss, but at least he had the right people and it looked like a victory for the good guys. Ted was able to get Sarah into the front seat of his car. He would get her to the hospital for a physical check up, and then hopefully she would go home shortly afterwards.

Sarah sat quietly as she was driven away from this horrific scene. She looked at Jack lying in the street as they slowly maneuvered past the site of the shooting. The officers were unfurling blankets to cover his body. His eyes were open, but there was no life left in him. Jack looked to her as though he had finally found peace. "Thank you, Jack. May God forgive you."

Sarah couldn't cry anymore. She was completely drained. She looked at Ted Dalton and whispered, "Thank you." The officer just nodded in return. She praised God and thanked him under her breath. When she had the strength, she would shout his praises from the roof tops!

Chapter Twenty Eight

Ed and Jason had developed a plan they were comfortable with. Comfortable might not be quite accurate, but it was all they could come up with. They were low on resources as they only had each other. In addition to their meager two man team, they had Steve's continual petitions to God. They were counting on those prayers most of all. Jason had to go to the warehouse to meet Simon, and Ed was bound and determined to end this. They didn't know who to trust in the police department, and they weren't about to ask Pastor Steve to stick his neck into this noose. Ed would get to the warehouse hours in advance. He would park blocks away and work his way in by foot. His plan was to find a hiding spot so that he could watch who Simon brought with him. If it was possible, Ed planned to take Simon down tonight. He believed that if they could get Simon, the organization would fall apart. With Simon in custody, Ed felt they would be able to get a search warrant for Simon's residence. He was confident they would be able to discover who was helping Simon in this endeavor and then start taking the organization apart. Jason was just supposed to go to the warehouse as planned. He would know that Ed was there covering his back, but he wasn't to take part in any of the arrests or violence if it turned to that. His job was to carry on the charade. Ed's job was to do the rest.

"Well, Jason, I think we have a plan. Any concerns?

Questions?"

"I have a ton of concerns, Ed, but no questions. It is the best plan we could come up with given the time and resources. I'm sorry I got you into this, Ed."

"Don't be silly, Jason; this is what I live for. It is my purpose in life. Now, my wife might agree with you. She's not too happy about these extra curricular activities. As for me, I want to bring this group, and especially Simon, down. I have been waiting a long time for this, and it will be a pleasure to see their faces when I point my 9 mm at them and tell them they are under arrest."

Ed stood smiling at Jason when his cell phone rang. He grabbed it without diverting his attention to Jason. "Ed Lancing here"

"Ed, it's Ted Dalton. We got her, Ed. She is safe and sound. We had to take her. They were starting to move. There was a gun battle and we killed the guy that was holding her. We found another one of them dead in their cabin. Someone slit his throat."

"Oh my God! Ted, you better not be pulling my chain! Are you giving it to me straight?"

"Straight as I know how, Ed. Mrs. Shepard is just now starting to talk to us. She is fine, but she went through a lot. She is being treated at the hospital for shock as we speak."

"Great news, Ted. Awesome job! But I do need one more favor from you."

"Name it, Ed. By the way, the kidnapping case hit the wire just in the nick of time. Actually it was a little later than the nick of time, but creative writing will clear that up. What do you need now?"

"I don't want you to notify my department of what you've got yet. I need a few hours, Ted."

"What? Why, Ed? You're killing me here! How am I not supposed to notify a neighboring department that I have solved their kidnapping case, recovered the car, and oh yeah, brought the victim home safely?"

"Ted, I think a cop is in on this, or at least someone from the department. If they find out you have Sarah, it will blow the sting we have set up tonight. You got a player, Ted. I want the brains. I just need till about 7pm. No more. What do you say?"

"Okay, Ed. I must be a sucker. I don't know how I'm going to do it yet, but I'll do it. Give them hell, boy. You owe me big time, Ed, and I'm going to hold you to it."

"I owe you more than you can know, Ted. I'll be back in touch soon. Thanks for the call and thanks for the good work. All your people okay?"

"We came out fine. We've just got a ream of paperwork to complete, but the good guys 1; the bad guys 0."

"Well done, my friend. I'll call you soon."

Ed looked up at Jason who had obviously heard parts of the conversation. Jason knew the call was about Sarah, but he couldn't decipher the details from only one side of the conversation. He knew it was good news based on Ed's reaction, but how good?

"What's going on, Ed? Have they found Sarah?"

"Not only found her, Jason. They have her safe and sound."

"Oh, Lord, she's safe? Is she okay? Why didn't you let me talk to her? Where is she?"

"She's fine, Jason. They have taken her to the hospital to treat her for shock. She has obviously been through a lot. I couldn't let you talk to her because she wasn't with my friend, Ted Dalton. They had to kill the guy that was holding her, but they found her in a cabin just like she described to you on the phone."

"I want to go to her, Ed. She needs me. I need to be with her, she needs me, especially now. Let's scrub this plan and get our butts up there and see Sarah. I want her to meet you."

"We can't do that, Jason. I know it's what you want more than anything, but we have to play this out. If we let Simon go, they will come back after you. They won't be so kind the next time. They will eliminate you and your family and try again with the next plant manager. The guy that came after me, and I'll bet the one that was holding your wife, were trained killers. I don't know the details of how your wife got away, but she is very lucky. We have to destroy this thing now, Jason. We have to crush it at the head. Otherwise it won't stop and your family will never be safe."

There was silence for a time. Jason knew that Ed was speaking the truth. He had to play this out. He wished he could talk to Sarah, but if he did, she would want him to come to her and she wouldn't understand why he couldn't. Maybe this was better. Jason was relieved that she was safe, but he was getting angrier by the minute. Simon and this gang of thugs had killed his friend, terrorized his family and horrified his wife. He needed to go through with it. He wanted to take the whole lot of them down and end this. He knew he wasn't trained at this, and he knew they were killers and he wasn't; but God would show them the way. Jason was convinced that God had been involved from early on. He brought Ed into the game and saved Sarah. How could he not go through with this? God deserved praise and thanks for all He had done, but Jason would have to save that for later. He had to focus on one last event. He needed God because he knew that he was no match for the opposition without Him.

"I'm with you, Ed. You're right. I will follow this thing through until the end."

"Good to hear you say that, Jason. I was worried you might chuck it all and head for the hills. Look, I need to get going. I really want to get into place at the warehouse hours before they show up. I'm sure they will be dropping some folks in there early as well, but nobody gets on site before

Ed Lancing. I want to see who comes and goes before you arrive. We don't have the upper hand here, so we need some breaks. I better go. Good luck, Jason."

"Ed, I know you're not comfortable with prayer, but I think it would be a good idea if we prayed together right now. I can do the praying, but I would appreciate it if you were here with me?"

Ed was nervous but agreed. He bowed his head and Jason gave thanks to God for all that had happened so far, for the safety of Sarah, and for all the unseen movements of God. He also asked for God's help tonight. "We will be out numbered, God. We need your help again. We have faith in you, Lord, and we trust in your wisdom. Be with us and help us win this battle for your glory. Amen."

"Amen." Ed responded. "Okay, Jason. I've got to go. See you there."

With that, Ed was gone. What the heck was I supposed to do for the next several hours? I had to stay quiet and wait. This was going to be the most painful wait I could ever remember: painful and scary. I had no idea how many people Simon would bring. I didn't know whether Ed would try to make a move tonight or not. The key was for me to keep Simon talking and to find out his identity, if possible. Ed had a theory, but it was just so hard for me to accept. Whether I knew the identity of Simon or not, I knew it wouldn't change what I had to do. My job wasn't to be the cop; my job was to be the live bait. Not very comforting, but it was reality.

Time ticked by slowly. I filled much of the time in prayer, just as I had promised God. I knew God was behind our successes so far. I knew that a lot of people had worked very hard to bring Sarah home, but God was guiding Ed, and God had led Ed's friends to her. I couldn't wait until I could see Sarah again. I wanted to hold her and comfort her. I was hopeful that she was going to be able to put this behind her when it was all over. I wasn't sure how I was going to accomplish that, though, and it would be 100 times tougher for Sarah. Tears came to my eyes as I thought of the horror that she must have endured. "Thank you, God. Thank you for bringing her home."

Finally, it was time to roll. I went across the street and said hello to Ralph and Carol and told them that I was going to be gone for a while. I didn't tell them that Sarah was now safe, because I still had reservations about who was good and who was bad. I trusted Ralph and Carol now, but I didn't know who they might talk to. It would only take one slip up. If Simon knew Sarah was free, I knew I would be a dead man. Simon would know that I was just playing along, and I'm sure Simon would kill me. Well, there was no use belaboring the point. It was time to go and I knew what I had to do. My friends were praying for me, the congregation was praying for me, and I believed that God was with me. I couldn't get cocky, but I believed that if God was with me, I had more than just a fighting chance. If God willed it, there would be victory.

I pulled out in my car and headed downtown. I wondered how Ed was doing and whether he was safely in place. I would be there in fifteen minutes. I was anxious to get on with it. I just wanted an end to this.

Ed walked for about three blocks from where he parked to the warehouse. He used back alleys and went through businesses along the way to break up his path. He had no fear that he was being followed. They probably assumed that he was dead by now, or that their guy was already following me. They wouldn't be concerned about me, and that, as small as it might be, was an advantage. Ed went through a side window into the warehouse. Even though it was early and light outside, it was dark in the warehouse. Once he was inside, he stood silently. He listened and waited to see if anyone was present. He didn't think so. He was several hours early. Once he was comfortable with the fact that he was alone, he checked the place out from one end to the other. He wanted to find a good spot to hide, but one that would allow him to see the bulk of the warehouse. If Simon's people came early, he wanted to know how many, and where they were positioned. He didn't know how big their team was, but they must have put a good dent in it. They had captured the guy that was sent to kill Ed, they had killed one of the guys that had taken Sarah Shepard, and they found another one dead inside the motel room. That was three down, and that had to hurt their numbers. Ed didn't believe the group could be all that big. He knew they had some people in strategic positions, but he didn't think they had a sizeable team. At least he was counting on that right now.

Ed's eyes had adjusted to the warehouse light, and he had found a spot on the ground level that he felt was secure and yet gave him good visibility. He would usually try to pick a spot above the action if he was going to want a bird's eye view, but he also might have to be the cavalry here too, so he didn't want to get too far away from where the fight might be. Now, he had to wait. It was part of what made Ed Lancing a good cop. A lot of guys get impatient and bored. Ed didn't. He could out wait the best of them and remain alert during the process. No newspapers, coffee, or donuts on his stake outs. He was there for a purpose, and he was all business.

About an hour and a half after Ed had taken his position, he heard some movement near the front of the warehouse. Two men walked in and stood looking around. They made no attempt to conceal themselves and gave no thought to the fact that someone might be watching them.

"Okay, I want you to take a spot up there in the loft. You need to be able to get a good look and a good shot if I need you. Take your time and use the scope of your rifle to help you pick out your spot. I will go stand in the spot that Simon has chosen. You dial me in. Once you get into position, you've got to be absolutely silent. I don't want Jason Shepard to know we have a gun on him. Got it?"

"Yep, I got it." The second man bounded up to the loft above the warehouse floor and moved around for a while until he settled in to a chosen spot.

Ed watched the first man take a Simon's position. They had chosen a spot so that Simon could stand in the shadows. Ed wasn't sure why, because by the time everyone got there, the place would almost all be shadows. This group had shown their planning was suspect on several other points of this exercise, and this may be another flaw in their thought process. He studied the shooter in the loft and was glad to see that he was in pretty good shape right where he was sitting. Two men. Was that the extent of Simon's entourage?

As though on cue, the man on the warehouse floor yelled up to the man in the loft,

"Okay, that looks good from here. I will be at Simon's side. Jack is supposed to be here right after he does away with Sarah Shepard, so I will keep him down on the floor here, maybe somewhere over there. The man was pointing in Ed's general direction. Ed wasn't concerned though. He knew what they didn't know. Jack wouldn't be showing up. Jack was dead.

So that was it: two plus Simon. Ed felt as if he had caught a break. Things were looking up. He thought his chances of success were looking better. Ed believed this was even truer if Simon was who Ed thought Simon was. If he was right, Ed didn't think Simon would be much of a fighter. Deadly, yes. That was a proven point, but deadly by the hands of others. If he was right, Ed felt that he would have a chance to take out the other two if he had to. If he was wrong, well, if he was wrong, things could go south pretty fast. He wouldn't make a move unless he had to, or unless he felt he could protect Jason and make the arrest at the same time. It wouldn't be good to save Sarah and lose Jason in the process.

It was almost time. The wait had been worth it. He knew the opposition, and he knew their locations. A car pulled up to the rear of the warehouse and the man on the floor opened the door to let someone in. At first Ed got nervous thinking that someone else might have shown up and that they might send someone over to where Ed was hiding; but very quickly he realized that Simon had just entered the room. Ed only caught a quick glimpse of Simon coming through the door. Ed spotted the outfit and not the person. It was unusual, and Ed believed it had to be worn by the one they call Simon. Simon wore a dark full length cape with a hood. You could not see the face or features of the one hidden beneath. The outfit looked like Simon was trying to imitate the character we imagine when we refer to the "Grim Reaper." Simon stood by the back wall while the man in charge of security updated him on the situation.

"We got Frankie upstairs in position. I'll be at your side. Jack hasn't shown yet, but if he gets here soon, I will put him over there. If he doesn't, we will go without him. I don't think we are going to need any of this based on what you've told me, but better to be safe than sorry."

Ed only saw Simon's hood move up and down in agreement. Simon did not speak. They remained silent for several minutes when a car pulled up front. Frankie yelled down from the loft that it was Jason's car and that he was on time and following instructions to the tee. The head of security acknowledged him, and then told him to shut up and keep quiet. The man stepped to the position that he was holding before in the middle of the floor, and Ed could hear the man in the loft move slightly as he was probably raising his rifle.

I walked through the door and slowly approached the middle of the warehouse floor.

"Over here, Mr. Shepard."

I spotted the man that had beckoned me over and I moved to my right to meet the man as he had directed.

"Are you Simon?"

"No, I am not Simon. Did you come alone?"

"Yes, I'm alone. I've got to believe that your people are watching me and probably have been since I left the house. You know I came alone."

Simon smiled at this remark from the shadows. Jason believed that they were even more powerful than they were. Simon enjoyed that. That is exactly where the power comes from; fear. People will someday believe that Satan's Den is everywhere and that they have eyes and ears on everything. This will keep them in line. Jason's words and behavior were living proof. Simon enjoyed being proven right.

"Raise your arms, Mr. Shepard. I want to make sure you didn't bring any unauthorized toys with you."

I raised my arms and remained silent as the man searched me. When he was done, I put my hands down and then replied, "If you're not Simon, where is he? I came here to meet with Simon."

The man took a step back and out of the shadows came Simon.

I felt a chill go down my spine. This person was evil, no matter what his real identity turned out to be. The dark cloak and hood only emphasized it even more. Simon stood silently in front of me with the man that searched me standing to his right and one step behind. I waited for Simon to speak, but nothing came. I couldn't stand the silence. "Well, I assume you are Simon. I'm here as you have requested."

Simon snapped the fingers on his right hand, and the man stepped up next to Simon. "He's alone and unarmed. It appears that he has come just as you instructed him to. The warehouse is clean, the meeting is yours." With that, the man stepped back obediently. He stood a step behind Simon and slightly to his right. This must be part of their little game, I thought. They would want to give Simon a look of superiority. I had seen similar types of behavior in business. It was a silly game, but right now it was Simon's to play.

Simon spoke. "I am very glad you followed instructions so well, Jason. It proves to me that you not only can be trusted, but you can lead as well. Discipline and organization are the keys. You seem to have them both."

The voice! Ed Lancing was right! I knew the voice. I knew the identity of Simon!

"Are you surprised to hear my voice, Jason? Did you think I was someone else, a man maybe?" With that Simon laughed out loud. The man behind him stood stoic, but Simon enjoyed the mystique.

"I know who you are, but I am having a hard time believing it. I'm trying to understand your motivation; what drove you to kill your own husband, Abigail? What motivated you to track me down and destroy my life?"

Abigail pulled back her hood and stepped closer to Jason. "Oh, Jason, it is good to see you again. I know this is confusing to you; but as I promised, I will make it all clear for you."

"Abigail, you're part of the group or maybe even the leader of the group that mercilessly killed your own husband? How can that be possible? You kidnapped my wife? I thought I knew you, but obviously I have no idea who you really are.

"I had my husband killed, yes. It was unfortunate, but he would not play ball. He resisted everything. He fought me every step of the way, and then finally, he vowed to turn me in and destroy the group. Of course you understand I couldn't let that happen. Joe signed his own death certificate. I only carried out the execution. I had expected that Gene Rikes would have taken his place. I felt that Gene would have been easy to manipulate, but they gave the job to you. I didn't want to hurt you, but I had to get your attention. Sarah accomplished that. Even you admit that. I am happy you are here, Jason. I know that once you have heard everything, you will love the possibilities. I think you should forget Sarah. You can have all the women, money and power you can handle. Sarah will only be an anchor to you. Imagine the possibilities, Jason, can you?"

"Oh, you can't even know how much I have been visualizing the possibilities, Abigail. I had a friend tell me you were Simon, but I didn't believe it. Now I know he was right."

"First of all, you cannot call me Abigail. You must call me Simon. That is my new given name. Secondly, I am very interested to know what friend of yours knew I was Simon."

"You must know who I'm talking about. You know Ed Lancing don't you?"

Abigail/Simon smiled, "Well, he was very resourceful. Closer than I thought if he told you I was Simon. Unfortunately for him, his resourcefulness cost him his life today." Simon watched for my shocked reaction, but when I didn't give it to her, she was puzzled. She enjoyed surprising people, and she loved acting as though she was all knowing and all seeing. I refuse to give her the satisfaction.

Ed saw it coming. Jason was testing and toying with Simon, and that would lead to trouble. Jason couldn't stand being in her presence. She had caused so much pain and heartache, and it was all just a game to her. Ed coiled, ready to strike. He wasn't sure what his move would be, but he was ready and assumed that Simon or her head of security would make the first move. Ed silently gloated knowing that he was right about Abigail. He couldn't understand how he had missed it for so many years, but it finally jumped out at him. While he listened to Simon and Jason, he remembered the prayer that he prayed the day that he figured out who Simon was. Did God answer that prayer? Ed wasn't sure and right now he didn't have time to think about it. He hoped God answered it and that he heard the prayer he and Jason had prayed tonight as well. They were going to need all the help they could get.

"I didn't see any reaction from you, Jason. I thought you would be surprised by Officer Lancing's demise."

"I am surprised, but I'm surprised by your lack of knowledge, Simon. I just talked to Officer Lancing, and he's not dead. In fact, the man you sent to kill him is over in the county jail."

Concern fell across Simon's face. Ed noticed that the security man was getting nervous and clearly didn't like the way things were progressing.

"Well, that is a surprise, but just a little setback. The outcome will be the same in the long run."

"Well, I guess I should let you in on another little secret, Abigail. Sarah is safe and she's free. Your man Jack is dead. How am I doing, Abigail. Am I surprising you?

"Don't call me, Abigail. I'm Simon! You are surprising me, and I wonder why. If you are correct, you have your precious wife back, and Officer Lancing is still alive. I have you, Jason. Did you forget about that?" Abigail smiled at Jason, but Jason smiled right back. This infuriated Abigail/Simon.

Ed saw the anger building in Simon's face and the nervousness in her security team. He began to get concerned that the man in the loft may be given a secret signal to kill Jason. Ed couldn't wait for that to happen. He had to move soon.

"What other surprises do you have for me, Jason? Do you think that someone is going to come to your rescue? My team swept this place before you arrived. We are the only ones here. There's you, me, and my Angel of Death here. Of course, we have our man with the rifle in the loft. Frankie, do you want to say hi to Jason?"

Ed knew this was his chance. Frankie couldn't yell down without disturbing his line of site, even just slightly. This was the opening Ed was looking for. As small as it was, it was all he had. As soon as Frankie began his hellos, Ed moved.

"Hello, Jason. I'm up here looking at you through a rifle scope."

By the time Frankie got to the "I'm up here," Ed had come out low and fast behind the pillar he was hiding behind. The chief of Security looked shocked and began to pull his weapon. Ed fired off two rounds that struck the man and took him down immediately. Ed then tackled Jason to get him out of the line of site of the sniper. When they were on the floor, Ed could still hear the end of the man's speech, "rifle scope." The fool was so busy showing off that he had missed the fact that Ed was there and had shot his boss. Ed could hear the man scrambling in the loft to take a better position, but Ed had moved Jason out of site with his running tackle.

Simon stood without moving through all of this. She seemed unflinching as her security man fell dead to the ground. Ed was recovering from the flying tackle and was surprised to see Simon still standing in the middle of the warehouse. Ed rolled over to protect himself from Simon, but it was too late. Out from her cloak, Abigail pointed a 38 caliber revolver at Ed. Without hesitation, she fired two rounds that struck him in the chest. He fell back flat on his back dropping the gun as he went. He was losing consciousness, and he knew that Jason was in trouble. Ed knew he had failed. He had underestimated Abigail. Ed Lancing's last thoughts were of Marion. Then the darkness came.

Abigail stood over Ed Lancing smiling. "You have been a pest, Officer Lancing; but enough is enough. May you find Satan in the afterworld!" Abigail raised her weapon one last time to put a final bullet in Officer Lancing's head. She never saw Jason coming. Jason hit her at a dead run and she flew five yards sliding across the warehouse floor dropping the weapon as she went. The blow dazed Jason, but his weight nearly knocked Abigail out. Jason regained his senses and moved toward her. He was careful not to give the man in the loft an open shot. Abigail was moving again, but slowly. Jason scooped up her revolver, and then grabbed her by the arm and pulled her out of the shooter's sight under the loft.

She looked at Jason from the floor with amazement and fear. "Why would you do this, Jason? I promised you everything!"

"You didn't have everything to give, Abigail. It is only for God to give. You will pay for the evil you have chosen. You will suffer by the hands of men, and you will suffer the judgment of God. Satan cannot help you now. God is with us."

"You are a fool, Jason, just like my husband was a fool. You saw what happened to him and what happened to your precious Officer Lancing. Your fate will be the same if you choose this path?"

I had forgotten about Ed for just a few seconds. I looked over at him and I saw no evidence of life. My anger began to rise again, and I wanted to kill Simon right there and then. I moved a few feet towards Ed and called his name, but I got no response. While I was looking for life in Ed, Abigail made her move. She jumped up and ran across to the opposite side of the warehouse. I raised my gun, not knowing if I could actually shoot; but I never got the chance. Two shots rang out from the loft above and Abigail was violently thrown to the floor. I heard the man upstairs scream when he realized what he had done. He had just shot Simon. He had killed the one he followed. The man was screaming and asking for forgiveness. He was calling to Simon and asking Satan why he had let him shoot the wrong person. Jason remained still as he listened to the man in the loft call out in fear and remorse. Seconds later another shot rang out from the loft and I heard a body hit the floor. There was only silence now.

I moved slowly and cautiously to Abigail. She was dead. Abigail had been shot in the head. She was dead before she hit the floor. She would take many secrets to her grave with her, but mostly she would take her love for Satan to the throne of God. She would pay the ultimate price for her sin. I couldn't even fathom what that would be like. I had to get back to Ed, but I needed to know if the man in the loft was really dead. I moved up the stairs and saw the body lying in the middle of the floor. The man had apparently put the rifle in his mouth and pulled the trigger. There was nothing left to look at. I wasn't sure how he could pulled the trigger with the gun in his mouth like that, but that was a job for the police not me. I hurried back down the stairs to Ed.

It seemed like hours had passed, but in reality help had come quickly once Jason had called for reinforcements on Ed's phone. Jason felt guilty because he knew he had brought all of this on. He let his anger at Simon affect his behavior, and it cost Ed dearly. Ed Lancing had saved Jason's life and had saved his wife's life too. The warehouse was now a bee hive of activity. Police units, detectives, coroners, and paramedics were all here scouring the warehouse and examining the bodies that were lying about. I was the only one left standing. I was the only one to walk away from all of this, and because of that I felt guilty. I had to confess that I was glad when I saw Simon hit the floor. I wanted her dead. I had even wanted to be the one who killed her. I knew I probably wouldn't have been able to do it, but I had to confess my anger and the hate I felt in my heart. The rest of the people were pawns, so I didn't have the same level of hate for them. Abigail was evil incarnate. I would never know what drove her to it or why she gave up on God, but she would pay for it for eternity.

"Jason, remember me. I'm Detective Kyle. I'm going to need a full statement from you."

"How is Ed Lancing? Is he going to make it?"

"I wouldn't count on it, Jason. He was hit twice in the chest. He bled a lot. He is where he needs to be right now, but I don't think his odds are very good. I'm sorry."

I gave the detective what I could. I thought it was a pretty good summary of events for the condition I was in. He was surprised when I told him that Sarah was safe and in the hands of the County Sheriff's Department. I had to promise that I would meet with him again the next day. He just couldn't understand everything that had happened and he wanted to run through it all again. I couldn't blame him though. I didn't think I understood it all either. All I knew was that I had to get out of here. I needed to get to my wife. I needed to spend some quality time in prayer for Ed. I also needed to check on my children. I hadn't spoken to them in a few days, and I needed to hear their little voices.

God had delivered me on this day. He had also delivered Sarah from the hands of Abigail and her followers. I know that I could not have survived without Him. I know that my wife would not have survived without Him. I was so thankful for what God had done, but I just needed one more prayer answered. "Please, Lord, give Officer Ed Lancing his life. He did your will and sacrificed himself for your children. Give him life, Lord, so that he may glorify you."

Chapter Twenty Nine

Four weeks have gone by since that infamous Sunday and the return of Sarah to her home and loved ones. She has been recovering steadily since she has gotten back home, but she still will not drive the car by herself. She had not yet returned to work either, but Sarah appeared to have regained her joy, and was on her way to a full recovery. We had sold her car as soon as it was returned by the police. Sarah wanted nothing to do with it once the police gave it back. It was a constant reminder of the terror of that fateful evening and the following horror filled days. Even though Sarah wasn't driving without me yet, we were still going out after church today to find her a new car. "Something sporty. Something fun." Those were her requests, along with "preferably no trunk!" I think I understand that one. I had gone back to work and was keeping busy trying to manage the business. It was almost a full time job managing the constant questions and inquiries from friends and acquaintances, while working closely with the police on the follow up investigation. I was fine. The hard work and busy schedule helped put the past behind me quickly. The children were back home and they seemed as happy as ever. They were happier now because they had their mother home. Having Sarah stay home for good is something we are discussing together. Staying home is an option, but Sarah wants it on her own terms, not because she is afraid. She has a lot of reasons she wants to stay home, but she won't allow fear to keep her there. Sarah refuses to let evil win. If Sarah stayed home because she was afraid to drive or afraid to work, evil would win. She wasn't about to live her life like that. Staying home was an option, but it was an option that was yet to be firmly exercised. Sarah would decide when she was ready. The children were enjoying Sarah's time at home for now. They had been kept away from most of the chaos, so they seemed to get back to their normal routines relatively quickly. They had enjoyed their surprise trips to visit to see their cousins; and by the time they got home, Mommy was there and life was relatively normal again. Life in the Shepard household would level off and return to some level of normalcy again. I was convinced of it.

Miraculously, Ed Lancing pulled through. He survived when no one gave him much of a chance. He left the hospital a week ago and is doing remarkably well considering he has two bullet holes in his chest and some bullet fragments lodged against his spine. For the present he is in a wheel chair, but the doctors believe he will walk again. They said that if he was tough enough to survive being shot, and strong enough to survive the resulting surgery, he was tough enough to get out of the wheel chair and walk again. Knowing Ed I had to agree with them. The medical staff didn't want to go in and get the bullet fragments now because they were too close to the spinal chord. The doctors hoped that his therapy and continued exercise would free the fragments and move them far enough away from the spinal chord so that at a later date they could go in and remove them. Ed was indeed a fortunate man. The bullets had not done any permanent damage to his spinal chord. The metal pieces were pressed against the chord causing pain and limiting Ed's leg movements. If they could get the pieces to move, or preferably get them out altogether, his mobility will return and his pain will ease. For now Ed is confined to a wheelchair, but you wouldn't know it by his spirits. Marion has been right by his side through the whole thing. She has been strong for him, and she has provided just the support he needed to help him keep looking at the bright side of life. Because of this, Ed's spirits are high. He takes great satisfaction in the fact that he solved this case. He is even happier because his department and his colleagues know he solved it. Ed is happiest of all knowing that Sarah is home safe and sound. Through all of this Ed and Marion are becoming close friends to Sarah and I. We have been through a lot together, and I thank God for both of them. I thank God for bringing Ed back to us from the throws of death. Not many gave Ed a chance of survival, but Pastor Steve and I never gave up hope. Their doubts weren't their fault. After all, none of them knew what we knew. God was working on that Sunday just like he always worked. For some reason he chose to reveal a piece of himself to a few of his children that day. I was blessed by the experience. I knew he would bring Ed back home, and God proved me right once again.

Ralph and Carol were doing great. They were thrilled to have the children back. They had been watching them frequently while Sarah was participating in grief and trauma counseling. Ralph and I had grown much closer since the ordeal, and I appreciate both of them so much more now. Why is it that so often we have to be drawn into a crisis before we recognize what we have and who our true friends are? Now I know, and I pray I never take it for granted again.

The police had found the apartment that Abigail used as a headquarter for the group she called Satan's Den. They found her files and computer, and they were slowly making their way through all of the evidence. This evidence lead to several arrests, including Ed's friend, Laura Brown, from the police department. She turned out to be the inside influence with Abigail's group. She had apparently been approached by the group after her husband was killed, and she was vulnerable enough to fall for their story. Because of her, Sarah had almost been killed. I didn't have much compassion for her. Ironically, Sarah has been the one helping me work on my compassion. It has been difficult to say the least but God gives me plenty of opportunity to work on it. A few other arrests have been made, including a teacher from our children's school. I don't know what motivated each of them, and I doubt that most of them knew the extent of violence and crime this group was involved in, but the results are the same; they turned their backs on God. I have prayed that God will forgive them, but that is between them and God. Prayer was all I could offer. The police had yet to uncover what led this group to want to conduct worship services at the plant. The belief that it was "sacred ground" seemed contained in the mind of Abigail alone and thus died with her. There was one unusual twist that the police had not yet resolved. Frankie, the man in the loft, was not killed by his own gun. I assumed that he had killed himself, but the police had determined that not only was it virtually impossible with the rifle he was carrying, but the bullet that killed him did not come from his gun. If that is true, then where did it come from? Who shot the last man between me and safety? Was there someone else in the warehouse, or was there a Guardian Angel sent by God to avenge and protect his people. I know what I believe, but the police were still looking for clues and were still deeply engaged in their investigation.

Abigail was dead. Simon no longer existed. The "Den" was crumbling. Members were being arrested, and the history of the crimes the group committed was now public. No one would really know why she did what she did. Her secret died with her. She caused the deaths of many people, and she robbed and hurt many others. She had given herself over to evil, but God would deal with that. What lured her down that path and away from God was the question that haunted me. In the past Abigail and Joe attended church with Sarah and me. What would cause her to reject the truth and attack the very people she claimed to befriend and love? I will never know. I have to let it go and give it to God. It is important that I allow God to remove the stain in my life that Abigail has left behind. Letting her memory go is one step towards that goal.

Steve was right there by our side during the first trying weeks. I should say that he is still there. The congregation has come through for us. Their love and support, whether it is meals, rides, counseling, or shoulders to lean on, has been endless. The church family really came together for Sarah and me, and we know that we couldn't have made it without them. Steve and I began praying together consistently about two weeks ago and it has been one of the most rewarding and Spirit filled times of my life. I have been blessed by his maturity in Christ and his love for the lost. I hope to learn and grow from the relationship that God has allowed to evolve from these trying times.

My walk with God has become strong and deep. I have seen the Lord work and have seen the power of prayer. Because of this Sarah and I have both grown and matured over the past few weeks. We have both rededicated our lives to our Heavenly Father. We have also recommitted our devotion to each other as well as our commitment to raise our children in the teachings of the Lord.

This Sunday morning is hectic just like every Sunday. Everyone is running around getting ready for church. There is a difference in this house now. We know why we attend. We always went to church to worship and hear a good sermon, but now it's different. We look forward to going, to thanking God, to being with believers. It is a subtle difference to those who know us, but it is substantial to us. We finally pull ourselves together this morning and head out the door for worship. We sing praises on the way and we look forward to hearing Pastor Steve challenge us in our walk with God.

Today is a beautiful crisp morning and it is good to be alive. At church we visit with the many friends who are always checking on how the family is progressing and endlessly seek to find ways to serve us. Before services we find ourselves standing near the front of the auditorium talking with Pastor Steve. The congregation is filing in and picking their seats. I look back to the double doors and see Marion Lancing walking through the doors pushing Ed in his chair. I turn to Steve and his big grin tells me that he sees them too. It is exciting to see them because I know God has just answered another one of my prayers. God is good, and He is faithful. I move up the aisle with Sarah by my side and I capture Ed's attention. His smile and wave send chills up the back of my neck. This moment fills me with such joy, that I can hardly contain myself. I almost run to greet them.

There are no guarantees in this life. Whether a Christian believer or not, tragedy can strike anyone of us at any time. I have learned through these recent trials and tribulations that even though there is evil among us, for the believer, God is right here by our side. He wants to love and protect his children. God wants his people to call on him, to be faithful to him, and to trust in him. He is waiting to help us; waiting to answer our prayers. Sometimes we just forget to ask.

ws

Printed in the United States
28479LVS00003B/55-510

9 781597 812627